Delayed Justice

Also by Arthur Haberman

The Making of the Modern Age
Impressionism and Post-Impressionism: Private Lives/Public
Worlds (co-author, Fran Cohen)
Civilizations: A Cultural Atlas
(senior editor and author)
The West and the World: Contacts, Conflicts, Connections
(co-author, Adrian Shubert)
1930: Europe in the Shadow of the Beast
Europe, 1859: In the Ebb and Flow of Modernity

Toronto Justice Series
Blind Justice
Careless Justice
Poetic Justice
Social Justice
Wild Justice

Anthologies
The Making of the Modern Age, Ideas in Western Civilization
On The Edge: Literature and Imagination
(co-editor, Fran Cohen)
The West and the World, Selected Readings
(co-editor, Adrian Shubert)

Delayed Justice

Arthur Haberman

Viaduct
Press

Library and Archives Canada Cataloguing in Publication

CIP data on file with the National Library and Archives

ISBN e-book edition 978-1-55483-520-1
ISBN trade paperback edition 978-1-55483-519-5

"To no one will we sell,
to no one will we deny or
delay right or justice."

— *Magna Carta*, clause 40

To Mike O'Connor

Part One

I

It was Canada Day, July 1, 2021. Gabriella Agostini and Danny Miller were dining on the patio of their regular restaurant, *Elena's*, on the Danforth.

Unlike other years, it was a muted and ambiguous Canada Day for many people in Toronto. The good news was that Ontario was opening up as the third wave of Covid was subsiding. Restaurants, hair salons, and retail stores had opened the day before, with careful rules about masks and distancing. Vaccination rates were moving up and both Danny and Gabriella had received their second jab of Pfizer only a few days ago.

The sad news was the recent revelation of mass graves of indigenous people, many children, at some of the former Residential Schools run by the government and various churches from 1828 to 1997. The country was still absorbing the fact that not only did it formerly have a policy of destroying indigenous identity and culture, but it was also complicit in what many termed genocide.

The effects of the pandemic were many, all of them concerning: elder care was revealed to be very poor and even life-threatening in many homes for the aged; schooling was missed by everyone, more so by poor and racialized young people; family relations were interrupted; young people were deprived of social interaction. The country's colonial treatment of its indigenous people added to the gloomy mood of Canadian society.

Gabriella and Danny arrived at the restaurant early, at 5:45, in order to have a conversation with the proprietor, Constantine. He took care of the patrons, while his wife, Elena, managed the excellent kitchen.

Constantine, masked, hugged both of them, something he hadn't done for fifteen months, and showed them to one of the seven outdoor tables on the Danforth.

"I hope it's over for you, Constantine," said Gabriella. "You've had a rough time."

"Maestra," replied Constantine, "it has been awful. But for you, too. You have not been able to conduct or play with others. I don't know how you musicians manage."

"I'll be all right," said Gabriella. "I'm beginning to pre-pare for concerts in the Fall. I'll admit I wondered if I would ever again play great music with others. What happens to you now?"

"We are not sure. You know the province opened, then closed, opened again, then closed again. Finally, we can have some tables outside. We could never have survived in business if loyal people like you and the Inspector hadn't ordered take-out regularly. I apologize for the qual-ity of the food when you ate it at home. Not everything we do travels all that well. It's like some wine."

"It was wonderful," said Danny. "We at least felt close to you and Elena while eating your food. And you don't know that Gabriella is a wonderful cook. She duplicated some of Elena's creations."

"I'm pleased," said Constantine. "I only hope we remain open, that soon we can have you indoors."

"That will happen," said Danny. "The numbers of people who are ill are moving down. And the number of those vaccinated are up. I'm optimistic."

"Remember, Danny," said Gabriella, "you worked. You solved crimes and caught murderers. Constantine and Elena and I languished, as the feeling has been called. Sometimes I wondered about who I would be if I were not doing music. I'll bet, Constantine, that you and Elena also questioned your identity in the last several months."

"You caught it, Maestra. We did. But now let me get you an aperitif and an *amuse bouche*, and let's get back to being civilized human beings."

"I wish we could talk about small things, Danny," said Gabriella as Constantine left, "but we have to get the last fifteen months out of our system. It's true. I had several people call me, colleagues or folks from Bloor Street, some weeping about what was happening to them. 'Who am I?' asked Benny, 'without my clarinet.' 'I'm deteriorating,' said Lydia, 'I need to play with others,' said Sheila."

Constantine came with some kir, made with Aligoté and crème de cassis, and two small plates of goat cheese with chives.

"Elena is still at her best," said Danny after tasting the *amuse bouche*.

"I agree," said Gabriella. "But are you at your best as a

violinist in a very good amateur Baroque orchestra? Am I as good a flautist as I can be? Can I still conduct well?"

"I won't answer for you, my love, but I am lousy, nowhere near where I should be if the Bloor Street group gets together again. I practice, but I need to play with others. I need to breathe with others in the moment. Playing together on zoom is not playing together. I do it and make believe something is happening, but it's not music as I know it."

"No argument, Danny. It's going to take me time to play the flute as well as I did before the pandemic. It will take time to conduct well again. And any orchestra I work with in the Fall will be rough for a while. We're like athletes who are in the top class but who haven't performed in a long while."

"People applauded us for going on Zoom, but that was just a façade of real music."

"Totally. You breathe together in ensemble work, as you said. It can't happen online. You don't have that sixth sense of being together. The psychological distance is overwhelming."

"We'll all need to be patient," said Danny. "we'll get there, but we'll be unhappy in the beginning."

"At Bloor Street we can rehearse as long as we want. But in a professional orchestra you're changing programs weekly. It will be tough."

"OK," said Danny. "Enough lamentation. Let's talk about when we can travel and where. We haven't anticipated anything in a long time. Anticipation is a pleasure we can begin to indulge again."

Constantine appeared with menus. "Tell us what Elena has prepared," asked Gabriella.

"There are two specials, both of which the Inspector can eat. One is a traditional chicken cacciatore with onions, peppers, lots of garlic, carrots and olives. The other is a grilled salmon with small potatoes and beans."

Danny and Gabriella looked at each other and silently weighed the options. "You decide for us," said Danny.

"I'll have the chicken and Danny will have the salmon. And we'll share. Tell Elena to make whatever small salad she thinks is right. You choose some white wine for us and join us for a toast."

Constantine smiled. "Now I think we can talk about getting back to normal," he said.

The meal was delightful. As Danny said when they were finishing, "Normal is now exciting." Gabriella added, "There are things I'll never take for granted ever again in my life."

II

Molly Muldoon was trying to keep it all together this summer. Molly was the executive director of Tessa's House, the largest and most prominent women's shelter in the city, probably in the country, located at Queen and Broadview. She was well known because over the years—she was forty-eight now—she had become one of the most articulate and important spokespersons for the homeless, the battered and the needy. By now, she was someone contacted by the media when there was a story about one of her people, and she was trusted by all the beleaguered women and the homeless of the city.

Molly was also a person who knew virtually everything occurring on the street because she had an army of informants who came to her with news. When Duncan MacNeil, who lived on the street and in the ravines, was killed, it was Molly who first said to the media that it likely was not done by a street person but by, as she put it, "an upstanding citizen with a grievance in his heart." She was proven right.

Molly looked like the fair Irish lasses of her ancestry. She was slender, not skinny, very fair in complexion, with a face that could be found on the streets of Dublin or the green countryside of her isle. She had a slight accent because she came to Canada with her parents when she was eight. Her hair, once light red, was now grey, and she wore it in a bun which was never perfect, so that some strands curled over her forehead and around her ears. She had once been married, but she divorced the man, causing him some facial damage, when she realized soon after the wedding that he liked beating her up. Molly since had a succession of men 'friends', ranging from a professor of psychology at the University of Toronto to a reporter for Maclean's to a street person, an eccentric and brilliant poet.

Covid made her job more difficult and more necessary. Demand for shelter for women and children rose to the point where some called domestic violence from March 2020 forward a 'pandemic within a pandemic'.

Before Covid Tessa's and other shelters already couldn't handle all the safety and transition issues that arose in people's lives as a result of the maiming of women and children, psychologically as well as physically. Now, it was impossible to cope.

They did what they could. The city also provided some assistance. But it was clear it was not enough. Molly pushed as hard as she could but, like many frontline health care workers, she was overwhelmed.

An added difficulty at the moment was something she could only share with the chair and vice-chair of the board of Tessa's Place.

Five months ago, out of the blue, Molly was contacted by a couple, Vivian Blakestone and Gary Gerrity, both five or six years older than she. They asked to meet with her privately on Zoom and then made what was the surprise of Molly's administrative life.

They explained that they had long admired what was being done at Tessa's House. Moreover, Blakestone said she had a daughter who had been in an abusive relationship and had in the past sought and found refuge for herself and her son at Tessa's. Gerrity said he had recently been told that he had oesophageal cancer and that he was being treated at the cancer centre of Toronto, Princess Margaret Hospital.

"I don't yet know if anything can be done about it," said Gerrity. "There's some hope. But it has caused me to think about things, though I'm not really an old man yet. What I'd like to do is to donate five million dollars to Tessa's House. Vivian and I want to talk with you and whoever else is in charge in order to discuss what you would do with the money."

Molly was both staggered and gratified. After they talked further, she arranged a virtual meeting of the two donors with the Chair of the Board, Eva Rotenstein, and the Vice-Chair, Geoffrey Keller.

The annual operating budget of Tessa's was now just over a million dollars. Moreover, Tessa's building needed a lot of work—a new roof, paint, better windows, and more. Since its inception, Molly was always struggling to get enough money to meet the needs of the hospice. Now she would have the cushion she needed.

Molly even fantasized that it might be possible to expand the support so desperately needed in the city. She knew the present Tessa's should not grow, lest it become the kind of institution that ignored the personal relationships so necessary for its clients. But she thought a second Tessa's might even be possible. When she informed the officers of the Board, she described it as something like winning the lottery.

Gerrity and Blakestone made some requests. They wanted Blakestone to join the Board and to have signing authority for all monies dispersed from their contribution. They asked about new programs and wanted to be presented with a set of alternatives in order to decide what to support.

The Zoom meetings dragged on. When, after three months, Molly and her two board members expressed some impatience, Gerrity took out his chequebook and wrote a cheque for the sum of five hundred thousand dollars. "This is a sign of goodwill," he said. "A down payment." He added he would mail the cheque and asked that Molly not deposit it until the negotiations were complete.

The rest of the Board, ten others, were brought into the discussions, Blakestone officially joined the Board, and it seemed they were concluding.

Then, at the beginning of June, Gerrity met alone at Tessa's with Molly and told her he was dying. "The disease has spread," he said, and he lowered his mask. "I have maybe six months. You'll understand that this has thrown me. I have a lot to take care of now. It may take longer to complete our arrangements than I thought." He also brought up some apparent slights he felt had come from some board members, especially from three members who he said, "seemed to challenge my sincerity." I want them off the board, he said.

Molly met on Zoom with the three members who had queried Gerrity. They were Janet Knapp, who was the chief executive of a health-care consulting firm, Samuel Parkel, a professor in the Department of Psychology at York University, and Debra Castle, a prominent librarian. Molly talked about the delicacy of the matter, especially now in light of Gerrity's prognosis.

"Frankly, Molly," said Knapp, "I'm willing to bet that all this is nonsense. I remember that you told us that Gerrity said he had some support from other donors. Who are they?"

"He said they wanted to be anonymous," said Molly. "One, he said, was from the States."

"So we can't check them out," said Castle. "Do they really exist?"

"You're implying that it's all made up?" asked Molly.

"We're implying it," said Parkel. "We don't have hard evidence. Where's the money? How about cashing that cheque?"

"Gary said there wasn't enough money in the account. He'd fix it when he gave us the balance."

"I am willing to say," said Castle, "that I believe there's an eighty per cent chance that this is all a fraud."

"I didn't want to go there," responded Molly. "I've thought about it once or twice at four in the morning. Why would anyone do such a thing?"

"Who knows?" answered Knapp. "Attention. Authority. Power."

"Add cruelty and control," said Parkel.

"Have you ever heard of anything like this?" asked Molly.

"I've not seen one go this far," said Knapp. "I have seen donors withdraw for strange reasons."

"This occurs at the university as well," added Parkel. "Donors withdraw, usually saying they thought they'd have more control over their money. Who knows if their offers were legitimate in the first place?"

"What do I do?" asked Molly.

"Have you ever talked to Blackstone alone?" said Castle.

Molly thought and then said it had never happened.

"Well, that's the first thing to do. Is he using her and her daughter?"

"I do know that Vivian talks a lot about her daughter. She's still not in good shape. She says Gary is helping her."

"We're happy to be wrong," said Castle. "I hope we're wrong. We'll remain on the sidelines while you go about finding out more."

Molly arranged a masked person-to-person meeting with Vivian the next week.

It began pleasantly, with Molly noting how pleased everyone was with the donation, and Vivian saying all the right things with some humility.

"There's a problem, Vivian," continued Molly.

Vivian blinked and her body posture changed from one that was straight to being a bit bent. "I don't know what you mean."

"I'll be direct," said Molly. "There are some Board members who are worried."

"About what?"

"They think that Gary may be playing us along. He has asked for a lot of cooperation, though we haven't seen a dollar of his promised contribution."

"Gary's sick. He wants the donation to be right."

"Did you tell us that Gary was being treated for oeso-phageal cancer at PMH?"

"That's right."

"And I assume you accompany him to the hospital some of the time, if not for every visit?"

"Yes. But I can't go in with him. I wait outside."

"Well, I have some contacts at the hospital and they tell me that there's no patient named Gary Gerrity." Molly was bluffing. No one outside the hospital could get hold of that information, at least legally.

"Something must be wrong," said Vivian.

"Vivian, is Gary a patient at PMH? Is Gary a person with millions of dollars?"

Vivian began to weep. Molly told herself she should be ashamed of doing this, but she decided she'd be ashamed and make it up to Vivian if her bluff was in error.

Vivian wept for a short while and then looked up at Molly. "He's been helping my daughter financially. She has a good place to live and she's able to get professional psychological help. He helps me."

"Is he using you, Vivian? Is he abusing you for his own reasons? Is he making you dependent on him?"

Vivian broke down. Molly went to sit near her and she took her hand, the first time she had touched anyone like that in a long time.

When things were calm, Molly continued. "I can find help for you and your daughter. This guy is sick, Vivian, and he's hurting you and he's hurting us."

Between sobs, Vivian commented: "I can't live the lie anymore. I need help. My daughter needs help."

"We will find help for you. You need to leave this abusive person. He is abusing you and your daughter and now he is hurting Tessa's."

"Can I rely on you?"

"Other people do. You'll have a tough journey. So will your daughter. But now you're in a kind of mental prison. He'll never let you go. You have to decide to do it."

"I know, but I'm afraid."

"You're right to be afraid. But think about staying with Gary forever."

Vivian seemed to be waiting for this moment, for she took the plunge. She informed Molly that Gerrity had money, but not millions. The whole episode of pretending to make a donation was designed to boost his ego and his self-importance. Moreover, he was healthy. The cancer story was a lie to further obtain pity and to manipulate the circumstances. He would have found a way eventually to terminate his relationship with Tessa's.

Molly did what had to be done. She found support for Vivian and her daughter. She informed Gerry Keller and Eva Rotenstein, and together they called Sachs LLP, the law firm that gave time to Tessa's Place pro bono.

Within twenty-four hours a registered letter was sent to Gerrity informing him that "Tessa's House has come to the realization that your representations regarding a significant donation to Tessa's House have been false, and that you have fabricated a number of matters in your discussions." It went on to tell him that Tessa's House would no longer have any contact with him. He was told that should he go to the premises of Tessa's he would be regarded as trespassing and he would be reported to the police. He was instructed to contact the lawyer from Sachs, Irwin Feldman, if he wanted to respond to the letter and not to communicate or copy any person from Tessa's. Feldman noted that Tessa's reserved the right "to pursue further legal remedies."

The Board had a special meeting to discuss the matter and came to a unanimous decision. They had important work to do and had lost planning time while anticipating the donation. Now it was necessary to get on with their mission.

Molly had a lot of support from members of the Board and especially from Janet Knapp, whom she had known for two decades. Still, she beat herself up at night and took a few weeks to get back to normal. Now she had a lot of work to catch up on.

III

On Friday, July 9th, Danny finished his work at the station at 4:30 and did something he had not done for over a year. He drove to his sister's home near Bathurst and Glencairn for a Friday night family dinner to celebrate the beginning of the Sabbath.

Danny had divorced over a decade ago and since then, until Covid, he had spent every Friday evening with his sister and brother-in-law, Ruth and Irwin Feldman. The two Feldman children, now in their twenties, were always present when they were in Toronto, and Danny's son Avi, nineteen, spent every other weekend at their home. Gabriella joined the group five years ago when she and Danny became a couple. There were always anywhere from two to eight guests.

'Finally,' thought Danny as he started his car and took off his mask, 'Finally. It's time.'

As he had done for all those years, he parked his car several blocks from the Feldman home, put on his fedora, and walked to the house, finding this a meaningful personal ritual to signal the transition from work to Shabbat.

He let himself into the house with his key, as he had always done, and went into the kitchen. Ruth was preparing the meal and looked at Danny with a big grin. They stared at one another for several seconds, this sister and brother who had communicated by phone, text, email and Zoom almost daily since the middle of March 2020, and who had met regularly at a distance in the Feldman's backyard for the last few months. Then they hugged for a long time.

Danny sat at a small table and Ruth brought him a nosh, some chopped liver with some challah. "We forgot how important this is," said Ruth. "It's time to find whatever the new normal will be."

"It won't be the old normal," said Danny. "But Shabbat has been normal for our tribe for over three thousand years. Some things don't need to change. Are there any guests tonight?"

"No, just the six of us. You me, Irwin, Gabriella, Deborah and Avi. We just wanted the close family for the first opportunity. In fact, we are only permitted to be five indoors. So we'll eat outside on the deck. But next week we can have a larger Shabbat indoors."

"How is Leo doing?," asked Danny, referring to his twenty-four-year-old nephew who was completing a two-year stint in the *Tzahal*, the Israeli armed forces.

"He's fine. He wrote yesterday. He's currently in the Negev helping to train new recruits. He's a veteran by now."

"And how are you doing?" Ruth was four years older than Danny. He had always said that she was his rock since their parents had died. But like many on the planet, Ruth and the necessities surrounding Covid did not get along well together. She found herself moody and unhappy and Danny was someone she could talk with about it.

"I'm getting out of the funk," answered Ruth. "Now I can see my loved ones, I can do more volunteer charity work, I can get on with life. At least I expect so. Heaven forbid that we need another shutdown."

The long hugs were repeated as the others came to the house. Deborah, the Feldmans' daughter, now twenty-six, and Gabriella had developed a close relationship and the two of them huddled in a corner of the kitchen, just pleased to be together in the same place. "Zoom is not adequate for musicians," said Gabriella. "It is also inadequate for personal relationships. Nothing substitutes for being together."

A half-hour later the six gathered together in the kitchen, held hands in a circle, and sang *Zemirot*, starting with *Sholom Aleichem*, to welcome the Sabbath. They then went outside to sit at the table. Irwin recited the blessing for Shabbat, and Deborah gave the blessing over the bread.

"Now let's catch up in person," said Irwin as they began the meal. "I'm going into the office for a few days a week nowadays, and I'm seeing clients, masked." Irwin was a senior partner of the downtown law firm, Sachs LLP. "I'm even going to synagogue tomorrow morning for the first time since this pandemic began." He looked at Avi. "What's happening with you?"

Avi swallowed some chicken and looked up. "I'm off to Montreal in early September. Back to McGill. Last year was online, but this year will be in-person. I'm glad. I didn't learn as much as I should have last year."

"Are you still going to major in mathematics?" asked Deborah.

"Absolutely. Maybe with a minor in philosophy. They used to go together a few centuries ago, before the age of specialization."

"Wasn't mathematics a branch of philosophy once?" asked Ruth.

"It was," said Avi , "at the time of Descartes and Pascal. But then everything was thought of as a branch of philosophy, just as it had been a branch of theology before that. The British liked to divide knowledge into what they called natural philosophy, what we call the sciences, and moral philosophy, which included literature, history and the humanities."

"Well," said Danny, "they overlap. For example, natural science has given us the vaccines. Moral philosophy has raised lots of questions. Who gets it first? How do we share with others? What do you do with someone who refuses to get vaccinated? What can you require?"

"Let's not go there tonight," said Ruth. "Let's just be together. That's one of my greatest pleasures. We can solve the big moral questions another time."

They moved to talking about the family, telling stories about their parents and grandparents, the oral history of many families. They laughed together a lot, something that Gabriella felt was very much part of the healing from the difficulties of the last sixteen months.

On the way home, both Gabriella and Danny were peacefully quiet, a pleasurable silence that was part of their relationship. Every so often Danny took his right hand off the wheel and put it on Gabriella's left hand. Both still could not imagine how they had lived without the other for so long, until they had found one another in maturity.

IV

As was customary, Danny met with his senior aide, Sergeant Sara Borelli, on Monday morning.

In Homicide, about two years before, there had been a significant change in personnel. Danny's long-time associate, Ron Murphy, retired. Ron was the administrator of the squad, in an arrangement that was unusual. It permitted Danny, even as Head of Homicide, to get deeply involved in the occasional murder case, as well as to work with other areas, particularly the Major Crimes squad headed by his former boss and friend, Sydney McIntyre.

Ron Murphy had a serene temperament, a reputation as a cop's cop, very fine management skills, and an attention to detail which never lost sight of the larger picture. Danny and the Chief of Police, John Kingston, knew he couldn't be replaced. Moreover, there was no one in Homicide who seemed to have the qualities needed for the job.

As a result, Sergeant Serafina Bellucci, known to all as Sara, moved from her position in the regular force to become the administrator of Homicide. Sara was well-known to Danny, for she had worked in the same building and on occasion he had consulted with her on some matters. He found her directness stimulating, and he had a lot of respect for her intellect.

Bellucci was now forty-two, dark, short and round, with a personality that was determined, bright and on occasion blunt. Yet she was popular with her subordinates because she was fair and she stood up for them when necessary. Danny knew that he could never find another Ron Murphy and he decided that Sara's administrative skills and his comfort level with her would be fine. He also bet on Sara's capacity to learn and grow, hoping that within a short time she would also be the kind of colleague he went to when he needed some advice.

Sara worked hard, played no favorites, admitted what she didn't know, and gained the confidence of the detectives she was supervising. 'So far, so good', Danny said to himself.

However, the change meant that Danny needed to be in the office a lot more during the long transition and the adjustments needed because of Covid. For what he believed was too lengthy a time he had taken on fewer cases. He felt a need to get back into the street and convinced himself that soon he could do so. He was waiting for a case that would attract his attention and perhaps need his well-developed skills.

The two colleagues reviewed the last week and what cases they knew were active and/or coming up. At the end of their review, Sara raised the fact that Sergeant Nadiri Rahimi was transferring as of this day back to Homicide from Major Crimes.

Nadiri and Danny had become partners over six years

ago, when he was a sergeant and she had joined Homicide as a Constable. They became the most successful team in the city, and during that time Danny became known in Toronto and beyond as something of a public personality because of his meetings with the media on many cases. Moreover, Sara knew that partners could become friends, as had happened with the two of them.

"There's nothing special to discuss, Sara. Nadiri's moving back as a Sergeant and as a senior person. As much as I liked partnering with her, that can't happen now, and Nadiri knows that. She's really talented and we need to find a junior partner for her."

"I like her a lot, Danny. You remember I supervised her on the missing persons case. I just wondered if there was anything I should know."

"There's no subtext to her moving back. She's told a lot of people that Major Crimes didn't suit her. She likes the edge of being on Homicide."

"So just treat it as a normal move?"

"Absolutely. She's a professional. We've had our own private discussion and we're on the same page."

Sara nodded. Then she asked, "I'd like to talk to you, Danny, about the job."

"Any problems?"

"No, nothing that's not normal and that I didn't encounter working in the regular squad."

"You're not happy?"

"I'm fine." She smiled. "Especially working for the brilliant Homicide chief."

"C'mon Sara. We've been good colleagues and friends

for a while. You know I don't think of myself that way."

"Of course." She smiled. "I just thought part of the job is making sure you don't get a big head."

"I've got plenty of women who look after that. My sister, and my wonderful and tough niece. Even my partner occasionally lets me know I'm fallible. I'll add you to the list."

"I'm honored. A good group. You happen to be one of the few males I know who understands how women rule the world."

"Not a problem for me, Sara. We males haven't done a very good job. Most of the work of the homicide squad is the result of male behaviour one way or another. Now, what do you want to talk about?"

"I feel that I'm doing an OK job as your administrator and second-in-command."

"Me, too. Better than OK. And you have the confidence of our colleagues. You learned quickly."

"Not quickly enough, Danny."

"What do you mean?"

"I came here after being a sergeant and running things in the regular police. I still don't really know how things are for people on the squad on a day-to-day basis. I think I need some experience in the field, on a case or two, to get that knowledge. It would help me to assign people more carefully and to appreciate some of the subtleties of the job."

"Let me think about it. I can't argue with you. Ron did the job really well and he came up from the squad, not a transfer, like you. So you may be right."

"It would mean you might have to do a bit more administration for a while, which you really dislike."

"Not only do I dislike it, I told the Chief I wouldn't be a full-time administrator. I need to get out on the street occasionally, more than has happened since you moved here. But if you're right, then you getting experience on the street would help in the long run because you would be able to do your job better."

"That's what I'm thinking. I'm not asking for a transfer or to be a regular homicide detective. I like what I'm doing. I even find it exciting at times. I'm asking to get some experience so I can do the administrative job better."

"Let me sleep on it. And we should have another conversation soon."

"Sounds good to me, Danny. I'll get back to work."

V

Many journalists and other commentators in Toronto welcomed the move in Ontario to Stage Three at the end of June, hoping it would signal a better time when people could again socialize, shop, visit one another, and just live a life that could anticipate the future instead of being in the eternal present, what some felt was the eternal void, of Covid.

Not only did the revelations from Residential Schools make news. An incident in London, Ontario, five weeks earlier shook the nation. The driver of a pickup truck deliberately struck five pedestrians who belonged to one family, killing four of them. "There is evidence that this was a planned, premeditated act and that the family was targeted because of their Muslim faith," said a spokesperson for the London police.

The shock caused many to wonder if Canada was losing one of its most cherished qualities, the peace and civility of its public life. No longer did people take for granted that Toronto and Canada were immune to some of the madness that was part of everyday life in many parts of the world. Civic minded people began to organize and to pressure for gun controls and new laws.

Then an event in Toronto gave further pause: a murder which seemed a hate crime.

The case began in a normal manner. On a Wednesday afternoon following the beginning of Stage 3, the Homicide Squad received a call from 14 Division informing them that a person had been murdered on Baldwin Street, just west of Spadina, in the Kensington Market area of the city. Sara Bellucci received the call and immediately informed Danny.

"There's a murder on Baldwin near Spadina," she said. "Do you want to take it?"

"No, you take it."

"Really?"

"Sure. You asked about taking a case to get a feel for how we work. This is a good opportunity."

"But who will do my job?"

"I'll do your job. I'll stay in the office while you're outside. Take Nadiri as your partner. She has the experience you might need. It's time anyway for a female team to appear."

"What do I do?"

"Go immediately and take over. I'll find Nadiri and send her down. She'll help you."

Sara drove the short distance to the site of the crime. She found the area taped off and two police cars, an emergency medical team and an ambulance. She showed her identity and went to the officer in charge.

She looked at his uniform. "What's happening, Kruger?"

"We got a call a short while ago. We found two people on the ground, the body of a man, and a woman who was beaten and is being taken care of by the medical team. Their two kids, daughters, are in one of the police cars being looked after by my partner. We called to get social workers here."

"Anybody touch anything?"

"We left it for you. Forensics are on their way."

Sara went to look at the body. She found a male of about forty lying on his back. His head was bashed in and he had bled from both the head and his torso. There didn't seem to be a weapon involved. She found his wallet. He was Haris Bashera.

Nadiri appeared. They nodded to one another and Sara briefed Nadiri as they looked at the body. Two minutes later Emily Chow and her forensics team arrived.

"We'll let you do your job," said Sara. "Let us know when you're done and we can talk."

The two then put on their masks and went to the Emergency Medical vehicle. In it were two paramedics treating a woman in a niqab. She had a bandage on her cheek and one arm was in a sling.

"*Wa 'alaykum al-salaam*," said Nadiri.

The woman gave a rueful smile. "No peace, Officer. There is no peace in my life. Where are my children?"

"They are with an officer and are being looked after," said Sara.

"And where is my husband? Have they taken him to hospital?"

Sara swallowed hard and looked at Nadiri, who nodded.

"We are sorry to tell you that your husband is dead," said Sara. Nadiri added, "He was looked after by a doctor."

The woman broke into uncontrollable sobbing, overcome by grief. Neither Sara nor Nadiri knew what they could do, other than just be there.

After some minutes, Sara asked of the woman. "Can you tell us what happened?"

The woman composed herself as best she could. "Yes, I will tell you."

"Tell it your way."

"I'm Diana Bashara. We drove from our apartment in Thorncliffe Park to Kensington Market for an outing and some shopping." Diana stopped in order to get herself together. "I don't know if I can do this. I'll make it short for now."

"Whatever you can do will help," said Nadiri.

"There's no help, Officer. You know that. Let me tell it fast and then I must see my children."

"Go on."

"When we got to this street from Spadina, two men were crossing. In the middle of the street. They didn't look and were walking in the street. My husband gave a short honk on the horn. They turned and saw us. First one, then the other, came and kicked the car. The first one said, 'You fucking Arab, go home to your country. Don't tell me what to do.' They pounded on the window near my husband and continued kicking the car. They shouted obscenities. They even said that if I wanted to stay in Canada, I should burn my niqab. They called it a head covering. My husband opened the door. They pulled him out and beat him and kicked him. Then they pulled me out and hit me in the face and twisted my arm. One kicked me in the ribs when I was on the ground. Our children were crying and yelling. One person came and tried to get the men to stop. They called him an Arab lover and told him to go live in Iraq."

She stopped. "I can't go on. Another time. I have to see my children."

"Of course," said Sara. "Let me take you to them."

As they walked the few steps to get to the children, Nadiri asked, "What is your husband's name?"

"Haris."

"And," added Nadiri, "where were you born?"

"I was born in North York General Hospital."

After they made certain that Diana and her children were looked after, Sara and Nadiri had witnesses to interview. The most important seemed to be Jon Normanson, the person who had intervened and tried to help.

Normanson was in his late twenties, blond, short hair, clean shaven, and dressed casually and nicely. His partner, Rose Chan, accompanied him. The four went into a local coffee shop and found a quiet corner. Nadiri took orders, brought back hot coffee and lattes, and they began.

"Tell us what happened as you understand it, Mr. Normanson," said Nadiri. "Then we'll ask some questions."

"Rose and I were walking to the market from our apartment on Madison Avenue in the Annex. We turned onto Baldwin and saw that two men were hitting and kicking a woman on the ground. Next to her a man who was badly beaten was lying on the ground, not moving. What happened to him, by the way?"

"He died from the wounds. The men not only beat him, they killed him."

Rose gasped. Jon said "That's terrible. I've never experienced anything close to as bad as this."

"I know, Mr. Normanson," said Nadiri. "This is a terrible thing. But we need your story if we are to catch the men."

Jon took a sip of his coffee and continued. "OK. Where was I?"

"You came upon the scene," said Sara. "And you saw two men beating the woman."

"I ran up to the men and yelled, asking them to stop. They turned and said 'Mind your own fucking business. We're sticking up for you.' I yelled again, 'Stop'. One of them called me an Arab lover. He pushed me away and I banged into the car. Then Rose yelled 'The police are here. Help. Help.' The men ran away. Someone had called 911. Police cars then did come and we tried to help the man and woman. That's it."

"No," said Rose. "When they left after I yelled, they looked at me and one of them said, 'Fuck you, you yellow bitch. Long live the white man.' Then they pushed me so hard that I fell down as they left."

"Can you describe the men?"

Rose answered first. "White. In their twenties, probably around the same age as us. No beards or moustaches but they didn't shave today. Maybe even two days of growth on their faces. Both wore headbands. One of them was plain black, the other was grey and had a 'We the North' statement on it.

"You mean a Raptors headband?"

"If that's their slogan, I guess so. The one with the Raptors headband wore a black shirt and jeans."

"Was anything on the shirt?" asked Sara. "Any words, any insignia?"

"I didn't notice."

"You're doing fine. Keep going."

"The one with the black headband also wore jeans, but his were torn at the knees. His shirt was checked. Mainly red.

"Anything else?" asked Sara.

Both were silent and shook their heads. Nadiri then asked, "What I want you to do is to close your eyes. I want you to think about the faces of the two men. Is there anything you can tell us about how they looked? For example, was one taller than the other? Did one weigh more than the other? Did you see their eyes? Does one of them have high cheekbones? Or a scar? Rose, you start."

Rose closed her eyes and they gave her several seconds to think. Then she said, "One was about Jon's height, almost six feet, the other was about five eight."

"Good," said Nadiri. "Which headband was on the tall guy?"

"The one with the Raptors slogan. He was the guy who called me a yellow bitch. I don't know why, but I got the feeling he was the leader. I don't remember much about their faces other than the stubble. It happened fast. The tall one had a big nose. The smaller one seemed scared, even though he was beating people up."

They then asked Jon to close his eyes. "I don't remember much more," he said. "Rose is always more perceptive than I am about visual things."

They asked the two to provide identification and their email addresses and telephone numbers. They learned that Rose did illustrations for medical textbooks for a publisher and Jon was a securities analyst for the Bank of Montreal.

"We'll be back in touch," said Sara. "We'll need a written statement from each of you."

"Whatever we can do," said Rose. "We feel terrible for that family."

There were two other witnesses, including an elderly woman who had called 911. Their stories were similar, and they agreed on how the two men were dressed.

Finally, they had a discussion with Emily Chow after she had finished her examination of the body.

"He was killed by either the blows to the head or by the fall when his head hit the pavement or a combination of both. I'll know more when I do the autopsy. No need to speculate about time of death. It occurred about an hour ago, at two in the afternoon on a nice summer's day. Tell me the story about what happened."

Nadiri told Chow what they knew in as condensed a form as possible.

"Sometimes," responded Emily Chow, "this job does get to me."

Sara and Nadiri agreed that they should report immediately to Danny. They wanted his advice and they knew that he would be dealing with the press and with others who needed to be fully informed.

Danny was waiting for them when they returned to the

station at four. They met in his office and he was silent as they related what they knew.

When they had finished, he said, "A bad business. I already have had calls from CBC, CTV, The Star and the Sun. I promised a statement this evening. We can't wait until tomorrow. This is a very sensitive case, one which will bother a lot of people in a city which is already a bit on edge. First, I want you to know that when we finish, I'll be calling the Chief and Inspector McIntyre for advice."

"Why? It's a homicide," said Sara.

"In my view, given what you've told me, it's also a hate crime. That needs to be said right away. At minimum we need to say we're investigating it as both. The Chief will need to issue a statement in addition to my own."

"Where do we go, sir?" asked Nadiri. "We have four witnesses, no clear identity, two guys in their late twenties, one taller than the other, the taller one wearing a headband with 'We the North' on it. That means we could arrest a lot of people."

"I know what you're saying, Nadiri. Of course, if they have the money, they could be anywhere in the world tomorrow, though I doubt that will happen. Let's ask your question it another way. What do we have, besides the witnesses and a loose description?"

"They are racists," said Sara. "Ugly, nasty bigots."

"Well," said Danny, "that narrows it down. You're not going to arrest good people, like the couple who tried to help. What else?"

Both Sara and Nadiri looked puzzled. "Not much," said Sara. "They could be found anywhere."

"Here's what I'm thinking," said Danny. "I'd like you to call the woman who was so perceptive, the medical illustrator. I think we need to get some confirmation of the information she gave you."

"Why?" asked Nadiri.

"Humour me," answered Danny. "Nothing may come of this, but I'd like to confirm something."

Sara took out her phone and dialled the number given to them by Rose Chan. When Rose answered, she explained that Inspector Daniel Miller, who was in charge of Homicide, wanted to have a word with her. She gave the phone to Danny.

"Ms. Chan, I want to thank you and Mr. Normanson for what you did and for your help." A pause. "Yes, I know that's only what any good citizen would do, but you did it, and we appreciate that. Can I ask you a few questions?"

"Good. Can you put your phone on speaker? If so, put it on so that Mr. Normanson can take part." As he said this, Danny activated the speaker on Sara's phone and put it on the desk.

"All set? Good. What I need you to do is to remember exactly what the two men said. I know you reported that to Officers Bellucci and Rahimi. I need to hear it again from the both of you. Mr. Normanson, could you start."

"Sure," said Jon. "Not complicated. They told me to mind my own fucking business and they said they were doing it for me."

"I need their exact words, Mr. Normanson. If you can remember them."

"'Mind your own fucking business. We're sticking up

for you.' That's it."

"Thanks. Now, Ms. Chan, what was said to you. Exactly as it was said if possible."

"No problem," said Rose, "I think it was the taller one, but I'm not one hundred per cent sure. He said 'Fuck you, you yellow bitch. Long live the white man.'"

"Think now, the both of you. What happened after one of them pushed Rose and said what he said."

"Nothing," said Rose. "They ran away. Towards Spadina."

"How did they run?"

"Like everybody runs. As fast as they could, with their feet."

"OK. You said 'like everybody runs'. When I run I run with my feet and my arms move in rhythm at my side."

"I get it," said Rose. "They ran with one arm in the air."

"That's right," said Jon. "I remember now. I thought it odd."

"Which arm?" asked Danny.

"The right arm," said Jon. "Yes, that's correct," said Rose.

"How high in the air?" asked Danny.

"It wasn't straight up," answered Rose. "It wasn't at a ninety degree angle. More like seventy-five degrees. I deal with angles all the time in my work."

"Thanks to both of you. We'll get back to you."

Danny ended the call and turned to his computer. "Give me a few minutes. I'm searching."

Sara and Nadiri knew what was happening and just remained silent as Danny searched.

Then, "Got it," said Danny. "At least I think I've got it."

"Tell us," said Sara.

"I'm on the site of an Ontario group called the White Canadian Front. Let me read the first few sentences of their mission statement. 'We're sticking up for you. The white race is in danger. End immigration. Keep the race pure. Long live the white man.' I won't go further other than to note they proudly claim to be associated with other Canadian and US racist and Nazi groups."

"Clever, Danny," said Sara. "You're teaching me how to think about homicides."

"As Nadiri will tell you, Sara, there's not one way to think. In this case we need to enter the heads of those two vile human beings. Bad, bad stuff."

"Yes, Boss, but now we know where to start."

VI

It was almost seven o'clock by the time Danny spoke with the Chief and Sydney McIntyre, drew up a press release and then cleared it through the Communications people, which he always found annoying. His last act before leaving the office was to call Gabriella to let her know he would be late.

As part of the Stage Three opening, musical groups could now rehearse and perform indoors. For the last dozen years Danny had belonged to what came to be called the Bloor Street Chamber Group. They were amateurs devoted to the Baroque repertory, and they met weekly at the Royal Conservatory, where a number of the group taught. As well, they were composed of the owner of small grocery store in Parkdale, a cop, a psychiatrist who had studied at the Curtis Institute in Philadelphia, a few retirees, and others.

The small orchestra of thirty of so players gave a concert annually at the end of June and had played at the St. Jacob's Music Festival. For the three years before Covid *Toronto Life* designated them the best amateur music group in the city, an evaluation echoed by others, including *The Whole Note* magazine.

Danny and Gabriella had met at Bloor Street. Gabriella had been their principal flautist and six years ago became their conductor, chosen by the group. Danny was one of ten violinists, sitting in the last row of that section. He often had doubts about whether he belonged to this very fine group, especially as, under Gabriella, it attracted better musicians and much recognition. But he had learned to set those concerns aside and practice a lot to keep up his level.

Gabriella rose in stature over those years to become a visiting conductor, first in Canada, and then with fine groups in the United States, France, Italy and Britain. As well, she now taught flute and conducting at the Conservatory. In late 2019 she had turned over the conducting responsibilities to their then first violinist, Grigori Lapuchenkov, becoming Conductor Emerita, because she was on the road for more time each year and felt she couldn't do the job well anymore. When she was in town she would bring her flute and would occasionally conduct.

Just before Covid, in mid-January 2020, Gabriella was asked at the last minute to conduct the Toronto Symphony in a program including Haydn, Mozart, Stravinsky and Gershwin, replacing someone who in China had caught what was then said to be the flu, but turned out to be Covid. Her reviews were outstanding and brought even more conducting requests to her agent.

Then, everything suddenly shut down. Gabriella's career and development seemed stuck. Musical performances were cancelled for the next sixteen months. What teaching was done through the Conservatory was online. However, the lead time for orchestral music and opera is very long, and Gabriella was now heavily booked as a conductor, occasionally also playing a flute concerto, from the coming September. She, and hundreds—tens of thousands really—of other professional musicians only hoped the opening up of Covid restrictions would happen.

Danny drove quickly to his house on the Danforth to get his violin. Before leaving he made himself a salami sandwich, forgetting to put on the mustard, to eat in the car as he drove to the Royal Conservatory. He usually found a parking spot only after a search, but today he immediately parked in the public lot two streets away.

He entered the auditorium and quietly went to his chair at the back of the violin section, next to Olga Nevsky. Surprisingly, Gabriella was doing the conducting, and Grigori was in the violin section. They were rehearsing the very familiar first movement of Vivaldi's *Four Seasons*, *Spring*. Grigori had informed everyone about the Vivaldi, asked them to prepare, noting he wanted to start with something well known to all.

Danny had prepared for this night and he easily integrated into the group, finishing the second slow movement and moving into the third, designated *Allegro pastorale*.

When they finished, it was clear there was a lot of unhappiness. Benny Grunbaum said "*oy, veh*" out loud, Olga simply stared downwards, Grigori banged his hand onto his forehead.

Gabriella usually talked at this point, but now she asked a question. "OK, dear friends, what's the problem?"

She got lots of spontaneous responses, including "We're terrible," "This is like Grade 12 at ESA," "Zoom isn't much worse," "What happened to us?"

Gabriella responded. "You know, we're like good athletes who haven't played our game in over a year. A hockey player who skated by himself, a basketball player who never had to take a challenged three-pointer, a Blue Jay who never had a real game. We're all rough. We need to learn again to be together, to breathe together, to converse with our instruments.

"That's the bad news. The only good news is that everyone else is in the same position. I'm conducting the *Orchestre National du Capitole de Toulouse* early in September for a week. I have no idea what I'll find. They, too, haven't played together very much.

"So don't get down on yourselves. We have something many groups don't have." She paused and then said, "Time." She paused again. "We can take our time to get where we want to go. Which is to make great music and enjoy being together. Many places I've conducted don't have that. They go relentlessly to a new program every week, with limited rehearsal time. I promise you we'll get where we want to be. Covid didn't take away our talent. It took away our time being together. We are going to get it back. Soon.

"Now," she added. "Let's go from the top and think about the sound we need for *Spring*. Also, let's play it a touch faster and with joy. After all, it's Spring."

They all relaxed and by the time the session ended everyone felt they had made a lot of progress with both

Spring and *Summer*. Afterward, many stayed around, simply to get a hug from some of their colleagues and to catch up.

It was 10:30 by the time Danny and Gabriella got to the car for the short ride to both their homes.

When they got out of the parking lot and onto Bloor Street, Danny said, "That was really good. A pleasure. Even if we need to work to get back in shape. How come you were conducting?"

"Grigori was being kind. He said I'd need some conducting work before starting all my visiting in September. I'll be here for the rest of the summer, so we'll share the conducting for a while."

"I felt we improved over the evening. We began to be one again. Not quite, but we'll get there."

"Danny, tonight proved what we all felt. Online group rehearsals and performances don't work. The sound is awful. The players, because of the technology, can't be in synch. I know now that online there is no such thing as an ensemble. We made believe, but we were better tonight than at any time online, and we were not very good tonight."

"We're not alone, you know."

"I do know. But conducting now will help me through some rough spots when things open up in September. Now, what made you late?"

"A very ugly killing and hate crime in one." Danny briefly told Gabriella about the murder on Baldwin Street, for the drive to Gabriella's place near the Castle Frank Subway Station was a short one. "You'll read about it and hear about it. There's a press conference tomorrow morning with the Chief and me attending."

"Any leads?"

"One possible one. We'll know more soon. Toronto is going to have to absorb another bad killing."

VII

The press conference was led by Chief John Kingston, with Danny in the background. The crime was the focus, but the questions were broader, concerned with what was happening more generally in the city.

"Do you think," asked Ted Drangle of *The Star*, "that the city is becoming more violent?"

"The statistics say no," replied Kingston, "but there is a lot going on. We've absorbed a bunch of different horrible events, from a van running down people, to a random shooting, and now a hate crime that killed a good citizen. We're not immune to what is going on in the world."

"Chief, people want it to stop," said the CTV reporter.

"I want it to stop. We're looking into getting guns off the street. We need to go further and get hate off the street."

"How do you do that?" was the follow up.

"You educate people. You build a community that respects others. I know we're all upset by what is happening. I don't have some magic solution that stops two people from behaving in a terrible manner. The problem is deep."

"Yes, but right now, how are you going to find the out who committed the Baldwin Street murder?" asked Rosalie Daniels from the CBC.

Kingston turned to Danny and gave him the microphone.

"We have a lead," he said, "not something I can talk about, and we will be relentless. This is a racist act, a hate crime, and a murder. We won't let it go. At this moment, two of my best people are on it full-time and others are assisting."

Daniels persisted. "Inspector, do you agree with the Chief that racism and violence are a very difficult matters, something hard to control?"

Danny thought for a moment and then decided to speak his mind. "I agree with the Chief. However, I'd like to add a word or two." Danny saw the communications person at the rear of the room shaking her head. He went on anyway.

"We are part of a larger world, one in which a lot of people these days are invoking racial nationalism, part of what has come to be called populism. This is occurring in Europe, in Russia, in parts of Latin America and, as we all read every day, in the United States. It has enabled some people to say things that were not acceptable several years ago. And maybe it has encouraged people to behave in ways that would not have been part of public life several years ago. Public life has been coarsened these last several years. This is something that goes deep socially. It can happen here."

"What do we do about it, Inspector?" asked Patterson.

"We continue to support civic decency, equality, and the idea that we are responsible for one another. We don't let the people who hate think they can win. We live by a code of civic responsibility."

"Nice words, Inspector," said Daniels. "But a citizen was just killed on the street by people who hated him because of his background."

"And we then invoke the law," said Danny, "and tell our police chief and the homicide inspector to act. But that's not enough. We have a larger problem that all of us must address if we are to continue to be the peaceable country we love. It's not only my responsibility, Rosalie. It's yours, as journalists and citizens, and it's everyone else's as well."

Kingston permitted this exchange to happen, but now he felt he needed to end the press conference. He took the microphone and simply said, "It's time for us to get back to work. Thank you, everyone."

As the room emptied and Danny and Kingston were exchanging a few words, the communications person, Thelma Leighton, walked to the front to speak with them. "What the hell are you doing, Danny? Can't you stick to the script? Now we're going to have to reply to all sorts of people, here and elsewhere."

"I think we need to talk about these political and social issues. They affect our work."

"You might as well have just said you think what's happening in the States is awful and violence is crossing over the border."

"I didn't say that. The problem really is that people who hate now feel enabled because of what's happening in the States and elsewhere. We need to support our sense of what a good civic life should be."

"Well, we're going to get a lot of questions."

"That's your job. Maybe you should tell the people who ask questions that you're busy now doing police work and trying to catch the bad guys, and you've given up being a public relations person."

"That's enough, you two," interpolated Kingston. "We don't need this. It doesn't help. Cool it. You're both on the same side. I have enough crap to deal with. I don't need this."

Both Danny and Leighton nodded. But Leighton persisted. "I want an apology, Danny. You need to work with us."

"You won't get one, Thelma. If any Canadian has to apologize for saying what I said then our country is in big trouble."

"Stop it," yelled Kingston, in a tone Danny had never heard from him. "We're all stressed. I'll speak with each of you separately when I have time. Go do your work."

VIII

Neither Sara nor Nadiri attended the press conference. They were busy finding out about the White Canadian Front. It had a web-site which openly supported a 'white Canada,' claiming among other things that this vision was embedded in Canadian history. The Front was headed by Robert Dozier and its office was in his home on Coxwell Avenue, near Monarch Park. They needed to find the identity of the two men but decided not to show up at Dozier's door. Instead they would ask a Justice of the Peace for a warrant. Without it, Sara believed that they might be denied entry and then records could be destroyed. The warrant was carefully worded to conform to the *Charter of Rights* and to show that, as the law states, the police needed entry to "locate, examine and preserve all the evidence relevant to events which may have given rise to criminal liability."

Nadiri explained the Islamic funeral customs to Sara and indicated that, if possible, they should keep a distance from the family until Haris Bashara was buried, "probably today," she said, as at least three days of mourning had passed. They then got in touch with the family of Diana

Bashara and the imam of the mosque the family attended on Thorncliffe Park Drive. The family asked that they call back the next day to discuss when they might speak again to Diana.

While waiting impatiently for the warrant to be approved, Sara and Nadiri surfed the net to find information about other openly racist groups. They were disturbed to discover a number of them. However, Nadiri remarked, "Do you remember four years ago when the Inspector was shot at by two bikers who belonged to a hate group? Well, it turns out that their group was about twenty people, most of them drug addicts or alcoholics. Or both. So let's not overreact. Any idiot can put up a website and any idiot can make any kind of claim about his following."

Their waiting ended just after two in the afternoon. The warrant was granted.

As they drove along the Danforth to Coxwell and then south for four blocks, Sara said, "I'll bet that a lot of nice, decent middle class families live all around here. The homes aren't fancy, but they are kept by house-proud people."

"You're right," said Nadiri. "I know the area. My partner lives a little further out on the Danforth and I live south and a bit east in Leslieville. A good part of the city. Where do you live?"

"Near College and Clinton, naturally. This nice Italian girl didn't stray far from her roots. Did you know that my first name is Serafina? Like you, my name is part of my story."

"What does it mean?"

"It comes from the Hebrew, of all things, even though we are practicing Italian Catholics. The seraphim were powerful angels who were supposed to be very fiery and bright. In the bible Isaiah said they had six wings each. I found out when I was a kid that it was also the name of a saint who made clothes for the poor. I can relate to that."

Nadiri smiled. "A lot of us think you are fiery and bright. You're one of the women we look to."

"That's kind, Nadiri. But I just wish I was thin. I just want to go to sleep and wake up six inches taller and thirty pounds lighter. What's Nadiri mean?"

"I was really named Nadira. Which means gift of God. When we left Iran and got to Germany, the immigration officer heard Nadiri and that was what he wrote on my papers. I got called Nadiri in school and adopted the name. I kind of like it."

Nadiri parked the car about twenty meters from Dozier's house. "All right," said Sara, "let's go and look at the place that stands against everything this neighborhood is about."

They put on their masks, rang the bell and the door was opened by a man in his forties, well-groomed and impeccably dressed, the kind of person who Nadiri thought could only be found in the British Isles two generations ago, a male who wore a tie and jacket when alone in the house.

They identified themselves and then Sara said, "We're looking for Mr. Robert Dozier.

"I'm Robert Dozier."

"We have a warrant to search the records of the White Canadian Front." Sara took the warrant and gave it to Dozier.

"Why do you need to do this?"

"A crime has been committed and we believe that the records of your organization might help us to find the criminals."

"Being in the White Canadian Front is not a crime."

"You are correct, sir," said Nadiri. "You have a right to your beliefs and to peacefully practice what you believe. We are not investigating your organization. We have good reason to believe your records will help us to find some people who have committed a crime. That's it."

"What crime has been committed?"

"We're not at liberty to reveal that," answered Nadiri. "The court has approved a search warrant. We would like to get started. The sooner we do this, the sooner we'll be gone. Again, we are not investigating your organization."

"I'd like to call my lawyer."

"Mr. Dozier, this is a legal warrant," said Sara. "Your lawyer will tell you that you must comply."

"I'd still like to call my lawyer."

"We'll give you five minutes, Mr. Dozier. Then we will come in and do the search. In the meanwhile, we'll let you call your lawyer in our presence."

"You're violating my rights."

"Absolute nonsense, Mr. Dozier. And I expect you know that. Now, will you call your lawyer before we get moving or do we just come in and search?"

"I'll call my lawyer." Dozier had them come in to the entry area. He took out his cell phone and called. They only heard his side of the conversation, but it was clear he was unhappy. Finally, he ended the call and waved them in.

There were files. Dozier lived as he dressed, in an orderly and neat manner. More significantly, thought Sara and Nadiri, there were images of White Canadian Front rallies and even some social events. Now they had material from with which Diana Bashara, Rose Chan and John Normanson might identify who had killed Haris Bashara.

IX

Molly Malone met with Anna Crowe and Joe Grace that morning in order to move Tessa's into Stage 3.

"I welcome the opening," she said. "Now we can get our art classes and others going again. We have a lot to do. We need to have an art show in the Fall in order to signal the start of a better year. And we need to begin raising some money from our group of donors."

Anna Crowe was one of many volunteers at Tessa's Place. She was employed as the manager of the Stenbrook Gallery in the Distillery District, an art gallery specializing in Quebecois and Canadian art. She was the volunteer coordinator of the art classes at Tessa's and taught the class that met every Monday morning.

Joe Grace worked with Anna regularly in the art class in addition to teaching literacy to some of Tessa's clients. They became friends. Joe was a street person, with no fixed address or home. Molly knew some of his story and had great respect for Joe's intelligence and sensibility. Joe had, some two years ago, organized and put into action a truck which went out five nights a week providing food, blankets, medical help, and other support to some of the many homeless in the city. In addition, he had helped Danny Miller on a case in which a homeless person was killed by a member of the police.

"I've gotten in touch with our teachers," said Anna. "They're ready to come back at any time."

"Sounds good," said Molly. "What about you Joe?"

"I've been teaching online, which stinks. I'll start regular classes next week."

"All good," answered Molly. "What's happening on the truck?"

"We were as necessary in Covid as we were when we began a little over two years ago," said Joe. "The city did some stuff, but it doesn't reach everyone"

"As well" said Anna, "a lot of street people are just that, street people. They don't want to go to a hotel or a place where they feel confined. And in the hotels, we know that the danger of overdosing on drugs is greater than catching Covid. The truck is part of a lot of peoples' lives now. For example, the city just cleared out Trinity-Bellwoods Park. So now there's a tent city near Lamport Stadium. Those folks know Joe and Rob Dubois, who has been teaming with Joe. They trust the truck."

"How do you know all this?" asked Molly.

"I go out on the truck occasionally," said Anna. "It's important to have women working with the truck."

Molly raised her eyebrows. "Be careful, Anna. Don't overstretch yourself."

"Look who's talking," was the reply. "You're not exactly a good role model for a balanced life."

Molly moved on. "One more thing. Will we have enough

works to put on an art show come September? Also, I think, Anna, your friend Debra, who has joined the Board, could learn something if she was involved in the show."

"We'll have enough pieces by September if we get started next week," said Anna. "There are also works in storage that have never been shown. I'll be glad to have Debra involved. She's not only wonderful, she's smart."

Molly turned to Joe. "We'll need another *Joe Made It Happen.* Its popularity at the last three shows went a long way to making them successful. There will be an expectation of another one."

Joe winced. "I'd like another title," he said. "I like working with the group to include everyone in making an image, a large abstract painting, but I don't like the title."

"That's what it is, Joe," said Anna. "There were three versions in the three past shows. Now we need number four. People found them innovative and interesting. It will help attract a lot more people."

Joe nodded. "I went from being a bum to being a teacher and having my name on a work of art. Soon I'll buy a suit and tie."

"Are we OK?" asked Molly.

"We're fine," said Anna. "Let's get on with life coming out of Covid. If we have another shutdown, I'll go crazy."

Anna and Joe went to the art room to set it up for the classes which would begin the next week.

"You know, Anna," said Joe. "I really think sometimes of just going back to where I was three years ago. I'm a bum with what seems to be a career. I just want to be a bum sometimes."

"Joe, I think now—and I didn't think this three years ago—that life is better if you have a purpose. I don't mean making money, I mean trying to make the world a better place. It's corny, but it means something to me now after the trauma of being kidnapped and assaulted."

Joe paused, remembering what had happened to Anna. "I know," he said, as he put out supplies of paper and art materials. "But there's a lot of stuff that goes with having a 'purpose' that's a pain in the ass. Like raising money for the truck."

"In a perfect world, we wouldn't need the truck. Or *Joe Made It Happen*. Or even Tessa's."

Joe shrugged. "We'll never get that far. I told you. The normal world hides a lot of ugliness beneath its veneer of civility. Look at the graves at Residential Schools. Run by churches. The street is lousy, but at least it knows it's lousy. The normal world is also lousy for a lot of folks, but people make believe it's wonderful."

"You know what Gandhi said about Western civilization?" asked Anna.

"I know who Gandhi was, a kind of saint, but I don't know the answer to your question."

"He was asked what he thought about Western civilization. He replied that he believed it would be a good idea."

Joe laughed. "He was right then, and he would be right now."

In summer, the truck was easier to operate than in the harsh, bitter winter months. It carried sandwiches, but didn't need the warm soup that was offered in the cold. Instead of soup, the truck had fresh fruit. It also had blankets and socks, but there was less need for them now. However, the medical help—tending to some wounds, dealing with sores and coughs, the bandaging that was required—was still useful. As well, the volunteers sometimes heard stories that enabled them to ask for necessary social assistance from various city agencies.

This evening Rob Dubois was in charge, and he went out with two hired graduate students from the University of Toronto, Fatma Noor and Ernesto Garcia, known to everyone as Che. Rob, a former Roman Catholic priest (though only Joe knew this), was now a teacher of French and History at Riverdale Collegiate. Fatma was a Syrian refugee doing a masters in Social Work. Che was of Cuban background working on a doctorate in Economics. Rob had volunteered from the beginning of the truck's existence.

They made four or five visits a night, sometimes to a park where there were tents, often to a place in several of Toronto's ravines where there were tent cities. By now they were recognized by many of the homeless and accepted as part of their lives.

Covid added another dimension to the help the truck offered. Tonight the first visit was to a tent city under the Gerrard Street Bridge. It was still light when the truck arrived, in contrast to winter when the light faded early. Rob parked the truck nearby and the three went to the edge of the camp. Rob recognized several people.

"Hi Ellie, hi Willy, hi everyone. We're back to see if you need anything. We have food, sandwiches and fresh apples, tangerines and pears, and we have tea and water if you'd like some.

They were interrupted. "Rob, we need someone to tell the cops to leave us alone."

"I'm sorry," said Rob, "We haven't met yet. I don't know your name."

"Ronnie."

"Tell me what's happening, Ronnie." As this conversation was going on, Fatma and Che distributed food. When they finished, Fatma sat with the three women in the camp, and Che joined a group of men.

"The bastard cops come around and break us up. They try to get us to go into what they call a nice hotel. We don't want their hotel. We're fine here. Like everybody in this shitty world, they think they know what's best for us. We don't bother anybody. Leave us alone."

"You make a good point, Ronnie. I'll get in touch with the cops and the social services and deliver your message."

"Rob," said Willie. "There's one cop who pushes us around. He likes shoving us and even using his stick."

"Who is it?"

"I didn't get his name. His badge number is 6052."

"Thanks, Willie. I'll look after that."

"Does anyone need more food?" asked Rob. Two of the fifteen raised their hands and were looked after.

"What about medicine? Any problems, sores, scrapes?"

One of the women and two men raised their hands. They were tended to by Fatma and Rob.

"I have one more thing I'd like to ask, if you don't mind," said Rob.

Ronnie responded. "Do we have to thank Jesus for your help?"

"No," said Rob. "Your friends here will tell you we don't ask for anything. We just like to help."

Ronnie's face was skeptical, but he sat down.

"The thing I'd like to talk about is vaccines. There are vaccines available for Covid. And all the evidence is that they work very well. Covid could hurt you. It could kill you. If anyone needs a vaccine, we will arrange to get you one. It costs nothing. You're entitled to this as a person."

"There was a silence which Rob interpreted as one which needed some attention. "All right. How many of you have one shot of the vaccine?"

Two people raised their hands.

"This is not good, friends. In Ontario now over fifty percent have two shots. Over seventy percent have one shot."

"It's just another bullshit thing," was one reply.

Rob looked directly at the speaker. "It's Tom. Is that right?" A nod.

"Tom, it's not bullshit. It's the same thing as taking a polio shot so you don't get polio. We have evidence. It works. Not a hundred percent. Ninety-five percent."

"I still think it's bullshit."

"Tell me why?"

"Because a lot of people don't want it. And because a few people are making a lot of money from it. It's like war. Some people like war because they can get rich from it."

"You're not wrong, Tom. But your example doesn't apply here. You can get very sick without the vaccine."

"It's bullshit. Like the hotel being a great place. It's a great place to overdose, that's what it is."

"We'll agree to disagree. I don't want to make anyone do anything. If anyone wants a vaccine shot, you need to let us know. We'll fix something up for you."

Fatma spoke to one of the women. "I want it," said Ellie.

"OK. Fatma will arrange it. Anyone else?"

Two others signalled they wanted it. Che went to get their details.

"Thanks, everyone. We have some more stops to make. We'll be back next week."

Rob, Fatma and Che returned to the truck to move to their next site, a tent camp in the Cedarvale ravine.

As they were driving, Fatma asked, "What do we do about those who won't get the vaccine?"

"We do the same as we would do for anyone. We keep bringing it up and point to some facts."

"That doesn't work with the far right," said Che.

"Not really relevant, Che," answered Rob. "The far right behave like a movement. Lying and denying are what they do. Our people need to be convinced it can do more good than the trouble it takes to get it. We keep going."

X

Sara called Jon Normanson and Rose Chan and arranged to meet with them in her office on Friday morning, distancing as best she could. "I know you're working," she said. "But we need to identify the two men as quickly as possible."

When Rose and Jon arrived, there was coffee waiting to be poured and some donuts from Tim Horton's. "It's not as fancy as what you would get at a lawyers' office," commented Nadiri. "We did want to let you know that we appreciate your taking time out of work to help."

"Not a problem," said Rose. "We're glad we can help. It's a terrible thing that happened."

"We want you to look at a bunch of images," said Sara. "Some are pictures, some are taken from publications or a web site. Please go slowly. We are asking if you can identify one or both of the two men who committed the crime. Don't feel you have to identify anyone unless you're reasonably certain. Accuracy is very important."

"Can we look at them together?" asked Jon.

"Yes. Just put aside those images in which you think one or both of the men appear. You can even have three piles. Yes, No, and Maybe."

The couple looked carefully. Nadiri reminded them again to go slowly. They made three piles for the eighty-seven images. Fourteen were in the Yes pile, five in the Maybe, and the remainder were No.

"We're done," said Rose.

"Now," said Sara, let's all four of us look at them together and you tell us what you see. The Yes pile first."

Jon picked out an image of a rally. "Let's take this one first, because it's is the most obvious to me." "Me too," added Rose. Sara and Nadiri felt good about this, for they had found the same image as the clearest.

"They're both in the image," said Jon. "Absolutely" added Rose.

Rose continued, "They are wearing the same headbands we saw and the same shirts. You can see that. The tall one has the Raptors headband, the "We the North" slogan on it, and a black shirt.

"And," Jon continued, "the smaller one has on the black headband and a checkered shirt. His jeans are even torn at the knee."

"You can spot them in some of the others, even without those same clothes," said Rose. She picked out one of the images taken from the website. "Here, they are both in the background."

"I'm curious," said Jon, "what are these images about?"

"They are images of some people belonging to a group called the White Canadian Front," said Nadiri.

"Is that a racist group?" asked Rose.

Nadiri answered. "A lot of people call them that. Let's say, Rose, that you and I, according to these people, don't belong in Canada. You could easily look them up on the web."

"Who's the guy in front, the one with the suit?"

"The head of the organization. John Dozier."

"I've heard of him," said Jon. "He invited the American Richard Spencer to speak at one of their events. It got a lot of press."

"That's the guy."

"Let's remember, people," said Sara, "that we are here to identify killers. We can get into politics some other time."

"Well, that's them," said Jon.

They looked at the whole Yes pile and it was very clear that the same two men were in another ten images. Two of the images were blurry enough that Sara moved them to the Maybe pile. The rest of the Maybe images were either blurry or the two men were so far in the background that identification was uncertain.

"What are their names?" asked Rose.

"We don't know," said Nadiri. "Don't worry. We will know very soon. One other question. Would you be able to go to court and identify these men under oath?"

"Yes." "Absolutely."

They relaxed for ten minutes and chatted about the case and the city. Sara and Nadiri thanked the couple and they left.

The next day, the two detectives, as arranged, went to Thorncliffe Park, to the apartment of the Bashera family, to speak with Diana. They drove up Bayview to Millwood and went east on Overlea Boulevard to Thorncliffe Park Drive. They travelled past the single family homes and neat shops of Leaside to an area of high-rise apartments that became increasingly ethnic as they moved east.

Exactly on time, at ten in the morning, they found Diana sitting in a corner quietly, with relatives and friends gathered even this early, all in mourning. A sister of Diana, Emily, was looking for them. The four women went into a bedroom where they could have some privacy.

"We remain horrified at what has happened, Ms. Bashera," said Nadiri. "The whole city is upset."

"Thank you," said Diana. "I'm somewhat in shock. I hardly remember speaking to you two days ago."

"You were very brave," said Sara. "You helped a lot."

"What would you want Diana to do now?" asked Emily.

"If possible," said Nadiri, "we would like you to look at some images. We want to know if you can see the two men in any of the images we will show you."

Emily looked at Diana. "You don't have to do this."

"I do have to do this. We can't let those men walk around and damage more families."

Again, Nadiri cautioned the witness to go slowly and to arrange three piles.

It took time, time that in the atmosphere of a house in mourning seemed endless and even somewhat heartless. At one point, Sara asked Diana if she wanted to continue. She nodded and concentrated.

Finally, she was done. The piles were very close to being the same as those of Rose and Jon. The identification of the two men was clear. Again, Sara asked if she would testify in court. Diana simply said, "Yes."

When they finished, both Sara and Nadiri stayed for a half hour, sitting among the mourners. Mainly, it was quiet. But they were asked a few questions by relatives about the investigation. Nadiri used what little Arabic she knew when she replied, mixing Arabic, some Farsi, and mainly English.

On the way home, Sara said, "We'll get them. I'm glad. I think I should leave a message for the boss."

"He'll be pleased. What happens now?"

"We have John Dozier coming in to the station tomorrow morning."

"Will he talk?"

"He'll talk. Not talking in this kind of matter is a crime. Obstruction of justice. He talks or we arrest him."

Dozier appeared with his lawyer, who identified himself as Allen Walker. Both Sara and Nadiri knew of Walker, the defender of holocaust deniers, white nationalists, violators of gun laws, and neo-Nazis.

They continued to be masked and physically distanced at interviews, playing it safe. After they identified themselves on the tape, Walker spoke. "What are you accusing my client of?"

"Nothing," replied Sara. "We are here as part of our investigation of the murder of Haris Bashera three days ago. Mr. Dozier has some information which is central to the investigation and we'd like to ask him about it."

"What kind of information?"

"We are going to ask Mr. Dozier to identify two men from images we will be showing him. Those photos were in his files and on the web site of the White Canadian Front. We have clear reason to suspect these two men of being the people who committed the crime."

"My client doesn't have to say anything. He has the protection of the *Charter*."

"I think you are not correct in this case, Mr. Walker," said Nadiri. "You know section 139 of the Canadian Criminal Code. I'll recite a piece of it for Mr. Dozier's benefit. 'Everyone who wilfully attempts in any manner…to obstruct, pervert or defeat the course of justice is guilty of an indictable offence and liable to imprisonment for a term not exceeding ten years.' For the record, I left out a reference to another section which is not relevant."

"Can we see the images?"

"Of course. That's the purpose of this meeting."

Sara took out the image of the rally and three others. "We need you to identify two men." She pointed to the two identified by Rose, Jon and Diana. "I will inform you that we have clear information that they were involved in the crime."

Dozier looked at the images. He was silent. Sara let some time pass and then asked, "Who are they, Mr. Dozier? You are in these images too. You know these men."

Finally, Dozier said, "Can I have a private conference with my lawyer?"

"We'll give you five minutes." Sara shut off the tape and she and Nadiri left the room.

Outside, Sara said, "Are they that stupid? If he refuses, we'll arrest him and the newspapers will dump on him and the Front. If we arrest the two men, he can claim rightly that he had no hand in the killing and he cooperated with the law."

"They're not that stupid, Sara. They just need time to talk it over."

At the five-minute mark, Sara and Nadiri returned to the room and the tape was resumed.

"Well, Mr. Dozier," asked Sara, "who are they?"

Dozier replied quietly, "They are Karl Geistmeier and Michael Yellen."

"Which is which?"

"The one with the 'We the North' headband is Geistmeier."

"Are they members of your organization?"

"They were. As of this moment they are expelled."

Nadiri asked, "Do they have nicknames?"

Dozier winced and looked to Walker, who nodded. "Geistmeier is known as Goebbels. Yellen is just Mikey."

"Do you have their addresses in your records?" asked Sara. "Remember that we can easily get another warrant."

Walker put his hand on Dozier's arm to stop him from replying and said, "We have an email address."

"That's not what I asked. Do you have their home addresses?"

"My client has the addresses they gave to him several years ago when they joined the organization."

"We will accompany you to your office, Mr. Dozier, in order to get those addresses."

"Is there anything else?" asked Walker.

"No. We'll drive Mr. Dozier home and we'll get the addresses and any other relevant information."

They ended the session and silently drove back to Coxwell Avenue. As both Sara and Nadiri suspected, Dozier's meticulous personal style carried over to his record-keeping. He had a hard-copy file card for each member. On it was the kind of personal information that any organization might require: name, address, telephone numbers, email address, and identification (both men used their Ontario driver's license). Geistmeier was listed as working for a roofing company. Yellen was said to be a plumber's helper.

Sara and Nadiri hastened back to the station and put into place all that was necessary to find the two men, from an all-points bulletin to other jurisdictions to a most wanted bulletin for Toronto and Ontario. The addresses of the two men were in the north-eastern edge of the city, Geistmeier in an apartment near Finch and Markham Road, Yellen several blocks north near McNicoll and Tapscott.

Both women took their guns with them as they drove to Scarborough.

They stopped first at Geistmeier's address, part of a high-rise apartment complex. They managed to get to the caretaker who informed them that he had no person named Geistmeier on the list of tenants.

"Did you know anyone by that name?" asked Sara.

"I only came here ten months ago. What I can do is look at the records on my machine." He did so and then added.

"He left here three years ago."

"Any forwarding address?"

"No. There's a note here saying that we didn't need to forward his mail."

"Did he cause any problems?"

"There's a bunch of complaints that the place is too noisy. Nothing else."

They thanked him and moved on to Yellen's place. It was a single high-rise with, as told by the many balconies, a large number of studio apartments. However, Mike Yellen was listed at the entryway index, with a code to call up.

The ringing of the call was answered. "Is this Mike Yellen?"

"Yeah. What do you want?"

"We have a delivery of a package. I was told to give it only to you. It's from a plumbing supply house."

"I didn't order anything."

"I don't know about that. It says on the package that this is a free gift from a new supplier. They don't list the apartment number."

"307." And the door buzzed.

Before they took the elevator Nadiri called 42 Division and asked for a car and police officers to help with a possible arrest in apartment 307. "Ten minutes" was the response.

They went to the apartment and knocked on the door. When it opened, Sara and Nadiri had their identification open for Yellen to see. He recoiled but couldn't manage to close the door and keep them out.

When they entered Nadiri simply said, "Mr. Michael Yellen. You are under arrest in connection with a murder and a beating on Baldwin Street three days ago. You have a right to call a lawyer."

Yellen panicked and tried to leave. Nadiri easily pinned his arm behind his back and Sara tripped him so that he was on the floor. Then Sara took out her gun. "Don't move, Mr. Yellen. You're in enough trouble already."

Yellen stayed on the floor and started to shiver. "I have rights," he shouted. "You can't do this to me."

"We will protect your rights," said Nadiri. "We have a clear identification of you being on Baldwin Street and beating a man and a woman. The man died. You are being charged at this moment with assault and suspicion of murder. We'll take you downtown and give you a phone. You don't have to say anything without having a lawyer present."

"Fuck you, you Arab bitch. You're ruining this country."

"And what are you doing, Mr. Yellen? This would be laughable if it wasn't tragic. A man died because you decided he didn't belong."

Sara signalled to Nadiri to let it go for the moment. By this time two officers had arrived. Yellen was given into their custody and they drove him downtown to the cells reserved for suspects.

Sara called Danny and put on the speaker phone so that Nadiri could hear and participate. "Good work," he said. "I suggest we give Yellen the time and opportunity to talk with a lawyer. Then he should be interviewed first thing tomorrow morning. Of course, put out information on Geistmeier in the GTA and a bit beyond."

"What about the press?"

"We can wait until tomorrow to announce that we have a suspect and whatever else we learn. I'll call a press conference for tomorrow afternoon. This is a big story. We don't have closure, but we do have a result in hand. By the afternoon, we may have more. We also may need to give the press information on Geistmeier and let them help us find him. Let's give all this some thought and we'll talk tomorrow morning."

Sara looked at Nadiri. She nodded. Sara gestured to Nadiri to speak. "Sounds good, sir. We'll arrange for legal aid if Yellen doesn't have counsel."

"Well done. Keep going and keep in touch."

"Will do."

XI

What Sara and Nadiri didn't know was that Danny had met in person the previous Friday afternoon with John Kingston, at the Chief's request, to discuss relations with communications and the press.

After they greeted one another, Danny said, "Am I being called on the carpet?"

"Not really, Danny," replied Kingston. "However, we need to talk about you and Communications. And there's something else I want to get your opinion about."

"John, I thought about it. I overreacted, admittedly. But I really think the Communications people have it wrong."

"I haven't yet had a conversation with Thelma. They do have a role, you know."

"I suppose," said Danny. "Let's just talk about our relations with the press and the media."

"Our relations with the press and the media are important. They shape how the public sees us. We need the public, let's say the mom and pop who work hard and put their kids through university, to feel good when they see us or encounter us. Otherwise, our job is ten times harder. Think about what happens in Chicago."

"You're correct. So what am I doing that hurts us?"

Kingston smiled. "Nothing, Danny. Other than getting into a public fight with a fellow officer."

"Sure, we both should have stifled it until we got into a back room. Agreed."

"Here's where I am on this. I've thought about why you are viewed by Thelma and others as a problem. You have differing views about the press."

"What do you mean?"

"I'll do something you do occasionally. Answer a question with a question. Tell me, how do you see the role of the press?"

"They can be a pain, but they are absolutely necessary. They hold us accountable, as they should do in a democracy. Sure, there are some of them that are annoying. There are also some of us that are annoying. But these days we have politicians like our premier trying to avoid them, much less the people down south who call the press enemies of the people. No, in a democracy they are as important as we are…."

Danny stopped and put up his hand. He thought for a moment. "Now I get it, John. Thelma and I have different views on what the press is doing."

"You got it," said Kingston. "She, and the whole Communications team, see them as adversaries. You see them as part of the democratic process. For them, the press is always a danger. For you it's necessary."

"Good thinking, John. Now I get why we clash. I'm uncomfortable sometimes with the press, but they have a very important job to do."

"That's also why the press seems to like you, Danny. You treat them as important to our well-being."

"That's because they are."

"I agree. Let me talk with Thelma. I think this can be sorted out. It may need a long meeting with Communications. We'll see. The one thing they can't deny is that you and I are regarded well by the media and the press. That certainly doesn't hurt the force."

"So, what am I supposed to do?"

"Be who you are. But also respect that other people might have an idea or two on this which would be useful."

"Fair enough."

"The other matter. Why are we experiencing more violent, random acts?"

"I sort of said it at the press conference. It's not just about Canada or Toronto. Politicians, mainly down south, a few here, are enabling people who are bigoted and violent with their words and deeds. Things like saying guns are owned by a lot of nice people, so don't take them away. Or code words for white power, as we see in the killing on Baldwin Street. Or in the very nasty demonstrations of anti-vaxxers. It's not that people didn't have these beliefs or feelings before. But now it's acceptable in some places to say things that couldn't be said before."

"I'm inclined to agree," said Kingston. "It's sad. And it's not only about Jews and Blacks. It includes Muslims, as we just experienced, and it's moving to include immigrants and refugees in general."

"I wish it weren't so. I thought of the right word for it. It's a coarsening of our public life."

Kingston sighed. "It's sad. I expect we have to keep on it. You know, there are over five million people in the GTA. It only takes a handful of them to destroy the peace of our public life which is more fragile than we think, Danny."

"We've learned, John, that civilized life is very fragile. Peace, order and good government are hard won."

"Thanks for the conversation, Danny. It doesn't make me happy but it helps me feel I understand it."

"Thank you, John. With any other chief, I'd be reprimanded."

"We're all on the same side, as I said. Even Thelma. Now let's get on with the important stuff."

"Will do," said Danny as he rose to leave.

As Danny was near the door, Kingston said, "Oh, I forgot something."

Danny turned. "Yes?"

"Shabbat Shalom, Danny."

Danny smiled. "Shalom Aleichem to you and your family, John. Peace be in the world."

"Amen."

XII

Sara and Nadiri interviewed Mikey Yellen on Monday morning, with Danny watching via the one-way mirror. He had called another press conference for the afternoon and wanted to have as close a feel for the case as possible.

Yellen arrived with a young lawyer, Kevin O'Hara. When O'Hara gave his card to Sara, she and Nadiri learned that he worked in the office of John Dozier's attorney, Alan Walker.

Sara opened the session. "Mr. Yellen, we believe that you and Mr. Geistmeier were responsible for the assault and murder that occurred on Baldwin Street several days ago. Do you have anything to say about the matter?"

O'Hara responded. "My client has no comment."

"We are charging you with both assault and manslaughter," said Nadiri. Can you tell us anything that may help you?"

"No comment," again replied O'Hara.

"Do you know where Karl Geistmeier lives?"

O'Hara let Yellen answer. "No. He lives in Scarborough. That's all I know."

"We are searching for him. Do you know where he might be hiding?"

"No."

"Can you can tell us anything that would help us find him?"

"No."

Sara then asked, "Are you and Mr. Geistmeier friends?"

But O'Hara again intervened with the ritual of "My client has no comment."

After trying several more questions, Sara gave up hoping they would learn anything and ended the session. Yellen was escorted back to his cell.

Danny, Sara and Nadiri walked silently back to Danny's office. When they were seated, Nadiri said, "The strategy is to protect Geistmeier."

"Yes," Danny said. "I wondered if they would try to throw Geistmeier to the wolves to protect Yellen. Not so. The point is that we are no closer to finding Geistmeier."

"Well, we'll just keep looking. Lots of people are on the search."

Danny leaned back. "So, Sara. How does it feel to be on a case?"

"It's interesting, even exciting. I get the tension. But it would have been harder if we hadn't had your insight. I sense that this isn't a normal case."

"From what I've learned," said Nadiri, "there are no normal cases. There are just cases. The simplest is the ugly domestic matter where one spouse kills another. But you have to look at each one with fresh eyes."

"I think, boss," said Sara, "that I should do this every so often. Maybe once or twice a year. It helps me to understand what happens on the squad. I think it also helps me choose better when I assign people to cases."

"No argument, Sara," said Danny. "We'll sort out how to do it. Later today I'd like both of you at the press conference. You may not have to speak but the public should know who's on the case."

At the press conference, Danny opened by narrating what led to discovering who killed Haris Bashera and assaulted Diana Bashera and noted that one of the two people, Michael Yellen, was under arrest. He acknowledged that the investigating team was led by Sara and Nadiri, and then opened the floor to questions.

"Do you know which person actually killed Haris?"

"We're gathering information. Both men hit him. That's clear."

"Is this something that was ordered by the White Canadian Front?" asked the CTV reporter.

"No, John. The two belonged to the Front. The leader of the Front, John Dozier, co-operated in helping us to identify them."

"Are you saying something nice about the Front?" This comment was made by the CBC.

"I'm telling you what happened. Mr. Dozier was asked to cooperate. His lawyer agreed that he was required to do so under the law or else face a charge of obstruction of justice which could lead to a jail sentence. He answered our questions."

"Do you think being in the Front contributed to the beating and the killing?"

Danny looked to the rear, where Thelma Leighton was standing. This time she didn't shake her head. She simply refused to look back at Danny and kept her head down.

"I can't answer that with a yes or a no, Rosalie. I can say that I believe—and this is me talking, not anyone else—that when hate is elevated to a norm, it contributes to a growing acceptance of this kind of behaviour."

"What about Geistmeier? Are you close to finding him?" asked *The Star*.

"That's one of the purposes of this press conference. We want your help in the press and in the media in general and we want the help of the public. We have distributed images of him and a description of the clothes he was wearing. He owns a ten year old Ford pick-up vehicle and we have distributed the license plate number. We will be monitoring his use of credit cards and his banking. We have a hot-line number for people to call."

"So you're not close?"

"He's not around the corner. You know how difficult it is to disappear these days for any length of time in our connected world. He'll be found. I have no doubt about it."

XIII

The next day Nadiri had dinner at the apartment of her partner, Debra Castle. It was located in the east end of the Greek part of the Danforth, in a house that had been turned into three units. Nadiri had taken it upon herself to try to teach Debra some basic cooking skills. Debra had none when they met three years ago, having been brought up on KD and canned pasta. By now, she could make roast chicken, eggs of different sorts, some interesting sandwiches, and some basic sauces. Tonight, the lesson was how to bread a cutlet and make a simple but elegant chicken Milanese.

Nadiri brought most of the ingredients because Debra still didn't keep much in the house. By now, she could rely on there being salt, pepper, olive oil, butter, eggs, and flour in Debra's fridge and cupboard, a big improvement on what she might have found some time ago when they began this monthly ritual.

Debra even had a food processor, which had been donated to her by their friend Anna Crowe when Anna stayed with Debra for several weeks, recovering from her ordeal of kidnapping and rape. Anna did the cooking for them both at that time and she would go to a kitchen store nearby on the Danforth to get things like the processor, a good frying pan, tongs and spatulas. When she was able to return to her own place, she insisted Debra keep those items. "Nadiri will teach you," she said, "and she'll be happy these things are here."

"First," said Nadiri, "we make basil oil." Nadiri insisted that Debra participate as part of the learning process, so she gave instructions, sometimes intervening to show how things were done.

"OK," she ordered. "Put about half a cup of olive oil and a cup of basil leaves into the processor." Debra managed. "Now, take a fat garlic clove…"

"Define fat," said Debra, a grin on her face.

"Cut it out. This is serious. Take the garlic bulb and get a fat one. If there's no fat one, get two medium ones. Dice them. Remember how to hold the garlic and the knife."

Debra obeyed, this time behaving seriously.

"Now put the garlic with the other stuff in the processor. Put in some salt. As much as you think will help. All of these kinds of recipes say…"

"Salt to taste. I know. Make sure I don't overdo it."

"Now, purée the mess until it's smooth."

"Done. Can I guess what happens now?"

"Sure."

"You brought cherry tomatoes and mozzarella. The basil oil goes on them."

"Good. What do you do first"

"You cut up the tomatoes and the cheese. Even I know that."

"You're getting there. Do it and set the salad aside."

"Now," continued Nadiri, "we make the chicken cutlets. Let's lay out the flour, egg and panko bread crumbs. I'll do the first one and you can follow."

They finished preparing and cooking the cutlets, put them on plates with the salad and lemon wedges, and took the plates to the table, on which there was a good bottle of sauvignon.

As they sat down, Debra said, "I'm getting it. You can make interesting food without having to be a gourmet chef. For the first time, I'm beginning to like this. I could easily make a version of this for myself."

"A lot nicer than Kraft Dinner. Let's eat."

After a few bites, and after praise for the food, Debra said, "I've been wanting to talk to you about my job."

"Any problems?"

"I don't know. I find the whole thing puzzling."

"How?"

"To put it simply, I've been 'Manager, Humanities, Literature, and User Education' at the Metro Library for the last year and a half and I haven't yet done the job. The whole system shut down two months after I moved to Metro. You know I became someone who was a troubleshooter. I stepped in as temporary head of several branches when people retired or got sick. But there was almost nothing to do. I got in touch with colleagues in branches who were at home to try to boost morale. Then, we spent a lot of time figuring out how to adjust to technology. Then, I continued to troubleshoot and pivoted into training."

"Didn't you have contact with the public?"

"Very little. A huge portion of the population lost access. We moved online. But some of the people who used the library regularly didn't have home computers, so moving to online programming was not only difficult, it was impossible for many. On top of this, the province flip-flopped a lot and this indecision contributed to uncertainty and chaos.

"So, for fourteen months we technically had curbside service sometimes and online access to books and films for those who wanted that. There was great frustration for colleagues and for the public. Wanda Eng, a friend at Leaside, told me…Debra lifted her hands to make quotation marks…'It's hard not being able to help people when that is your job.'"

"We had problems as police," commented Nadiri, "but nothing like that."

"You had your job. You didn't lose your identity." Then Debra smiled and added, "People still stole and killed. I'm not being cynical. Think about Gabriella. She could no longer do what was her identity. She couldn't play music with others or conduct in any meaningful way. Librarians were no longer doing what we are meant to do. There were massive accessibility issues. Librarians, like musicians, struggled to find what we could do. Did you know that some called regular senior clients at home? The frustration led to trying to find new ways to help people.

"I'll finish my rant soon," said Debra, as she drained her wine glass and put it out in the middle of the table. "More please, Nadiri.

"One more matter. We had lots of requests from parents

who were struggling to keep their kids reading. They reached out and we tried to help them. And the help we gave to people—at tax time, to assist in filling out forms for everything from immigration to pensions—simply ended. A lot of people regarded their library as part of their community. People lost a good part of their social lives. As soon as things opened even a little bit, when clients re-appeared they just wanted to talk. The librarian who watches everyone and says 'shh' with her finger to her lips doesn't exist anymore.

"Enough," she added. "I'll stop. I've been holding this in. Thanks for letting me vent."

"What are you going to do about the job?"

"I don't know. We're opening up slowly. Things will get better. You took a new job in Major Crimes and decided you didn't like it as much as Homicide. You did crime and found it boring. So, you moved back when you could."

"That's not quite it. I found it less interesting and less exciting than Homicide. Murder has an edge that stimulates me more than solving a bank robbery. I also find that sometimes in Homicide you really feel you are working on the side of justice, not only on the side of law."

"Well, I like being on the side of books. And I like helping people. I'll try this job out and if it satisfies me, that's good. If it doesn't, then I have some thinking to do."

XIV

Nadiri had a meeting scheduled with Sara Bellucci the next morning. She assumed it was about her role now that the Bashera case was solved. The police were actively looking for Karl Geistmeier but there was little if anything for Nadiri to do further on the matter. She hoped she would be assigned a new case.

When she entered Sara's office there were two people present, Sara and a young woman Nadiri had never met before. "Good morning, Sergeant," opened Sara. "I'd like to introduce you to Constable Katie Nelson."

Nelson rose and she and Nadiri bumped elbows. Nelson was slightly shorter than Nadiri's five and a half feet, blond and blue-eyed, of medium build. Her face was pleasant, a small nose, full lips, and, Nadiri noted, her skin seemed flawless. She wore a wedding band.

They sat distanced, still careful and in the habit of the last sixteen months, even though all were fully vaccinated and not required to do this in Stage Three.

"I brought you together," said Sara, "because the Inspector and I would like you to partner for a time." She looked at Nadiri. "Katie is joining the unit and she could benefit from being with a senior experienced person."

She then turned to Nelson. "Sergeant Rahimi was with us for several years, moved to Major Crimes and is now returning to Homicide. She has an exemplary record in both places and can help you get experience here."

"Thank you, ma'am," said Nelson. She then faced Nadiri. "I hope we'll work well together."

"So do I," responded Nadiri. "We'll get to know one another as we work together. What's your background?"

"I'm thirty. I have a degree in Law and Society from York and I have been with 42 Division in Scarborough since I came onto the force. I've had policing in my life since I was born. My father and grandfather were on the force and I have an uncle who is a member of the RCMP. I'd like to think I have policing in my DNA."

"I have a degree in sociology from the U of T," said Nadiri. "And lots of experience in both catching thieves and murderers. When I was here as a junior I partnered with Inspector Miller, a really good teacher."

They exchanged some small talk and the Nadiri asked Sara, "Do you have a case for us?"

"Not yet," replied Sara. "As you know, one will come up. Soon. In the meanwhile, you two can do some work on violent crimes, especially domestic ones. We have so many because of the restrictions and tensions of Covid."

When Katie and Nadiri left and sat down together at Nadiri's desk, Nadiri said, "You should start by reading some files of recent cases to get a feel for what we do and how cases are handled."

"Do I really need to do this?" asked Katie. I've been

hearing about cases at the kitchen table all my life."

"I think it will help you get oriented to your new work," replied Nadiri. "Everybody does this. We can talk about the cases and I can answer any questions you might have."

Katie pursed her lips just enough to show some annoyance. "Yes ma'am," she replied.

"I'll get you some files," replied Nadiri. She rose and went to the filing area. 'So now I'm a ma'am,' she thought. 'Let's see how this turns out. Remember to give her the benefit of the doubt. She's nervous. Let's see how she behaves on the job.'

For the next two days, Katie read files and they discussed how the cases were handled. "I don't see any formula," said Katie. "Am I missing something?"

"What do you mean by formula?"

"There's usually a process. As in a lot of what we do. This is the way you deal with someone who is speeding. This is the way to handle a break and enter. I don't get that from what I'm reading. Or maybe you guys don't have a formula."

"There are things we do, Katie, that follow a template. For example, we are required to tell people their rights. We can only hold someone in custody for a specific period of time. If someone wants a lawyer, we wait until she has one. We always call forensics. And more.

"But there is no formula for solving a murder. There are murders. Some are like others we have seen and that gives us some guidance. That's one of the reasons you're reading files. Experience does make a difference. But I firmly believe—and the boss does too—that you don't fit the murder into a formula. You figure out the best way to deal with the individual case in front of you."

"Aren't most cases alike?"

"No. You start with the case. For example, Sergeant Bellucci and I were on the recent case of a murder of an Islamic-Canadian at Kensington Market. Figuring out how to find the killers in that particular instance didn't fit any formula.

"There's one thing the Inspector insists on. You don't give up. He has a really nimble mind about homicides, but people forget that he is very, very determined. He has the best statistics because of that, not only because he's smart."

The two also went out on one domestic violence case. It was not at all complicated. Katie deferred to Nadiri and watched how it was handled.

Then they got their case. Sara called Nadiri. "There's a body on Dovercourt, near Bloor. It's yours."

Nadiri and Katie drove to the scene. "What do we do?" asked Katie.

"We wait for forensics to do their job. We wait for the medical people to examine the body. Then we see who is around and start asking questions. Go in with a fresh mind. Don't make any assumptions."

"It sounds like we don't know what to do."

"We'll know what to do when we get there."

"Well, there are a lot of immigrants in that area. Maybe that matters."

"And maybe it doesn't matter. We'll have to see."

"Are you an immigrant?"

"Does it matter?"

"Just asking."

By this time, they had arrived at a familiar scene. An area roped off, a small group of people behind a tape, an officer standing in front of a low storefront, in this case a local dental office.

Nadiri and Katie went to the officer at the scene. They showed their credentials and Nadiri asked Officer John Metexis what was happening.

"The person who opened up this morning went into the office and found a body. Someone shot. She called 911. The forensics people are already inside."

"Thanks," said Nadiri. "We'll go inside."

They entered a reception area for what Nadiri had noted from outside was an office for three dentists, Rui DaCosta, Stefano Locotelli, and James Marson. In a corner, two women and one man were seated alongside another officer.

Behind a French door were several small rooms with dental chairs, a place for storage and a separate office with two desks. Nadiri knocked on the French door and Dr. Emily Chow from forensics soon appeared.

"Hi, Nadiri."

Nadiri turned to Katie and introduced her. Then, she said, "What's happening?"

"A murder. One of the dentists, James Marson, was shot to death last night. We're almost finished. I'll let you know when you can come in."

Nadiri and Katie left to go back to the reception area. Nadiri asked Officer Brett Overholt what had been done so far.

"We got here about an hour ago," Overholt said and turned toward one of the waiting women. "Ms. Howard found the body a little before nine when she opened up. She called 911 and here we are."

"Thanks, Officer," said Nadiri. She turned to the three sitting together. "I'm Detective Sergeant Nadiri Rahimi and my partner is Detective Constable Katie Nelson. First, could you tell me who you are and why you're here."

"I'm Janet Howard," replied a woman of about thirty-five. I'm a receptionist here and I usually open up the office."

The other woman, slightly younger than Janet Howard, identified herself as a second receptionist, Amy Zhao. The man, about forty-five, said, "I'm Dr. Rui DaCosta. I'm one of the three partners in this office. I've known James since dental school. This is a terrible thing."

Emily Chow appeared and indicated she was finished. "Do you want to see the body? You can come in now."

Nadiri and Katie followed Chow into the interior area. To their left were four rooms with dental chairs and other apparatus, clearly used for patients. To the right was one other cubicle for patients, a small space for x-rays, a storage room and an office.

Chow took them to the office. On the floor beside a desk was the body of James Marson. A chair which had fallen was nearby. He was dressed in pants and a white shirt, now red with blood. His body was on its side, and Nadiri could see two bullet holes, one in his upper body and one in his head.

There were papers on the desk that Nadiri and Katie would soon get to. Nadiri looked at Emily Chow, asking the ordinary question with a facial expression.

Chow, as usual, was as economical and efficient with her report as she was with her doctoring. "He was killed with one of the two bullets. The other might have been insurance, just to make certain he was dead. I'll know more when I do the autopsy tomorrow. It was last night. I'll say now between seven and midnight. I might be able to be more specific tomorrow."

"Thanks, Emily." Nadiri then looked at Katie. "Anything you want to ask?"

"Do we know the gun?," asked Katie.

"Not yet," said Chow. "We'll know when I dig out the bullets."

"OK," said Nadiri. "Let's get the body to the morgue. Katie, we'll start with the person who found him."

They went with Janet Howard to the storage room, where there were also some chairs.

Howard was distraught and Nadiri went slowly. "If you could just tell us what happened when you opened up," she said, "that would help."

After wiping her eyes with a tissue, Howard replied. "There's not much to say. I opened up a little before nine, as usual. Everything seemed normal. I put away my bag and opened the computer. I printed out a bunch of the day's schedules. Then I went to the back to post the schedule in the rooms. I passed the office and there he was."

"Did you touch anything?"

"I did. I looked for pulse. Probably I shouldn't have done that, but I had to know. I thought maybe I could help him."

"You did the right thing," said Nadiri. "And then?"

"I called 911. I went out to the reception area and waited a short time. That's it."

"How long have you worked here?" asked Nadiri.

"Almost five years."

"Has anything arisen which might explain this?"

"Dr. Marson was a nice guy. We have some patients who get unhappy when they are told they need a lot of work, but that happens everywhere. It's an efficient office. All the doctors are busy and we have several dental assistants who clean patients' teeth."

"Are there any personal problems?" asked Katie.

"We get along. I work regularly with Amy. We're not close friends, but we like one another."

"Anybody here who would murder somebody?" said Katie.

Nadiri moved her chair a bit in order to put herself partly between Katie and Howard. "We'll get to that another time," she said. "Soon. Thanks, Ms. Howard. Please leave your phone number and personal email address with the officer outside." She then stood up to indicate the interview had ended and walked outside with Howard to the reception area.

"Give me a few minutes," she said to Amy Zhao and Rui DaCosta, and returned to the storage area and sat facing Katie.

"Katie, you can't do this. One of us takes the lead. Now it's me because I'm the experienced one. If you want to ask a question, give me a signal. Then as you did at first, you follow where the interview is going. You don't just ask someone who is emotional and upset if they know anyone in this office who would murder somebody."

"Why not? My grandfather told me of a case that he solved with that question. The person identified someone who turned out to be the killer."

"It's early days, Katie, and we are dealing with a difficult moment for the people we're interviewing. All that can do is throw them."

"My grandfather was an old-fashioned cop. He put people in a corner."

"We no longer do it that way. Please follow my lead."

"OK, ma'am. You're the boss."

They interviewed Zhao and DaCosta and got no further than the information given by Howard. Nadiri indicated to both that they would be speaking to them again soon.

Nadiri called Sara to ask if she should inform the family of Marson's death or if the squad might send someone to do it, after summing up what had happened.

"I know what you're asking," said Sara. "You stay and go through the office to see what we can get. I'll send someone to Marson's house on Dawlish Avenue in Lawrence Park. But you'll need to interview the family soon."

It made things easier that Marson had his own desk and the other one was shared by his partners. Nadiri had asked the three earlier if they knew the code to Marson's personal computer. They all replied negatively.

The desk had pictures of his family on top, his wife and two children. In the larger drawers there were only professional matters, copies of letters to various periodontists, endodontists, and others about patients, a few professional journals with some pages which had been saved with yellow stickers, and some notes he had retained for whatever reason. One small drawer was seemingly personal. It contained a lease for an apartment on Madison Avenue in the Annex, and some hydro bills for the last few months on which Marson noted the date of his payment. In addition, there was a copy of a will, signed only two months ago.

Nadiri and Katie left with Marson's computer in order to take it to the lab to open and see what they could get.

XV

The next Friday the Feldmans had their first 'normal' Friday night since early March 2020, after sixteen long and frustrating months.

Not only would Gabriella, Danny and Avi be there. Avi brought his girlfriend, Molly Gerber, and Deborah, who now had her own apartment on St. George Street, brought along her long-time boyfriend James Erman. Also invited were a couple from the Feldman's synagogue, Helene Gordon and Stephen Walter, who had attended one of the last Shabbat meals before the shutdown.

They all just wanted a kind of normality, and relished its possibility. When Danny arrived, Gabriella was already in the kitchen, her customary blue apron around her waist, helping Ruth prepare the meal. He hugged both women and sat at the table in order to receive his nosh, a piece of gefilte fish accompanied by a slice of rye bread *mit kimmel*, with seeds.

"I've longed for this," said Ruth. "We need our rituals and our connections with the world."

"Speaking of rituals and connections," added Gabriella, "did I tell you that Danny and I are again playing with

Bloor Street on Wednesdays?"

"How is it going?" asked Ruth.

"We're rusty," said Danny. "In fact, we're not close to where we were sixteen months ago. Playing with others is totally different from doing it online."

"You'll get there. Any chance of a public concert in the fall?"

"Unlikely," said Gabriella. "We'll just keep at it. We're already a lot better than we were two weeks ago."

"Danny," said Ruth, "Irwin asked that you go up to see him before dinner. He has something he wants to discuss with you."

"Another old ritual," said Danny. "Probably, we should be less self-conscious about life and just live it."

"No reason we can't do both," said Gabriella. "We live and think about how we live at the same time. Just as we did at our first gathering of music a few weeks ago and told ourselves it's time to get back in shape."

Danny went upstairs to Irwin's study and knocked on the open door. Irwin looked up and smiled. "Come in, Danny. It's time for us to schmooze together again."

The two brothers-in-law were now close friends, a friendship that developed after a very careful several years during which each had some skepticism about the other. They had reached an unspoken mutually agreed peace, bound together by their love for Ruth. Irwin, a modern Orthodox Jew and a partner and senior member of Sachs LLP, one of the biggest and most prestigious law firms in the country, thought Danny too casual with regard to his practice of Judaism and somewhat strange in his choice of profession. Danny found Irwin too rigid in his thinking and too sure of the rightness of his beliefs. As the years went on, each realized he was wrong about the other and they dropped their defenses and came to value the relationship and the other's judgment.

They exchanged small talk and then Irwin said, "I'd like to pass a thought by you. I don't need an answer, but I'd like your opinion now or after you have a chance to think about it."

"Sure. What is it?"

"I don't believe that everything can or should go back to where it was before Covid. We'll have a new normal. Some of it, like Shabbat, will be like the old normal. Some won't."

"I certainly agree with that."

"Well, I wonder how and what the big law firms should change, now that we've had the covid experience. Some partners say nothing should change, others say we must think about it."

"What side are you on?"

"We need to think about it. A lot. Covid revealed that the system doesn't have enough support for those who are needy or in trouble. We need to talk about what our obligations happen to be. The big law firms are too tied to those who have money, be they corporations or individuals."

"You're sounding like your daughter," said Danny with a smile on his face.

"You may be right. I told Deborah to get settled in a large Bay Street firm. But instead, with your support I have to say, she decided to go into a very good small firm that does a lot of pro bono work. Other young people are doing the same."

"You know," said Danny, "I told you some time ago that were I to need a lawyer I couldn't afford your firm. And I'm somewhere at the bottom of the top ten percent in my earnings. The best lawyers aren't working for most of us. In fact, they probably mostly work for big corporations."

"I never saw it as a problem," said Irwin, "until Deborah became the go-to person in her small five-person firm for pro bono work on cases related to Covid. They are many, too many."

"Let me try it on you this way, Irwin. If I need a new knee or a hip I use a health care system open to all. Since I live in Toronto I'll probably be operated on by a top surgeon, no matter what my means. If I believe a corporation has done me wrong, the corporation hires your firm and I hire someone who works on his own or is in a small firm. Not that there aren't good lawyers working independently on their own, but the corporation has resources I can't fathom."

"Do you think we should have a universal legal system?"

"No. Your implication is correct. The analogy isn't perfect. But it's not totally imperfect either. Lawyers are part of a legal system and, as you and others will agree, have responsibilities to the system. The question is, are you meeting those responsibilities? If not, how do you adjust?"

"A lot of lawyers in my firm don't want to adjust if it means they will make less money."

"That's part of it. But I agree that's it's worth thinking about one's obligations to society every so often. What happened during Covid might be a good time to do so."

At that moment there was a knock on the door. Gabriella appeared. "Our guests are here, gentlemen. Ruth said it's time to welcome Shabbat."

They went downstairs. Everyone greeted one another and they then welcomed the Sabbath with songs sung by their people for centuries. Irwin recited the traditional blessing, which includes the passages from Genesis establishing a day of rest after the Creation. Deborah recited the blessing of thanks over the challah.

When the fish was served and everyone was seated, Stephen Walter turned to Danny. "I read in the *Globe* that a dentist was murdered."

"Really?" said Gabriella, "I didn't know, Stephen, that dentists got murdered."

"They don't," said Walter, a prominent periodontist who also taught at the dental school at the University of Toronto. "That's why I'm asking. Dentists don't get murdered, they don't rob people, they're not lovers in life or in literature. We are not heroes or villains in films or TV series. We're anonymous."

"Even more anonymous than accountants," said Ruth.

"Absolutely," added Stephen. "We are the most boring of all the professionals." He looked around the room. "Detectives, musicians, lawyers, academics, even scientists like Helene, all get to be part of the drama of life."

"Maybe the murder means you're moving up in the world," said James.

"Let me say," said Danny, "that there was indeed a murder of a dentist. And add that this is also a first for me."

"Are you on it, Dad?" asked Avi.

"One of our best people is in charge. We'll see what happens."

"What if he was murdered by another dentist?" said Stephen.

Danny laughed. "That would be a double first. I've not experienced either in all my time on the force."

They then moved into several conversations. Stephen was known to have a deep interest in classical music and Ruth seated him across from Gabriella. Avi, Molly and James talked about their hopes for school in September. Helene, a professor of biology who also did research in the medical faculty, mainly on cardiovascular illness, was explaining to the others how she was drawn into some research on one of the Covid variants.

"Well, Helene," said Deborah, "now the big question is the issue of whether we mandate vaccines, for everyone or for certain groups of people. Two Februarys ago you predicted accurately the seriousness of the pandemic and the onset of the closedown. What now?"

"I'm a scientist, Deborah, not a philosopher or a social scientist. I'll just say I'm in favor of at least mandating it for all front-line workers, including teachers."

"Helene and I have discussed this," said Stephen. "I wonder if it is possible to mandate it in light of the *Charter* and the *Ontario Human Rights Code*."

"Deborah is the expert on all of this," said Irwin. He turned to his daughter, "What's the practice on this?"

"There's nothing in the *Charter of Rights* as it has been interpreted or in the *Ontario Code* which precludes a mandate, since it will be done for clear health reasons. Those who don't like a mandate will challenge it. The odds are heavy that a law properly written will be constitutional. I think the provincial government, or at least some of the cabinet, don't want to do this for political reasons, but it would be legal."

"I'm being devil's advocate," said James, who just obtained his doctorate in Social and Political Thought from York and taught in the Social Science Department. "Don't I have the right to choose? It's a populist argument. Aren't you taking away my freedom?"

"Yes," said Danny. "But we take away your freedom all of the time in civilized society. You can't hurt someone, you can't use hate speech, you're expected to look after your children, you can't pass a red light for that matter, unless of course you're a bicyclist. No political philosopher argues that we are free to do anything we wish to do in society."

"What," intervened Avi, "if I decide not to take the vaccine. Which, by the way, is not my position."

"Then," said Deborah, "you take the consequences of your refusal. What is happening is that employers are demanding you take the vaccine, theatres will not let you enter unless you're fully vaccinated. And so on. It will happen via employers, shopkeepers, and other venues if governments don't do it."

"There's another argument in the air," said Helene. "That's the one which says that not taking the vaccine poses a health risk to others and to the community. Refusing to comply is like saying you'll stop at red lights only if in your judgment it seems correct to do so. 'I'll use my own judgment,' says the person arguing his liberty, without regard for others…"

All turned to Deborah. "First, not having the vaccine is a risk to others, just like having some kids in an elementary school who have not taken the polio or measles shot. That risk justifies mandating the vaccine under the constitution. Second, as Uncle Danny said, society limits our freedom in all sorts of ways."

"James, what do the philosophers say?" asked Irwin, who seemed to be chairing what had turned into an interesting classroom.

"I would point to possibly the greatest defender of our liberty, John Stuart Mill. He wrote his *On Liberty* to protect us from the state, but he also gave examples of what he would do in certain circumstances. He would support the mandate. He'd argue that we should try to persuade those who won't take the vaccine, but if there is a pandemic, having the vaccine might need to be mandated. My guess is that eventually the provincial government will do so, with exclusions for religious reasons or health reasons, each case decided individually."

"Well, we ten are all fully vaccinated," said Ruth, "having achieved this at least fourteen days ago. I know this because I specifically asked those who were not family when I invited them."

"I'm glad you asked," said Stephen. "It made us far more comfortable."

"So, does that mean," asked Helene, "that Ruth has taken the law into her own hands?"

"I don't think so," replied Molly. "I think it means that Mrs. Feldman is taking her home into her own hands, which I believe she has every right to do."

"You're right, Molly," said James. "Who you invite to your home is your own business. But how you behave in matters related to others in society is a public matter. That's Mill's distinction."

"I read Mill decades ago, as an undergraduate majoring in Politics," said Danny. "He was also afraid of the power of the modern state."

"That's why we discuss it, Uncle Danny," said Deborah, "and try persuasion before going to a mandate. We may get a mandate, but I agree that the government should try to build a consensus rather than act quickly."

"Well, sixteen months ago, the federal and provincial governments closed down virtually everything," said Irwin. "Without asking."

"And they are now being blamed for not acting sooner," said Avi. "These are tough decisions."

"Another matter related to Mill," said James. "Of all the political philosophers he best defended the value of free and open discourse. That, he thought, was the way to reach important decisions in a liberal society."

"Do you think," said Molly, "that we should recommend to our premier that he read Mill?"

"Let's not go there tonight," said Irwin, smiling. "Dealing with the vaccine mandate is difficult enough."

They moved on to smaller group discussions and other topics. Then they ended the meal with the traditional grace.

XVI

Once the gurus in the lab hacked into Marson's computer, other avenues of interest besides his professional life got attention.

As Nadiri had guessed when she discovered the lease on a rented apartment in Marson's desk, his marriage was troubled. He and his wife had exchanged difficult emails over the last several months. They were sorting out what arrangements would be made after their separation last January, both financial and in terms of the care of their two children, a boy of 12, Jeremy, and a girl, two years younger, Jasmine. It seemed clear to Nadiri that a reconciliation was unlikely.

Perhaps of more significance, given the manner in which he had been murdered and likely targeted, reading the computer files revealed that James Marson was a gambler. He had private card games almost weekly at a place in North York, regularly played on the Ontario Lottery Corporation site, would bet on NBA basketball, and occasionally went to Woodbine racetrack for gaming. His wife, Caryn Easton, a partner in a public relations firm on Wellington Street, referred to his gambling as a major cause of the separation.

Further, two months ago Marson began a relationship with a patient, Norma Tennent, the owner of a dress shop on Bloor Street near the dental office.

As she was examining the computer material, Nadiri received a call from Emily Chow. "I just finished the autopsy," she said. "I can now put the time of death between 7:30 and 10:30. He was definitely killed by the first bullet in his brain. The second was probably just to make certain he was dead. The bullets came from a nine-millimeter Luger handgun."

"The Luger is small, but it's good at close range," said Nadiri.

"It's probably the most common handgun used. In this case, it did the job."

Nadiri decided to wait until after the funeral, two days hence, to speak with the family. "No need to rush or make any demands," she told Katie. "The odds are very high that we're not dealing with a serial killer or someone targeting others. Let's talk with his partners first."

A meeting was arranged at the station for two o'clock the next day. The dental offices were to be closed until after the burial.

The Toronto police policy guidelines for the covid period indicated that it was preferable that interviews be held in person, though they might also be done virtually, if necessary. Nadiri much preferred for them to be in person, even masked. Her sense of the others in the room was far deeper than when the exchange occurred on Zoom.

Stefano Locotelli arrived first, a few minutes early. He

was of medium height, balding, with brown eyes. He was dressed informally.

"We'll wait for Dr. DaCosta before we talk about what happened," said Nadiri. "Dr. DaCosta told us he had known Dr. Marson since dental school. Is that also the case with you?"

"Even before. We've been friends since our undergraduate days at York. It's been a long friendship and partnership."

"Where were you the evening he was killed?" asked Katie.

Nadiri looked at Katie and said, "We'll get to that soon. After Dr. DaCosta arrives." She then turned to Locotelli. "How long has the partnership been together?"

"Not quite ten years," answered Locotelli. "We three graduated, and each of us worked for other practices for a few years. Then we decided to get together. We rented the location at Bloor and Ossington, thinking there was a need for a local dentist office in that area. As well, Rui speaks Portuguese and I speak Italian, so that helped us get going."

"Are you an immigrant?" asked Katie.

"Technically, yes. I came here with my parents and sister when I was three years old."

Nadiri rose. "If you don't mind, Dr. Locotelli, my partner and I have something to attend to while we wait for Dr. DaCosta."

"No problem. I was early. I'm happy to wait here."

"Thanks," said Nadiri. She now looked at Katie. "Let's go."

Nadiri led Katie to an empty interview room and they sat down.

Katie opened the exchange. "Are you going to tell me again that I'm too tough?"

"I'm going to tell you that what you are doing is not going to work. I'm also going to tell you again to follow my lead. Actually, I am ordering you to follow my lead."

"I don't think you're going to get anywhere. You're too nice. People are usually nervous in front of the police. We should make use of that."

"I disagree. If this partnership is going to work, Katie, we have to be on the same page."

"Well, I don't like your page."

"It's not about liking it. It's about working together to get a result."

"Look, I dealt with a lot of immigrants in Scarborough. I know how to get their cooperation."

"We don't have time now, Katie, for a long exchange of method. For the moment, I'm asking you, as the senior in this partnership, to work with me."

"I know an order when I hear one, ma'am. I will follow that order."

"Thank you. Now, let's get back to work."

When they returned, Rui DaCosta was also present. He was slim, had black hair beginning to gray, and green eyes. He, too, was dressed informally, in chinos and a short-sleeved shirt.

"You said, Dr. DaCosta," began Nadiri, "that you had been in dental school with your partners. Did you also know Dr. Marson before then?"

"No, I met James and Stefano in dental school. We became friends and then partners in our clinic."

"We're at the beginning of our investigation," said Nadiri. "It's useful to get to know about the life of the victim, about his character and his history. Could one of you start to give us a sense of Dr. Marson as a person?"

The two dentists looked at one another. DaCosta asked, "Mind if I start?" He got a nod from his friend.

"James was a nice guy, a good friend. Frankly, he was probably the best dentist among the three of us, something we acknowledged regularly in consulting one another. He liked his work, liked helping people, and was someone who brought in business because of word of mouth in the neighborhood. He chatted with clients, got to know them. We work with a lot of families, not just one person. Once clients get to know us, we get to know their kids, sometimes even their parents. He helped us to become a real neighborhood institution."

As DaCosta paused, Locotelli entered. "James was a good personal friend. The three of us sometimes behaved as a family. Our kids know one another. We attend each other's celebrations. He and I have been playing tennis since we were undergrads."

"This all sounds like a nice Netflix series," said Nadiri. "What aren't you saying? I have friends who are close, but they also have lives which are varied, sometimes they are sad, unhappy. What I'm really asking is for you to give us a whole picture."

"James could sometimes be abrupt, if that's what you're asking," said Locotelli.

"I'm asking more. How was his marriage? Who liked him and who didn't like him? He was murdered. We don't think it was random. Tell us more about your friend."

"His marriage fell apart in the last year," said DaCosta. "It hurt him. He became very sad, sometimes even bitter."

"Do you have any idea," asked Nadiri, "why it fell apart?"

"His wife, Caryn, was unhappy," said Locotelli. "She told me she had put up a good front for years. Finally, she decided to end the marriage."

"Why? What was the front about? Did Dr. Marson abuse her? Did he get involved with women? You must have thought about this."

"Some of the trouble had to do with finances, for sure," said Locotelli.

"How come? You indicated this was a successful practice."

"They lived an expensive life," replied DaCosta. "They bought a house in Lawrence Heights, a big one. Their kids go to private schools, expensive ones. They liked European holidays."

"There's more to it, gentlemen," said Nadiri. "We've gotten into his email."

"We didn't want to go there," said Locotelli. "The dirty secret is not that James had lovers, not that he took drugs or something like that."

DaCosta interrupted. "He was a compulsive gambler. That was his....Achilles heel. Like most amateur gamblers, he lost. And when he lost, he gambled some more to try to get even. And he lost some more."

"He went through a lot of money," said Locotelli. "In the last two years, he worked here from nine to eight at night. He continually needed more money to keep his lifestyle going and to pay some of his markers. It just got worse and worse. He was deeply in debt. I don't know how much."

"He became scared," added DaCosta. "He felt that the people he owed would stop being patient. He got secretive."

"Do you know if people were after him?" said Nadiri.

"I don't know," answered DaCosta. "Maybe. He thought so. Maybe it was paranoia, but he believed it."

"Thanks for this. It helps," said Nadiri. "Is there anything else we should know?"

They told Nadiri and Katie what they knew already, that Marson had his own apartment and he had begun a relationship with Norma Tennent.

Locotelli summed it up. "He was a good guy, a good friend and a fine dentist. But he screwed up his life with his obsession for gambling."

"I need to ask you about two other matters," said Nadiri. "First, have you thought about who might have murdered him?"

They both responded that they had discussed it and no one came to mind. "He had people who might not have liked him," said DaCosta. "We all do. But this, a murderer, no."

"I also need to ask you both where you were on the evening of July 27?"

"Really?" asked a puzzled Locotelli.

"Don't be offended. We ask it of everyone at the beginning of an investigation. This is ordinary procedure."

"I was home," said DaCosta. "With my wife, kids and in-laws. We had dinner together and the grandparents read the kids to sleep."

"My wife and I were out," added Locotelli. "We had dinner with friends not far from here, in the Café Diplomatico, at College and Clinton.

"We'll need to ask the grandparents and the friends," said Nadiri. "That, too, is normal. This is a murder. No stone goes unturned." The two men nodded.

"Thanks to you both. We may need to speak with you again sometime soon."

"We're not going anywhere, Sergeant," said Locotelli. "We have a friend to bury and a practice to reorganize."

After they left, Nadiri asked Katie, "What have we learned?"

"Not much we didn't know," said Katie.

"We did learn that the gambling might the key to this. His friends didn't give us a lot more to look for."

"I don't know. Maybe they're hiding something."

"If so, we'll find out. In the meanwhile, can you follow up and check on their alibis?"

"Yes, ma'am."

XVII

It was near the end of July in the second year of Covid, 2021. Many felt both elation and disappointment. The high was being able to do some of the activities that had been missed, including listening to music indoors, having friends for coffee and dinner, walking around outside sometimes unmasked, and for Debra, having the libraries open to a wider clientele. Normal was, at first, after sixteen months, exciting, especially in a summer climate.

The disappointment was the dawning realization that Covid would not disappear, as many had either expected or hoped. The Delta variant meant the world was seeing a rise in cases. And the issue of mandated vaccinations gave rise to a lot of angst and emotion.

Danny and Gabriella decided to celebrate the return to 'normal' by going on Saturday to the St. Lawrence Market. The Market had been open throughout the pandemic, but the experience had changed. There were restrictions on how many people could be inside at any time, with lineups outside even longer than those at major grocery chains. People were encouraged to shop and leave, in order to let others enter, taking away one of the Market's pleasures, the joy of walking about, browsing, taking one's time, finding something new or tempting, bumping into people you might know.

Danny picked up Gabriella at nine o'clock. "You know," Gabriella said as they drove down Jarvis Street, "*National Geographic* has called the St. Lawrence Market the best public market in the world."

"How un-Canadian," said Danny. "We're supposed to be second or third. Or, like in the Olympics, get a lot of fourths. We're not a people totally comfortable with being first."

"Well, this market has made it. Actually, a lot of people in Europe and Asia might legitimately complain. There are great markets there. I know those in Barcelona and Naples. How do you leave out Paris?"

"Now that's more Canadian. We may be ranked first but we really don't deserve it."

She laughed. "OK. We're on King Street. Let's look for parking. I'd like to walk around the area first. I haven't seen the Flatiron Building for a while. I read some time ago that they re-did the park around it."

They were lucky and found a spot someone was vacating on Wellington Street, next to the building, bordering the park. They walked to the western edge of the park, away from the market, in order to get a good look at the building. "It's probably late nineteenth or early twentieth century," said Danny. "I still like it being here."

"It has character," said Gabriella. "It gives the area some tie with its past. And the trompe l'oeil mural is wonderful."

They walked into the park. There was a plaque telling about it. "I didn't know," said Gabriella, "that it has a name. Berczy Park. Who's Berczy?"

"No idea," said Danny. He walked closer to read the print on the sign and turned to Gabriella. "An early founder of this area. In Simcoe's time. And a painter."

"I do like the fountain they just put in," said Gabriella. "Any reason that there are so many sculptures of dogs as ornamentation? And a bone on top?"

"Another question I can't answer. Maybe it should have been pigs in honor of Hogtown, the nickname given to our fair city some time ago."

They strolled to the market, first going to the large street-sized tent that had been put up south of the market itself. The tent housed purveyors who had been in the north building, now demolished but not yet replaced.

As they were choosing which vegetable stand to buy from, Danny heard a familiar voice behind him. "Hi, Boss." Danny turned and saw Sara Bellucci, accompanied by a man in his mid-forties.

"Hi Sara. You meet everyone at the market."

"That's part of what markets are for," said Sara. "In Italy you go to the market to see people, to gossip, to get the news."

Gabriella overheard the exchange and broke into Italian. *"E per incontrare nuove persone."*

Sara responded, *"E per essere presentato ai loro partner."*

The two men looked at one another with raised eyebrows and hands in the air, indicating that neither of them understood what was being said.

"Boss," said Sara turning to Danny. "This is José Valdez."

"And this is Gabriella Agostini. Gabriella, Sara Bellucci, whom you have heard about, and José Valdez.

They exchanged some small talk and each couple went on their way.

"So that's the excellent Sara Bellucci," said Gabriella, "defender of women and defender of the law."

"How do you know she's a defender of women?"

"Nadiri told me about her as well. She really respects her."

"Glad to hear that."

"And she's right about going to the market for more than food. You know, there's a saying that if you want to know who slept with whom on Friday night in Toronto, go to the market on Saturday morning."

Danny laughed. "Well, it works in at least two cases here. I'll look at the many couples with new eyes now that I've heard that."

They bought their vegetables and went into the building to the north, still called the south market, to get some cheese and fish.

After they had finished shopping, Gabriella said, "Let's get a snack and some coffee. There's a good fish place where we can sit down."

They decided to share a halibut po' boy sandwich. When they were seated, Gabriella said, "I think I'm deciding, Danny."

"Deciding what?" he asked. "If you need something to decide, let me ask you if you will not be married to me for the rest of our lives."

She had a very wide smile. "Yes, Danny, I promise to not be married to you for eternity."

"I couldn't be happier. The rest is a coda."

"You're terrible, Danny. You're supposed to get me flowers, which by the way you don't do often enough, and get on your knee."

"I promise to do that."

"Soon, sir. Not sometime on the distant future."

"Yes, ma'am. Now what have you decided?"

"To not be married to you forever."

"And what else have you decided?"

"I've decided to continue the gamble and seriously pursue a conducting career. Even after the disappointment of Covid. That's who I am. Like others, I've questioned my identity these last sixteen months. Many will leave their worlds of music and the arts. Some have already left."

"I'll now be devil's advocate. You still have to eat."

"I thought about that too. I had a phone conversation with Helene Trappé at the Royal Conservatory. Nothing was settled, but she indicated she'd be happy to adjust my schedule at the Conservatory to fit with my guest appearances."

"You may be on the road a lot more."

"Helene said they could handle that. Others who are regular teachers are often away." She looked up. "And your next question will be about money."

"I didn't want to go there. I don't want money to be the final determinant. I told you I would help if you needed it. After all, we are now not wedded to one another for life."

"You're great, Danny. But we have to go there. Neither of us comes from money. We grew up in lower middle-class families that eventually became middle middle-class. As you know, I've managed through Covid by going through much of my savings, my cushion as I like to think about it. There's not much left. Here's what I've calculated. What with what I will earn, say next year, visiting orchestras and occasionally playing with them, and with the money I will earn teaching at the Conservatory—don't forget it is a contract position, which is what most everybody there has—I would earn about ninety per cent of what I would have earned staying at St. Mike's. That will do."

"I'm almost convinced. You know what you're losing?"

"Yes. I've thought about that too. I've already lost security by leaving a permanent teaching job at St. Mike's. And I've lost the very good teachers' pension scheme. I'll have to be very disciplined now that there is work again and put a certain amount very regularly into my RRSP."

"What do you gain?"

"You're tough. I gain an opportunity to stretch myself as a musician, and that is my passion. I gain a chance to see how good I can be. I gain a chance to work with great musicians and make beautiful music. And, to put a negative on it, I gain a chance to fail. I might fall on my face, Danny. So far, I haven't, even conducting the Toronto Symphony as a last-minute replacement. I don't want Covid to drive my development away. I feel now like a young person of twenty or so deciding to follow their passion."

Danny leaned back. He took a sip of coffee. "Then I'm on your side. Take the opportunity if the Conservatory works out."

She grabbed Danny's hand. "I knew you'd say that. It makes me stronger to have you on my side."

"Me, too. We entered a new world a little over five years ago. Let's keep inhabiting it."

XVIII

Nadiri had arranged to interview Caryn Easton on the afternoon of that same Saturday. She had seen the two receptionists the day before and learned little more to add to the information she had gathered from Marson's partners and his computer. She and Katie had also attended the funeral service and paid their respects to the family.

Now, she needed to get to what she thought was the core of the case as it was unfolding, Marson's gambling, his finances and those who might have reason to murder him, whether out of personal animosity or for 'business' reasons. She had asked Katie to join her, but Katie suggested Nadiri postpone the interview because she had another commitment that day. Nadiri decided to go ahead on her own.

The house on Dawlish Avenue was large, set back from the street among a number of other homes that were similar in style. The front lawns were well-kept, and the area had the feel of a quiet, well-off neighborhood, perhaps new money rather than old.

Caryn Easton was dressed in black pants and a black blouse. She had on little make-up, but was still a very attractive person. Her blonde hair was in a ponytail. Her eyes were green. She answered the door wearing a mask, but removed it after the two got settled in a corner of the living room. Her features were in proportion and she looked younger than her forty-four years.

"Would you like some tea or coffee, Sergeant?" she asked.

"I'm fine, Ms. Easton. Thanks."

"How can I help you deal with this terrible murder? Our children are devastated."

"It's hard to lose a parent at such a young age. And in such a violent manner."

"It is. They don't understand it. I really don't know what to tell them."

"What I would like, Ms. Easton, is to learn about your husband. Or perhaps you think of him as your former husband."

"As you undoubtedly know, we separated a little over six months ago. We were still negotiating the separation arrangements. Lawyer to lawyer. So, you're right on both counts. By now, I think of him as my former husband, though legally we are still married. As you saw from the notice and the funeral, James has two siblings. We made the arrangements together."

"Tell me about him. About his character, his personality. The more I get to know about Mr. Marson, the better I can do my job and find the murderer."

Easton took some time and shifted in her chair. "Is this confidential? I work in public relations and I really don't want what I will be saying to be in the media or on something like Twitter."

"It's not confidential in that I work with others. And there's a file which will contain my summary of this conversation. It will not be available to the media or anyone else outside of my colleagues. And I don't talk about this kind of conversation with anyone other than my colleagues. Like you, I imagine, there is a set of professional ethics about this."

"That's fine. Thanks. I've been tripped up before. That's why I ask."

"Now, just tell me about James. I'll ask more questions as we go along."

"James was smart, handsome, likeable, and a really good dentist. He liked playing tennis and was good at it. He, with one serious exception, was a good dad. Our marriage was a love match fifteen years ago. It turned into something else as we went along. That happens. It could still have been a decent marriage."

"What was the exception?"

"The exception was a major problem. It's still a major problem, even with James gone. Who have you talked with?"

"His partners and the two receptionists."

"Then Rui and Stef would have told you about James' gambling."

"Yes."

"He developed a gambling addiction. It became very serious about eight years ago. We consulted some medical people and he had a therapist who tried to help. It went the way this sometimes goes when it goes badly. James pretended he was getting over his addiction, and secretly he just continued to gamble."

"Did he lose a lot of money?"

Caryn sighed. "A lot. He made good money in his profession. We made good money. With the help of parents, we bought this house. Our kids go to good schools. We traveled. But we have been in debt for years. You want the truth? This house, which has only appreciated crazily like all of Toronto real estate, is now heavily mortgaged. James worked much more than most dentists because we were constantly on a financial edge. He tried to hide our difficulties, but his addiction became so terrible that it was eating up our relationship. I still don't know how much money he owed."

"What did you do?"

"I insisted we get couple's therapy. James continually promised to stop gambling, but he couldn't. Gambling to him, I said in one of our sessions, was like eating and sleeping to others. He couldn't do without it. In one way or another it cast a shadow on everything. Even his relationship with the kids. Gambling came first. Before the kids, before me."

Caryn had tears in her eyes. She rose and went to get a tissue from another room. When she sat again, she said, "So there you have it, Sergeant Rahimi. A few paragraphs to tell you how four lives were wrecked."

"Can you tell me who he owed money to?"

"Not *he* owed," said Caryn with bitterness in her tone. "*We* owed. It was a marriage. *We* owed the money."

"To whom?"

"To the bank. The house is mortgaged for over a million dollars. It's worth over two million. And then he owed a lot of money to some people in North York who run a gambling establishment, probably illegal, given that the province didn't license it."

"Who are these people?"

"I have a phone number. That's all."

"I'll need that before I leave." Caryn nodded. "Do you know how much he owes them?"

"No. It's a lot. We're talking in the hundreds of thousands. If James had a bit of money, he went to the Ontario Lottery Games site. And then he went to North York to lose a lot more."

Nadiri needed to move the conversation in another direction. However, she sensed Caryn could use a break. "May I ask for a glass of water?" she said.

"I'll get it. Will tap water do?"

"Yes. Thanks."

Nadiri stretched and looked around the living room, furnished with both good taste and comfort in mind. 'Behind the façade lies great sadness,' she thought. 'Danny would probably think about his beloved Balzac if he were here'.

Caryn returned with two glasses of water. Nadiri took a swallow and then said. "I need to ask. Do you know of anyone who might want James murdered?"

"I did think about that. I don't. He was liked. He didn't make enemies. He was a pleasant guy in everything but matters surrounding his gambling. Even when my parents learned about the gambling, they tried to help us and him. The only thing I can think of is that the murder's related to his debts. Maybe whoever did it wanted to make an example of him."

"Could be. We'll get to that right away. Is there anything else I should know?"

"I don't know. Do you think the people who James owed money to will get in touch with me? I'm frightened."

"I can't tell you. I don't think they will, but I'm not one hundred percent certain. It could be that the murder is how they decided to deal with the debt. And they need to remain quiet. If anyone does get in touch, I need to know immediately. Nadiri took out her card. "I'm putting my cell number on the back. Call me at any time.

"I need to ask one other question. We ask it of everyone, including Mr. Marson's partners and friends."

Caryn sighed. "I was wondering. No, I didn't kill him. I was here from six o'clock on. I made supper, ate with my children. They did homework and I watched something dumb on Netflix while doing a puzzle at the same time. Lights out for the kids is between nine and nine-thirty."

"Thanks."

Caryn seemed to not want the conversation to end. She asked Nadiri about her work and about how one becomes a detective. Nadiri asked about Caryn's work in public relations. "I help people negotiate the media and other matters. PR mainly deals with reputation," she added.

Both commented on the other's accent. Nadiri explained that she was born in Iran and lived as a child for six years in Iran, then three years in Germany before coming to Canada with her family. Caryn was raised in Kentucky. She and James met in their twenties at the wedding of a relative of James who was also a friend of Caryn.

After a time, Nadiri stood. "Thanks for your candor,"

she said. "I'm sorry for you and your family. We'll work hard to find the murderer."

"I'll be in touch if anything comes up."

It was the weekend, but when she got to her car Nadiri decided to call the phone number of the gambling establishment. No answer, and no invitation to leave a message.

XIX

On Monday morning Nadiri came in early and knocked on Sara's door. When Nadiri entered, holding several pages of typed material in her hand, Sara asked, "What's doing?"

"I'll get to that later," answered Nadiri, still standing. "Can I make an appointment to see you later this morning?"

"Sure. How about ten-thirty?"

"Thanks. If you have time, please read this," said Nadiri, as she handed the material to Sara.

When Katie came in at nine, Nadiri met with her and briefed her on the interview with Caryn Easton.

"What do you think?" asked Katie.

"We're not getting far. We need to keep interviewing people and finding out about Marson's life."

"I think we should look again at the partners," said Katie.

"Why?"

"It's just a feeling. I sense something funny, especially that Rui guy."

"We try to follow up leads that are clear. Is there anything tangible that might require our seeing the partners again."

"No, just a gut feeling. I've been right before when I have these doubts about someone." Katie paused and Nadiri didn't follow up. After a bit of silence, Katie added, "By the way, I'm sorry I couldn't be there on Saturday."

"That's OK. Life sometimes gets in the way."

"Definitely. I was at a private barbeque at the premier's house. My father is a neighbor and a friend. My husband and I live in the riding in Etobicoke, not far away. I've known the premier's family for years. It's not the kind of invitation you turn down."

"Let's get on with our work. What did you find about the alibis of the partners?"

"I'll get on it right away. I've been busy until now."

"Please do so. I'll follow up on the phone number."

Nadiri thought she may now have a way to find where James Marson gambled. She had Marson's phone, which the computer gurus had hacked. She knew that if you kept your phone on and you had the Google map app, Google tracked you wherever you went and kept a log of this information. The log is detailed—it tells you when you left for work, your route, even whether you drove, walked or took public transit. Google sent monthly reports to those they tracked. Nadiri found this creepy and had learned how to turn off the tracking, but maybe James Marson, like many, simply left it on.

She succeeded easily. Marson went most weeks on Wednesday evening to an address in North York, a home on Robinter Drive, not far from Bayview and Steeles. Given what she knew about Marson, she thought it was probably not a tryst, but a place he went to gamble.

At ten-thirty Nadiri went to see Sara, with yet another typed half page in hand. As she sat down, she passed it over to Sara. "Add this to the file, Sara. This morning."

"Are you making a formal complaint?" asked Sara. "If so, I have some forms for you fill out."

"No. I just came to you to tell you that it Katie has been a problem. I need advice about how to handle it."

"How have you been handling it?"

"I've been professional. Look Sara, I've had partners that were not like you and the Inspector. One was so touchy that I couldn't have a cup of coffee without his permission. Another was not that good a detective, but he tried. I don't need a friend. I need a colleague who works as part of a team. That's what worries me about Katie. She doesn't listen, she seems to show prejudice, she relies on her gut feelings, she doesn't seem to want to learn. I get along with everybody, and I'll get along with Katie. But so far, all that has happened is that she has gotten in the way."

"Let me look at your latest note." Sara read the page Nadiri had handed to her. "OK, so she didn't follow up right away with the alibis and decided being with the Premier was more important than being at an interview with Marson's wife. This fits with everything else you recorded."

"Can I ask a question which may be not my business?"

"You can ask. I may not answer."

"How did she get here? She doesn't strike me as a whiz at what we do. She has experience in only one area of the city. She's nothing like Louise or Alvin or many of our younger people."

"She was assigned. That's all I know. I'll learn more."

Sara paused and did some thinking. "Here's my advice for the moment. Leave it with me. Continue to be patient and professional. Behave as a mentor as much as you can. Don't lose your temper."

"What does this mean for the Marson murder?"

"Simply keep going as you've been doing. What I would like is your permission to show these notes to the boss. You've not made a formal complaint, but he does need to know about this."

"Of course. Thanks for asking. And thanks for listening. It helps to talk to someone about it."

The house on Robinter Drive had an owner, Ying Chan, who had an address on Lloydminster Crescent, several streets away. She looked him up on Google and found he was a property developer in North York and Markham. Nadiri obtained his telephone numbers. This time she got an answer.

Rather than try to get information on the phone, Nadiri believed she would be more likely to succeed in finding out how Chan might be involved in the case by interviewing him in person. She wanted the interview to be at the police station rather than in Chan's home.

"Can you come to the station for about an hour in the next few days?" she asked.

"It would be simpler if you came to me, Sergeant," replied Chan. "I'm a businessman and I don't have a lot of free time in my schedule."

"Mr. Chan, I'm investigating a homicide. It would be better if we talked about this at our offices. Tell me when you're free to come here and I'll do my best to accommodate you."

"I'm booked for the next four days of this week from ten to five."

"How about eight here on Wednesday morning?"

"Really, officer, this can't be that important."

"It's a homicide, Mr. Chan. They're all important."

"OK, but I'm protesting. Can't we do this on Zoom?"

"No, we can't. It's policy that interviews should be in person, if at all possible, masked if you prefer."

They made the date. When she had a chance, Nadiri informed Katie of the interview. Katie made a face when she heard eight o'clock, but didn't verbally complain. Meanwhile, they both got on with seeing people and checking alibis.

Chan arrived at the station on Wednesday a little before eight, accompanied by his lawyer who was introduced as Maggie Gruchuk. Nadiri recognized Gruchuk, in her mid-forties as was Nadiri, as one of the most prominent criminal lawyers in the province. She had a reputation as someone who was very smart and rarely lost a case. Katie joined them at eight in the interview room.

Once the introductions were over, Gruchuk didn't wait for Nadiri to begin. She immediately asked, "Is my client being charged with anything?"

"No. We need to speak with him about the killing of Dr. James Marson. I believe he can help us."

"Why are you in such a hurry?" said Gruchuk.

"All homicides, as I'm certain you know, counsellor, are important. We believe Mr. Chan can provide us with useful information." She looked directly at Gruchuk. "And now can we get to the subject at hand?" Gruchuk nodded.

"Mr. Chan, we believe you own a home on Robinter Drive. Is that correct?"

"Yes. I bought it as an investment. As you know, I live nearby."

"What happens at that house?"

Gruchuk took over. "What do you mean by what happens?"

"I'll rephrase it. Do you use the house for any personal matters?"

"I rent it. Through Airbnb and some other sites. Usually to people visiting Toronto or to a corporation wanting something comfortable for an overseas client or officer coming to Toronto. It's an investment property, as I said. I have a number of investments."

"Do you use the property for yourself?"

Gruchuk nodded, indicating to Chan that he should respond. Nadiri realized that Gruchuk and Chan had rehearsed his responses between her Monday call and this Wednesday morning.

"It's not always occupied by renters, especially during Covid. I sometimes have visiting relatives from BC stay there. I sometimes lend it to friends for their visitors. And, if it's available, friends and I meet there for a weekly poker game."

"Was James Marson one of those friends?"

"Yes. It's a terrible thing that happened. His family must be in shock."

"How many friends do you usually have for your gambling?"

"It's a social occasion, Sergeant," said Gruchuk. "It's friends getting together to have an evening to themselves."

"Were the stakes very high?" asked Nadiri.

"It wasn't a game played with nickels and dimes, if that's what you're asking," said Chan. "They are all successful people. We sometimes lowered the stakes and sometimes raised them. It depended on the mood of the evening. Let me add that I didn't attend every Wednesday, but I was happy to have friends use my property."

"Did Dr. Marson owe money to anyone? We know that he had a gambling habit."

"He might have. I don't know."

"How much might he have owed?"

Gruchuk again intervened. "You're fishing in the wrong waters, Sergeant. Mr. Chan invited friends for a weekly card game. That happens in tens of thousands of homes in this province. There is nothing illegal in this matter. Mr. Chan sometimes supplied refreshments to his guests, gratis. The house, as it is called in gambling establishments, was neutral. It did not benefit in any manner. The host never took a piece of the pot or any fee. There is nothing here."

"It would be useful if Mr. Chan could inform me if Dr. Marson owed money to anyone. Including the sum of money."

"Dr. Marson once owed my client a few thousand dollars. He paid his debt. My client has no knowledge of any other debt."

"Who else gambled there?"

"This was a private affair in a property owned by my client," said Gruchuk. "I don't believe we need to respond to that question. Frankly, Sergeant, we have told you what we know. I don't sense there is anything else to add."

Nadiri persisted, knowing it would be futile. "Can you tell us anything that might help us to find the murderer?"

"We have told you what we know," said Gruchuk. "Unless you are charging my client with a crime, I think we have cooperated and have nothing more to add."

Nadiri gave up, at least for the moment. "Thank you for coming. We appreciate your cooperation. This interview is now ended."

After Chan and Gruchuk left, Nadiri and Katie met with Sara, who had watched the interview on a screen.

"What do you think? Sara asked.

"I think we need to probe further into this, but I don't yet see how to do it," said Nadiri.

"They're running a gambling den," said Katie. "You should have been tougher on him and that high-priced lawyer who defends lots of scummy people. You're too nice."

"What would you have done, Katie?" asked Sara.

"I don't know. I just think we treat crooks and killers too nicely." She made a face. "We appreciate your cooperation, you said. Such bullshit."

"Tell me what you think Nadiri should have done," again asked Sara.

"I don't know. But if this is the way you treat scummy people like this bloody immigrant, it's a wonder you ever solve anything. Get tough. Policing isn't a tea party, my father said."

"OK," said Sara. "We're stymied and impatient. There's no clear path. This will be a tough case. Keep going, you two. Look at everything."

Part Two

XX

The first two weeks of August were frustrating for everyone on a number of levels. The joy of opening in late June turned into an abiding concern about the Delta variant of Covid and its consequences. Case numbers moved up, in Ontario and much of the world. *Toronto Life*, often somewhat behind the public sentiment by the time it published its monthly magazine, had on its September 2021 cover, released in mid-August, the words "The Great Reopening," with an image of an anonymous couple hugging as part of a vibrant urban street scene.

That's not how people felt. There were worries—Will this virus go on forever? What about my kids in schools? How do we keep safe without vaccine mandates? What kind of winter will it be? How do we relieve our health care workers?

Nadiri continued to work on the Marson case with Katie. She interviewed everyone associated with Marson again, but got nowhere. The only small consolation she received was when she saw Sara and asked about Katie. "We're working on it," said Sara. Though Sara would not comment further, Nadiri trusted her.

Danny was getting restless. Covid and Sara's request that she get some experience in dealing with cases kept him in the office for much longer than he liked. He had signalled to Sara that he was ready.

Danny's case came along the next week. Sara appeared at his office late one afternoon. "You told me you wanted to get back on the street," she said. "Something has come up that seems it might be for you."

"What's that?"

"There's been a murder in a public place. At the Regina Hotel and Jazz Spot on Queen near University. You could walk to it from here."

"What happened?"

"I don't know the details. A group was performing and a half hour ago someone came in and shot one of the performers. That's all I have."

"OK. Who's available to partner with me?

"Louise's partner, Steve Rangel, is on holiday"

"Very good. I'm going now. Get Louise to meet me there."

Louise Cartwright was one of several people who Danny chose to work with him when he needed to assemble a team. She was a veteran of several years on the squad, and had a reputation for solidity and reliability. She was a tall woman, nearly six feet, with a broad body, though Danny remarked to himself when he got to know her that she was very comfortable in her skin. Her face was round, but her features were proportionate and handsome, and she had a visage that was alive and bright. She was fluent in French, and Danny sometimes asked her help when he needed to liaise with colleagues in Quebec. She was intelligent, and was now one of the people who he would consider recommending for promotion when an opening arose.

Danny grabbed his coat and went out the door in a hurry. On the seven minute walk to the jazz place, he thought about what he knew about the venue.

It was the premier place in the city for jazz music. He and Gabriella had been there about two years ago, invited by one of their colleagues in the Bloor Street Chamber Group, Benny Grunbaum, to listen to a few sets that he and some friends were playing at the club.

Danny liked the place. The performer's area was slightly elevated, but it was close to the tables in the room, giving the whole atmosphere an intimacy you couldn't find in a concert hall. The club served drinks and food, but the audience was obviously there for the music and seemed to be very attentive and appreciative. Clearly, there were regulars, among them some of the jazz musicians he knew taught at the Conservatory. The quality of Benny's group and the one afterwards, for he and Gabriella decided to stay for a drink and some snacks, was very high.

When Danny reached the club, there was the familiar police presence and yellow tape. He went inside and found the officer guarding the body.

"What happened?" Danny asked.

"All we know," said the officer, "is that they were playing their music, and someone came through the back door with a gun and shot this guy."

"Any name?"

"Yes. Jimmy Chester."

Danny examined the body as best he could without contaminating the crime scene. Jimmy Chester, a trombone by his side, had been shot in the chest, at least twice. No need to look for a pulse. The bullets had pierced his heart.

By then, Louise appeared, masked, like everyone in the room. Danny briefed her and asked her to look after the group of customers that had been detained, to get as much information from them as possible at this time, noting that the police may want to speak with them again.

"I'm going to talk with the manager, staff and the other members of the group," Danny said. "Then let's put the information together and decide how to proceed."

The manager was Pauline Hecht, who Danny learned had been the day manager at The Regina for the last eight years.

Hecht and Danny found a corner. She was about fifty, five feet three inches, somewhat stout, very animated and cooperative.

"Tell me what happened," Danny asked.

"There's not much to tell," Hecht replied. "We opened indoors about six weeks ago. What a relief. Everything was normal, the tables were distanced, the band was doing its thing, and then all of a sudden there was a noise, three gunshots I think."

"Did you see the person who did the shooting?"

"Only from the rear. It was a male, dressed in pants and a jacket. He was leaving through the back, where he entered, as I looked up. As you can see, Inspector, this isn't a big place. The back door gives a good look at the stage."

"Any kind of description? Was he wearing a hat? Did he limp? Things like that."

"No hat. His hair was dark, brown or black. The pants were also dark, the jacket light. He had on a mask, so it's impossible to describe how he looked."

"Let me take another track. Has there been any trouble lately? Have there been any threats, or things of that sort?"

"Not that I know of. Not at all. You'll need to ask the owner and the night people, but I would have been told if anything like that had occurred."

"Nothing odd?"

"Nothing. We have a lot of regulars, Inspector. This is the best place to hear great jazz in the city. We have regular performers and regular patrons. Most came back in the last month."

"Thanks, Ms. Hecht. We'll be talking some more, but I'd like to get to the others."

Danny next interviewed the four wait staff and the barman together. They filled in what increasingly seemed to be a very simple scenario. Most agreed that the gunman had black hair. There was general agreement that he wore black pants and a plain blue jacket, no tie. As one of the waitresses remarked, "It happened in a matter of maybe twenty seconds. He came in, shot the trombone player three times, and left. I think one person chased him."

There were five others in the jazz group in addition to Jimmy Chester. The leader was the pianist Reginald Carruthers, who mainly spoke for the ensemble—a guitarist, a sax player, a bassist and a drummer.

"We're a group from an advanced adult class at the Conservatory," Carruthers reported. "We have a class on Saturday. Since before Covid. We were on Zoom, but lately we could meet to jam and practice. Sometimes we play here during the day. Frankly, we're good enough to be at the Regina, but not good enough to play in the evenings. We're just a bunch of older guys who love the music and want to get better at it."

"I was here some time ago," said Danny. "My wife is a musician and we listened to a group called the Highlights. One of our friends was playing. So I know what happens here."

The musicians relaxed with the realization that Danny had some understanding of who they were. However, they couldn't contribute any more to the description of the gunman.

"Let's get to Jimmy Chester," continued Danny. "Why would someone want to shoot him?"

"We talked about it," said Carruthers, "and we have no idea."

The guitarist, who identified himself as Antonio Adrainis, entered the conversation. "Jimmy was a sweet guy. He's a music and English teacher at Jarvis Collegiate. He played with us at times. He's married, loves his wife and two kids, and lives more regularly and quietly than most musicians."

The drummer, Kent Bradley, said, "He's a regular guy. A house, a family, a job. Everybody likes him."

By this time two other members of Danny's 'team' arrived, Detective Constable Taegen Brown and Constable Connor Smyth. Danny decided to end his interviewing and see what Louise had found out. He turned the manager, staff and the members of the band over to Taegen, who would take their information and any further remarks anyone might have.

Louise had Connor look after the patrons and she and Danny met. Louise brought one of the patrons along and introduced him. "Sir, this is Shawn Dennis, the person who chased the shooter."

They went to a quiet place in the rear to talk. "Mr. Dennis," Danny said, "I know you've spoken with Officer Cartwright. But I'd like to hear what happened directly from you as well."

Dennis, in his mid-twenties, replied, "Sure, Inspector. I told Officer Cartwright that I'm a law student at the University of Toronto. In my last year. I like jazz and now have gotten into the habit of walking over to the Regina about once a week for a beer or lunch to listen to whoever is playing. The place gets good groups."

"Where were you sitting?" Asked Danny.

"Not far from the back entrance. At a table with some friends near the door."

"What happened?"

"I didn't see the guy enter. People come in and out all the time. The group was playing a version of a Duke Ellington piece and I really liked what the pianist was doing. I heard the shots. I turned probably after the first one because I remember seeing him fire quickly two more times. Then he turned quickly. He didn't bother to look at the stage for any period of time, and he left. I ran after him."

"Where did he go?"

"He turned right…"

"How far behind him were you?"

"Officer Cartwright asked me the same question. I don't know. I'm not good at estimating distances. Maybe fifty feet behind. I yelled stop. Not that I thought he would stop, but I wanted to get the attention of the people on the street."

"Good thinking. What happened?"

"He jumped into a car parked on the side street and it sped away. It was a black car, four door, not big. I don't know the make. The driver was probably a male."

Louise intervened. "But tell the Inspector about the license plate."

"It was a BC plate. You know, one of those Beautiful British Columbia ones. The first two letters are CD. I didn't get the rest."

"Can you tell us what he looked like?"

"He was masked. I only saw him for a few seconds and then I saw his back. Dark hair, maybe in his thirties, dark pants and a light jacket."

"You've been very helpful, Mr. Dennis. Leave your address and phone number and email with us. We probably will need to have another conversation."

After Dennis left, Danny learned no more from Louise than the information he had already received from those he himself had interviewed.

"Now," he said to Louise, "we have the wretched task of telling Jimmy Chester's wife about what happened. Let's find out about him and get going."

XXI

Debra Castle had arranged to go to Tessa's Place that day. Anna Crowe would be there and they could talk together with Molly about the art show. As well, she wanted to get more familiar with the shelter and talk again with Molly about her responsibilities as a board member.

"It's different from a library," said Molly as Debra entered her office.

"Very different," said Debra. "But very important. Imagine not having a place for women and children at risk. It's bad enough that all this isn't funded by the city or the province."

"You're already talking like a Board member," said Molly. "We still have a way to go as a caring society. We Canadians are sometimes too smug about how nice we are."

"Well, we are nice. Tessa's exists. Sheena's Place exists. There are other shelters. Maybe a public-private partnership is a better model."

Molly laughed. "Now you're talking like one of the officers on the board. Watch out. Now, let's first talk with Anna. Do you want to see the art class she conducts? When she came here a few years ago I asked her to help with a class run by our art therapy person, Wanda Chu.

She's been so good that she now runs the Monday morning class herself."

"Yes, let's go. I know her as a jewellery maker and as a person who manages a gallery. This will be new."

"She's good at it. She has passion and she cares. All the people in the class can see that right away."

They went up two flights to a room overlooking Queen Street. There were about a dozen women at several tables working on their art. Debra saw Anna in a corner with three people and a somewhat seedy male in a second corner with two others.

"Hi everyone," said Mollie. "This is Debra. She's going to work with Anna on the art show."

Anna came to the front and she and Debra hugged. Anna said to the group, "We're going to meet about the art show. Molly, Debra, Irina and me." She looked at the male. "Joe, you're in charge."

As they went back down to Mollie's office, Anna introduced Irina Buruskana to Debra. "Irina's the class representative," she said. Debra and Irina touched elbows.

"Who's the male?" asked Debra.

"That's Joe," said Irina.

"Joe Grace," said Anna. "You've heard about him. He's a street person. And he has teaching skills. Mollie asked him to help one day and he comes around every Monday."

"He's OK," said Mollie.

"He's nice," said Irina. "Very respectful. He's strange, but good strange."

"That's a good way of describing him," said Molly. "We all have stuff. Joe has stuff. Sometimes people with a lot of stuff find Tessa's a safe place to be. He's a good guy."

The four women met in Molly's office. When they got settled, Irina said, "Some people will not want to show their work. They're shy or they feel it's private."

"That's fine," said Anna. "In fact, let's make certain people know that they can do that. No pressure on anyone."

"I think we should tie the show to the place in a deeper way," said Debra.

"What do you mean?" asked Molly.

"I'm not sure. I don't know the context as well as I'd like. But, for example, maybe we could get a sponsor for the show. Someone who wants to honor a loved one, or a group."

"Not hard to do," said Anna.

"I want to re-start slowly. Not too much," said Molly.

They discussed how the show would be put together as well as settling on the timing, which they decided would be the end of September. Then, Anna said, "One more thing. What's the policy if someone wants to purchase one of the images in the show? Is it the same as before?"

"Yes," answered Molly. "If someone is interested in buying a work, we put that someone in touch with the artist."

"That's good," said Irina. "But most of our people won't know how to handle it if they're asked about selling something. They have no experience in this."

"Good point," said Debra. "Anna has lots of experience. She should be there when the two meet and help to represent the artist."

"Easy to do," said Anna. "Important. I've done it before. I don't want anyone here to be uncomfortable.

Also,…" she looked at Molly… "with your permission I'm going to ask the people at the Faculty of Information at the university to assign one of their graduate students here to help. They do placements as part of their program."

"Fine with me," said Molly. "Do we get to interview the student before taking them on?"

"I can do that," said Debra. "I've seen students who work in libraries. Unless, Molly, you need to do it."

Molly smiled. "I see my reputation has traveled to you. I'm a bit of a control freak, but not that freaky. If she gets by you, then I'm OK."

"It might be a he, not a she."

"That's fine. It would be good to get more males involved in our work."

When they finished Molly and Debra stayed in the office to talk. Anna and Irina returned to the art room which had been rearranged in their absence. The four tables had been moved and everyone was seated, looking to the front where a huge canvas, some of it full of many colors, some of it empty, was hung on the wall. Joe Grace was in front of the canvas.

"Who wants to go now?" he said to the group. "Has everybody had a chance?"

"Susie needs to go," said one of the women.

"I don't know what to do," said Susie. "I might choose the wrong color and space."

"There are no wrong colors or spaces," said Joe. "There's only your color filling in a space that makes the canvas more interesting."

"C'mon Susie. Take a chance," said one of the women.

Susie was thinking. Then she said, "I want sky blue to go near the red in the middle."

"How big?" said Joe. "Come up and show me."

Susie went to the front and took a brush from Joe. She dipped it into the paint and put something close to a triangle on the canvas. The other women applauded.

"Now," Joe said, "everybody has contributed. What do you think? Is it finished?"

Susie spoke. "Irina hasn't had a chance."

"Go girl," said one. "Yeh, Irina" said another.

Irina asked, "What am I supposed to do?"

"We're making a work of art together," said Joe, "something we do before every show. It's abstract. Everyone is contributing some color and space. It's your turn, Irina."

Irina went up to the canvas and studied it. She then took a brush, dipped it into a pot of green and put a large stroke reminiscent of Jack Bush on the left side of the canvas.

"Why that?" asked Joe.

"I don't know," answered Irina. "I just felt it needed that for balance. And for color. It kind of works for me with the rest."

Joe stepped back to get a better look at the canvas. "Looks good, people. What do we do with the three small spaces we haven't filled in?"

A chorus of answers came: "Leave it empty." "Needs more green." "You decide."

"I don't decide," said Joe. "I don't like deciding. It's your painting. You have to decide."

A voice from the back was heard. "Make it white. Make all the small blank spaces white. White's a color."

"Thanks, Vinisha. An interesting solution. What do you think?"

"It would work." "Good idea." "Try it." "We can always paint over it."

"OK, Vinisha," responded Joe. "Make it white."

Vinisha walked to the front and filled in the white.

"Is it done?" asked Joe.

"Yeah." "White's good." "Looks done to me." "Finished." "Pretty good."

Anna stood at the back quietly, happily taking in all that was happening. She marvelled at the rapport Joe had with the women.

"We have a tough job, now," said Joe. "What do we call it? I'm tired of calling it "Joe Made It Happen. We have Joe I, Joe II, and Joe III. It's time to get another name."

Another chorus: "How about Class Painting?" "Number One." "Space and Color." "Tessa's Mess." "All Around the Mulberry Bush."

Anna spoke. "What about 'Broadview and Queen.'"

"You got it." "Yeah." "Perfect." "Good one."

"I don't think so," said Joe. "*You* made it. It should be about you."

"We like that name," said Irina. "This corner is Tessa's for the whole city."

Joe shrugged. "Anna's here. Let's take our break now."

Anna went up to Joe. "That was terrific, as always. You got a lot of energy going in the room. I kind of like the piece. It'll be the center of the show."

"Why," asked Joe, "do you leave me in charge sometimes?"

"It's obvious. You know what you're doing, people like you, you have their respect."

"I wonder if I know how to do this. I know how to teach literacy, but I'm just improvising with art."

"Joe, this is no big deal. Everybody had a good time and they bonded. What can be bad? They like you, Joe. You're good at this. In a way, I see you as a born teacher."

Joe let some time pass before replying. "Maybe not just born, Anna." He turned to leave the room. "I need to get some tea."

XXII

Jimmy Chester had lived in a small house in Parkdale, on Spencer Avenue near King and Dufferin. It was five-thirty in the evening by the time Danny and Louise arrived. His wife and two children were at home.

The next moments were by far the part of his job that Danny disliked most. How do you tell a family that their beloved husband and father had been killed? How do you console people whose lives are shattered for reasons you, at the moment, know nothing about? Danny was sensitive enough not to feel self-pity at this moment. He knew the family's grief was in a totally different and an immensely more difficult place than his own discomfort.

Susan Chester was inconsolable, as were the two children, Amy, 15, and Roger, 13. There was little Danny and Nadiri could do beyond making certain that relatives and friends were informed and that the family had support.

Susan's brother and sister-in-law, John and Faye Bomart, took charge.

"What are you going to do next?" Faye asked Danny.

"We're going to have to talk with Mrs. Chester. Perhaps the children as well."

"You can't talk now. The doctor is upstairs and I'm certain Susan will be sedated. The kids are simply overwhelmed. Their cousins are going to stay with them."

"Yes, I know that. Still, we need some information. It was murder, Ms. Bomart, cold-blooded murder. Can we ask you and your husband for some information?"

"I'd rather you left us alone, but I know you can't do that. Let me get John."

Danny took Faye and John to the kitchen, in order to get some privacy. The house was filling up with friends, relatives and neighbors, all of whom were already in mourning. He signalled to Louise to start the questioning.

"What can you tell us about Jimmy Chester? Give us a sense of who he was."

"He was a very nice guy," said Faye. "He was a teacher. John and I are teachers and Susan was a teacher. It's in the blood of this family. We like kids. We like to help."

"He was the epitome of the nice Canadian," said John. "He loved his work at Jarvis Collegiate. He was a good family man, a good neighbor. You won't find anyone here or at Jarvis who has a bad thing to say about him."

"I don't want to sound cruel," said Danny. "I have to ask. Tell me about his bad qualities. Tell me if he had any enemies. What could he have been involved in that caused someone to want to kill him?"

"If a bad quality is sometimes being stubborn," said Faye, "then that's as bad as it gets. He was a good guy. My kids adored him because he was a great uncle who gave them love."

"Like the rest of us, Inspector," added John, "some

people liked Jimmy more than others. But you'll have to look hard to find anyone who disliked him, much less hated him. What happened is a puzzle to all of us."

Faye then spoke, "Could it be that some crazy person just decided to kill someone and Jimmy was that person?"

"It could be," said Louise, "but it's not likely. This was a targeted killing." She paused. "It wasn't someone with a gun killing people randomly because he has a beef with the world. It's not about belief or god or whatever. Someone was hired to kill Jimmy. Why?"

"We can't answer that," said John.

"Think hard," said Danny. "You can't answer it or you don't want to answer it?"

"We can't answer it," Faye said. "This is a person without enemies, somebody who was a good citizen, whose family loved him, whose students respected him."

"Did he have money troubles?" asked Danny. "Did he have a flaw, such as a gambling problem?"

"When Susan left teaching to raise the boys," said John, "they lost one salary. She's been doing some supply teaching in the last few years to add some income. Like every middle-class couple with two kids in Toronto, they have a big mortgage. No Mommy and Daddy to give them capital. But they coped. My guess is that they don't have much in savings, but I'll bet they don't owe much other than the mortgage and maybe a monthly car payment."

"No big vices," added Faye. "At least none anybody knows about. And I'll bet our mortgage that there isn't a gambling problem or something like that. They didn't go on big holidays. We sometimes rented a cottage together for a few weeks in the summer. That's it."

"Thanks, Mr. and Ms. Bomart," said Danny. "We won't bother you any more at this time. We'll need to talk again, and I'll need to talk with Susan, but that can wait. I do have one difficult request."

Faye and John paused. "What's that?" asked John.

"It's necessary for someone to come to the morgue to formally identify the body. That's the law."

John said, "Susan should not have to do it. I'll do it." Faye nodded.

"It can wait until tomorrow, if you prefer," said Danny.

"No. I'll do it now."

"We need to stay here to talk with some other people. I'm going to call for a car and two officers will take you to the morgue and return you here. Is that all right?"

"If it has to be, it has to be," sighed John.

Danny and Louise spent the next two hours talking with some of the people who had come to the house. They learned little more about Jimmy Chester. People talked about his love of music, jazz and blues, and his love of literature, especially nineteenth century English novelists, Dickens, Eliot, and Trollope. They recounted his working with the school band and his occasionally giving private music lessons. He was portrayed as a good person, someone human, but without a major flaw. All were bewildered.

When they left, Louise did the driving. As she turned onto King Street to wend her way first to Danny's home on the Danforth, she said, "Not much to go on, sir. We'll need to dig a lot."

"Perhaps we'll get lucky," said Danny. "Maybe the license plate will help or something of that sort. Right now there's no good lead. We'll see. I think we might get some help from Ms. Chester."

After a silence, Danny added, "So now we have several files where there is not much information."

"I know we haven't yet caught the second person responsible for the murder of Haris Bashera, What else?"

"Among others, there's the Marson case, which Nadiri and Katie are working on. Not much evidence has turned up."

"Nadiri will find him. She's determined and smart."

"That she is, Louise, but we seem to have too many loose ends these days. Let's see. It might be useful to do a review."

XXIII

Joe Grace was having a tough time. He was concerned about all the commitments and relationships he was entering into. He worried that life was getting too complicated after some very spare years. However, now he was also disturbed by something that was happening in his home on the street, the small tent and cardboard 'village' in the ravine near the Castle Frank Subway Station.

On Friday, he went early to his teaching of literacy at Tessa's, hoping to speak with Molly Muldoon about his concerns. At 8:00 he found Molly in her office with Anna Crowe, talking about the plans for the forthcoming art show.

He poked his head in the door and Anna said, "Come on in Joe. We're discussing the show."

"Something's been bothering me about what's happening in my ravine. I need to talk to Molly."

"Joe, it's a very busy day." Molly looked at her watch. "Can we talk now for a few minutes?"

"Sure. Thanks. I think Anna can hear this. But it's private, Anna."

"I'm good at private, Joe," Anna replied.

"I know."

Joe sat down in a chair next to Anna and looked at Molly. "Something that's bothering me is going on in the ravine."

"Your tent home?"

"It's not mine. It's everyone's. There were eleven tents and cardboard homes. Now there are twelve."

"So?"

"He came a month or so ago. A guy named Charlie. Charlie Spirit, he calls himself. A made-up name like Joe Grace."

Joe then looked at Anna, who nodded.

"There's room, so that's not the problem. He talks a lot about the white race in Canada. He treats Moe and Lisa, who are Black, very badly. He insults them. They're old and they can't protect themselves. When Duffy told Charlie to stop, he pushed him and told him he'd beat the shit out of him. He doesn't follow the rules.

"Yeah, I know there are no rules, say some people, but that's wrong. They're just not laws or written down. There are ways you relate to people in tent villages and he's treating people like he's a god."

"I get it, Joe," said Molly. "What can I do?"

"No, Molly, what can I do? I know you can't just go there and tell him to behave. How do I get him out of there? We want peace. We'd move, but he might follow us. You know if I went to the police, they'd laugh at me. A bum can't ask the police to make someone behave."

"Why not?" asked Anna. "Bums are citizens."

"Don't be dumb, Anna. You're like Mr. Big. Miller thinks everyone is equal because he treats everyone equal.

That's not the way your world works. The wealthy and so-called normal people get different treatment than bums and street people. The normal world pretends that's not so. It's just a kind of hypocrisy."

"I don't have time for speeches, Joe," said Molly. "What do you want?"

"I want to know what to do. Who can I go to? How do I get this guy out of there?"

"Tough questions, Joe. Any chance for street justice? Any possibility of a group of people confronting him?"

"I thought of that. But this is a really terrible person. He'll get revenge. And he'll get revenge not on me, but on those who are weak."

"I have a strange thought," said Anna. "Do you remember the hate killing on Baldwin Street a while ago?"

"I don't watch or listen to news from the normal world," said Joe.

"I remember," said Molly, "Am I following you?"

"One guy got away. I was interested in the case because Joe's Mr. Big and my friend Nadiri were on it."

"You know Mr. Big and the partner?" asked Joe.

"I really don't know Inspector Miller. But he was terrific on something in the gallery a few years ago. Nadiri is a friend. That's not what I'm getting at. Molly, look up on google the name of the person who got away. They caught one of the two guys. The second one disappeared."

Molly got the name in under a minute. "Karl Geist-meier. So what good does that do?"

Anna smiled. "Remember, I'm not bad with languages. We'll play a game. What's the English for Karl?"

"Charles," answered Molly.

"And what does the word *Geist* mean in German?

Molly and Joe looked at one another and shrugged. Molly did the google thing again. "Wow, Anna. It means spirit or mind or ghost."

"I don't know what meier is in English," Anna said.

More google. "A bailiff or a steward. Could be a tenant on a farm."

"I don't think the meier is relevant then," said Anna. "This is really important, Joe."

"Why?"

"Because," said Anna, "I think your Charlie is the guy who murdered someone on Baldwin Street. There were two guys who belonged to…" She looked at Molly, who was working her machine.

"The White Canadian Front," said Molly. "A bunch of racists. Scum of the universe."

"Are there such organizations?" asked Joe.

"Yes, but let's not talk about that now," said Molly. "If Anna's right, we have to get to the Inspector and Anna's friend immediately."

Anna pulled out her phone. "I'm calling Nadiri at home. Hope she's there."

Nadiri answered on the third ring. Anna said, "Nadiri, something important just came up about the Baldwin Street murderer….O.K. I'll tell you the story."

After Anna related what had happened in the last ten minutes, the two women made an appointment to meet at the station at ten.

"Joe and I are meeting Nadiri, maybe also Inspector

Miller, at the station at ten. I'm sorry Molly, you'll have to figure out what to do with the art class. We can get the class started."

"No problem, as everyone says these days," said Molly. "We'll figure it out. I'd love to see the cops catch someone who exists in order to hate and beat up decent people."

"I don't want to go with you," said Joe.

"You must, Joe," said Molly. "You're the one who can identify the guy. And by the way, you'll have solved your ravine problem."

"Life's getting too complicated, Molly."

"That's life, Joe. You want peace, you have to work for it."

"C'mon, Joe," said Anna. "We'll get the class started. Then we'll get a cab to the station."

When they got to the station the person on the desk told them to go up to Danny's office. There they found Danny, Sara, Nadiri, and cardboard containers of Starbucks' coffee and some muffins.

Joe looked at Nadiri. "You remembered."

"Of course," she said. "In spite of your preference for the street you like a good cup of coffee."

"How are you, Anna?" asked Danny.

"Very good, Inspector. I'm finding myself. How are you doing?"

"The main stuff, family and loved ones, is fine. We're still looking for the bad guys."

"Maybe we found one for you," said Anna.

"If so, you've done the world a good deed," said Sara. "This is really a rotten person."

Danny turned to Joe. "And how are you doing?"

"I'm a little confused these days. But I really like teaching with Anna. And the truck is working."

"What are you teaching?"

"We run an art class at Tessa's. Anna runs the class. I help."

"I couldn't do it without you, Joe," said Anna. She turned to Nadiri. "He's a natural teacher."

"Bullshit, Anna," said Joe. "Nice bullshit, but bullshit."

"Let's start from the beginning," said Danny. "We're here to catch a murderer. I need the whole story."

"It started with something Joe told Molly Muldoon and me a few hours ago," said Anna.

Joe told his story of Charlie and his behaviour. Danny and Nadiri asked several questions and he gave more examples of Charlie's threats and rude manner.

"Then," said Anna,....

Danny interrupted. "Who's the language expert?"

"You got it Mr. Big," said Joe. "Anna figured it out."

"What do you mean?" asked Nadiri.

Danny looked at Anna. "You or me?"

"You," said Anna. "I took two years of German in university."

"I am, as you all probably know, Jewish," said Danny. "My parents often spoke Yiddish at home, so I picked it up. And we did some Yiddish in my Hebrew elementary school. So I understand some German as well."

Danny looked at Nadiri and Sara. "Karl is Charles in English. And *Geist* means spirit. The English cognate is ghost. *Meier* means someone responsible, a foreman or a manager of a farm."

Nadiri smiled and looked at Anna. "He also plays the violin, believe it or not."

"Let's be serious," said Danny. "Joe, Anna, you may have done what a lot of people haven't been able to do in two months. You may have found Karl Geistmeier, the most wanted person in Ontario, maybe the country."

"Do you need me to identify him?" asked Joe.

"Yes. We have several pictures of him."

Danny took three of the pictures from the folder and gave them to Joe.

"That's him," said Joe, pointing to Geistmeier. "What now, Mr. Big?"

"You and Anna are, as of this moment, out of it. We'll take it from here. Joe, I want you to stay away from the ravine until this is over. Do you think Geistmeier will be there now?"

"I don't know. Possibly."

"Good. Now we need to get organized. We'll let the two of you know what happens. Actually, you may learn from the media before you hear from us."

Danny took no chances. For the arrest, he called on the police Emergency Task Force unit which deals with high risk situations and is on-call 24-7. A tactical team of ten men and women, some specialists, all trained as assaulters, immediately went with Danny, Sara and Nadiri to the tent city in the ravine near Rosedale Valley Road.

They agreed that two of the unit would go in with Danny and Nadiri. Sara and the others would be spread about to be able to catch Geistmeier if he tried to run.

Nadiri made a suggestion when Danny and she were

discussing the process with the head of the unit, Allen Faulks. "I think it would work better if I went in alone," she said. "I'll just sit on a log. I'll wear clothing that's worn and ready for the clothing bin."

"Why?" asked Faulks.

"This guy is drawn to brown and black people. He loves to insult and harass them. Remember I had the honor of his buddy, Yellen, calling me an Arab bitch. He also believes that all men are superior to all women. I can be the bait that draws him. The others then go in and grab him."

"It may work better your way," said Danny. "Let's do it."

When they got to the ravine, Danny and two of the men stayed in the background behind some trees as Nadiri walked to the encampment. As is the custom in tent villages she sat down on the edge of a log. She even brought cigarettes with her, which she found disgusting, and lit one up.

Nothing happened for a time. Then a woman approached and sat on the other end of the log. After a time, Nadiri passed her a cigarette and matches. She lit up.

"You're new," the woman said. "What are you doing here?"

"I'm hanging around. I'm looking for Charlie."

"Are you sure you want to see Charlie? He's a real son of a bitch."

"I'm bringing a message. I won't hang around after that."

"Well, he's probably in his tent. It's the green one over there." She pointed to the tent.

At that moment, Geistmeier emerged from the tent and walked to the log. "What are you doing, Irna, talking to that brown bitch?" he said. "Get out of here, bitch," he said as he stared at Nadiri. "We don't want Arab people here."

Nadiri spotted Danny and the two specialists walking toward them behind Geistmeier's back. She held out her cigarette pack. "You want one?"

"Not from you. Anything you touch is dirty."

Nadiri smiled. "Aren't you nice? I have a message for you."

"What's that?"

By now Danny was only ten feet away.

"I think you're going to be in trouble."

"From who?"

"From me and my friends."

At that moment one of the specialists grabbed Geistmeier. The other put handcuffs on him.

Danny spoke. "Mr. Geistmeier, you are under arrest for the murder of Haris Bashera."

Geistmeier ranted and cursed, but by now there were four other specialists, each with guns, surrounding him. He was easily subdued.

As he was being taken to the wagon, Nadiri loudly called out. "Mr. Geistmeier." He turned. She said, "These are my friends."

As they always did, Danny, Sara and Nadiri summed up the end of the case.

"It was very clever of him, sir," said Sara, "to become a homeless person. An encampment is not somewhere we would ordinarily look."

"It was smart. Joe Grace is right. The homeless are invisible and out of sight. None of us thought to look there.

Joe and Anna are to be commended."

"Do you think," asked Nadiri, "that you'll tell the press that we caught Geistmeier because of the sensitivity of a street person?"

"I wouldn't mind it. He's a good citizen, is our Joe Grace. Speaking of that, I need to call Anna. I'll ask her to tell Joe since his only known address is 'somewhere in Toronto.' In any event, he'll find out from his friends at the tent city. Now he can go back to his life, the one he made for himself."

There was a quick press conference, ending the case. When Danny was asked how he found Karl Geistmeier, he answered, "I didn't. A good citizen found him. That person asked to be anonymous, so I can't reveal the name. I can tell you he is a street person who is deeply concerned about social justice and stood up for what's right. Folks, there's a lesson in that."

XXIV

Danny and Louise spent that Friday afternoon trying to get a handle on the killing of Jimmy Chester. The day before they had called the principal of Jarvis Collegiate, Estella Lopez, and arranged to meet first with her for a half hour and then with several teachers who knew Chester well.

"There is little to tell you," said Lopez. "I've been here for three plus years and haven't had a bad moment with Jimmy. He liked what he did and the students were in the main fond of him. Some of the union types found him annoying because he would not take direction in labour disputes. He saw himself as a dedicated professional. That was respected, in part because he was soft in his manner, not belligerent at all.

"He loved teaching music and he liked some of the English teaching. He had trouble with some of the ninth and tenth grade kids in English. Not trouble, just frustration. He wanted them to take literature more seriously. The music students choose to take those courses so they are really motivated. The English students are required to take those courses.

"The only time he got upset was when one of our vice-principals asked him to raise the grade of a student whose parents were complaining. That was the fault of the vice-principal because he seemed to order Jimmy to do it. Jimmy dug in. Rightly, may I add."

"Was there anyone who disliked him so much that they wanted him dead?" asked Louise.

"I can't believe that," said Lopez. "Besides, if I read the story correctly it was a targeted killing. Who's going to hire a hit-man to kill their teacher?"

"You make a good point," said Danny. "Do you know if he had outside interests or if he had any vices that could put him in danger, such as an addiction to gambling or drugs?"

"Unlikely. Over the years I've learned how to recognize a drug addiction and I'd bet he didn't have one. As for gambling, who knows? But I would doubt it."

The discussion with four of Chester's colleagues was similar. They liked him and saw him as a good role model for students. One of them said: "If you saw him teaching jazz or leading the school band, you'd want your kid in his class."

When they left, Louise again remarked that they were getting nowhere.

"You're right," said Danny. "We've hardly begun. The funeral is tomorrow and I'll speak with his widow next week. I think we should also take a look at the family finances. It may not get us anywhere but we can't overlook it."

"So now I have two big questions which could be titles of mystery novels," said Louise. First, there's 'Who Killed Jimmy Chester?' Second is 'Why Kill Jimmy Chester?' I remember that when I got to be a detective, I told myself that now things would be clear. There would be murder, a murderer, and a solution. Also, Nadiri has the Marson case still open. It too is murky, not clear at all."

Danny decided to have something like what he used to regard as a normal weekend. Now, during Covid, he often wondered if the 'abnormal' would become the normal. Covid had the capacity to destroy expectations as it mutated and again became dangerous. Numbers were moving up all over the world. The United Kingdom was seeing 30,000 cases a day, but seemed to disregard that or to simply accept it. Would that soon be the case in many other places? Would the new normal be to tolerate a certain amount of Covid rather than shut down activity? What troubled him most about civic life was what would be happening in schools to children who had already lost part of the social orientation and intellectual skills they would have normally developed.

On Saturday, Danny and Gabriella took a walk in the ravine connected to the Brickworks. They went from Gabriella's place to Milkman's Lane, walked down to the Saturday Brickworks Market, and then took the route into the long and lovely ravine. In what seemed only a few minutes, it was as if they were out of the city, on a country walk. There were others doing the same, but the ravine was not at all crowded. Sometimes they felt they had the place to themselves as they moved further inside the woodland. They passed ponds which had islands in them, covered with turtles and herons. They spied a fox and saw many rabbits.

"It's refreshing, Danny," said Gabriella, as they wandered along.

"A big change from traffic, crowding and murders. When we double back, let's get some lunch at one of the stands in the market. Now, remind me when and where you are going professionally."

"I'm heavily booked, to the point of having to say no to any request to play or conduct for the next six months. I go to Toulouse for a week in early September. Then to Boston at the end of that month. In October, it's London and Seattle. I'll give you the dates when we get home. There's more before the new year, Madrid, San Francisco, Winnipeg, and Naples. Naples, Florida, that is. I'm not entirely happy about going to Florida, but we accepted a while ago. And then, as we planned because you'll join me for part of it, there is my regular annual month in Victoria in January."

"And your teaching."

"And my teaching, as much in person as possible. What's happening with you? I saw the video of the press conference about catching that racist killer. You didn't say, but was it Joe Grace who helped?"

"He and Anna Crowe. Joe is becoming my version of a Baker Street Irregular."

"I'd like to meet him one day."

"He'll resist that. Joe isn't the kind of guy you make a date with. And let's not forget that he and his friends live in a ravine like this."

"We need to address that."

"I think the city is trying. We need to find some models

from elsewhere, maybe Finland, where they've had some housing success."

They turned back to return to the Brickworks, taking a different path.

On Sunday, as with Friday night dinner at the Feldmans, Danny did his best to revive the old normal. He went to the Y for his first squash game in about a year and a half. His partner was an old friend, Mike Ryan. They played hard, but as Mike said afterwards, they played badly. Mike won in five sets, but he told Danny afterwards, "This match shouldn't count. We stank."

"I thought my violin playing had deteriorated," replied Danny. "But this is far worse."

XXV

The funeral of Jimmy Chester was held in St. Hilda's Anglican Church in Parkdale. Danny and Louise attended, still trying to get the feel of a difficult case.

The one main lead they had, the BC license plate, turned out to be no lead at all. A visitor from BC reported his car stolen on the day of the murder and the car was found two days later, abandoned in a parking lot on Chesswood Drive in North York.

The service was held outdoors, under a large tent, in order to accommodate the many people who wanted to attend, including family, people from the neighbourhood, the jazz music community and from the school. Before the ceremony, as people entered the site, two jazz bands played, in preference to more traditional organ music. The first was a band composed of students from Jarvis Collegiate. The second was the band in which Chester had played at the Regina. The program noted that the two bands would be playing some of Chester's favourite music, including *Fly Me to the Moon*, *If I Were a Bell*, *What is This Thing Called Love* and Chester's top tune, *Take the A Train*. Danny noticed that the adult band had another trombone player and a second guitarist.

At the service, Chester was eulogized and again the two detectives got the impression of him as a solid citizen and a very decent person. Jazz again replaced the organ for the Recession.

Danny and Louise had arranged to meet Susan Chester the next day at her home. John and Faye Bomart were also present. Susan was distraught and still under sedation, but said she wanted to have the meeting.

"There's little to say to console you," said Danny. "I'm truly sorry for your loss and for what happened."

"Life is funny," Susan replied. "I know bad things happen, but I never thought anything like this would occur. There's no explaining it."

"We understand," said Louise. "We have little to go on, Ms. Chester. Nothing has come up which helps to explain it."

"Could it have been that horrible thing, just a random event?" asked Susan.

"We've thought about that," said Danny. "We're not ruling it out, but it's unlikely. The main point is that this looks like a targeted killing. The person entered, shot your husband and left. He got into a car which had been stolen only a few hours before. We've found the car and we've put our forensic people on it, but I'm not optimistic we will find anything. This seems professional."

"That's nuts," said John, "Jimmy was a good father, a good neighbor, a great brother-in-law. Who would target Jimmy?"

"That's the issue for the moment, Mr. Bomart. Who would want to do this to Jimmy?"

"Targeted killings are done for a reason," said Louise. "Usually there's something that the target has done that has violated some sort of agreement or code. Did Jimmy belong to any organizations that were secret? Did Jimmy hurt anyone? I'm sorry to ask this, because I know it seems odd, but we have to ask."

"I understand," said Susan. She then sat up very straight. "Jimmy wasn't a joiner. He joined bands. He took our son to his hockey games and our daughter to dance class. We pay our small dues to the neighbourhood association but we're not active. We belong to St. Hilda's. We go mostly on holidays."

"Did he have any habits that were dangerous?" said Danny. "Again, I'm sorry we have to ask. I feel awkward doing this, but it needs to be done, even to rule things out. So I'll ask. Did he gamble? Did he do drugs? Was he involved in something on the borderline of legality?"

"Inspector, this is too much," said Faye. "You're really offensive."

"I don't mean to be." Danny's voice was quiet and he spoke slowly. "I told you. We need to ask. If you say no, then we put that aside. If a relative of mine was targeted, the police would ask me the same questions.. If you want us to find the murderer, then we have to ask."

"Put that way, Inspector," said Susan, "I'll give you an answer. Jimmy gave up smoking cigarettes fifteen years ago, to please me. He was an open person. What you saw was what you got. A good Canadian, polite, kind, lots of quiet good traits, not flashy. He loved teaching, especially music, and you'll find he was admired by his fellow teachers and by his students…. What else did you ask?"

"Did he gamble? Could he have had gambling debts?"

"No. We have a mortgage and we occasionally would carry some credit card debt, though we tried to pay it off each month. Like any middle-class family that didn't inherit, we struggle at times, especially in Toronto. But nothing like that. I handled the family finances. Jimmy didn't like doing it. I teach math and history. I would know."

"Thanks, Ms. Chester," said Danny. "We won't bother you again about any of these matters."

"One last question," said Louise. "Another lousy question. The three of you would have thought about it. Who would want to hurt Jimmy? You must have given it some thought."

"I have. Faye and I have," said John. "We don't have an answer. No one is my answer."

"Mine too," said Susan.

"OK, Danny said, "Let's get off this bad track. We're not letting this case go. We want you to know that. We can't do much for Jimmy now, but we can bring his murderer to justice. We'll just keep going."

"What if you get nowhere?" asked Susan.

"That's not something we even think about at this stage. It's early days. We have no answers right now. This is tough, but we have a process and we'll be following it. Call us anytime. We'll probably get back to you anyway. This is the loss of a fine person, a loving husband and father. We owe it to him to find his killer."

"When you put it that way, I get it," said Faye. "Sorry for my early remarks."

"No need, Mrs. Bomart. I would have said the same thing in your circumstance."

They chatted about the children, just to get onto another, less difficult, topic. Then Danny and Louise left.

"It remains a puzzle," said Louise as she started the short drive to their office.

"That it is," said Danny with a sigh. "That's what it is."

XXVI

Little progress was made on the open cases, something that bothered Danny and most of the squad. He insisted they persist, as he was doing on the Jimmy Chester murder, though he was considering getting new people in for a fresh look.

On the first day of September, Sara summoned Nadiri to meet privately in her office. Nadiri was now working alone on the Marson case because Katie had taken vacation time for the two weeks around Labor Day.

"Grab a seat," said Sara as Nadiri entered, "I have some news for you."

"You caught the Marson killer?"

"Of course not."

"You're taking me off the case because we've gotten nowhere."

Sara laughed. "Not yet. You have a good track record."

"Then what?"

"As of this moment, you will be having a new partner."

Nadiri's eyes opened wide as she showed her surprise. "What caused this? My complaints were informal."

"The boss and I took them seriously. He took the matter

out of my hands. You'll have to ask him if you want any information about this, though I doubt you'll get much. Here's what I know. Katie is moving back to 42 Division when she ends her holidays. She's been informed. And I am assigning you a new partner."

"That's it?"

"That's what I know."

"Who's my new partner?"

"Alvin Wu. He's been informed and he's waiting for you to get in touch."

Nadiri smiled. "It's going from the ridiculous to the sublime. Maybe not sublime, but awfully good."

"Alvin's a good guy. You'll get along."

"Easily. We've exchanged thoughts on some cases. He's smart and on top of that, really nice."

"That's it."

"I'd like to know what happened."

"So would I. But you'll have to go see the boss."

Nadiri immediately got in touch with Alvin and they brought coffee to a small meeting room.

Alvin Wu was among the newer members of the Homicide Squad. Now thirty-one, he had an exemplary record as a Constable at 11 Division, in addition to a degree in Criminology from York. He had partnered with several people in his year on the squad, including Danny Miller, with whom he worked on the very public cases of the murders of a publisher and a journalist. Danny, after they finished working together, had written a very positive evaluation for Wu's file.

Alvin was five feet ten inches tall, lean in physique,

open in his countenance. He was the child of immigrants from China and he was fluent in Mandarin and had decent French. In his evaluation, Danny said he was impressed by Wu's careful preparation and the fact that he asked good questions.

Alvin became known around the squad for his unusual ties. Many days he simply wore a tie of one color, be it blue, red, purple, or any other. But some days he put on something special, celebrating whatever might be happening. He had worn a tie with Chinese characters on Chinese New Year. When asked he said the characters referred to the animal whose year was being celebrated. On St. Patrick's Day he wore a green tie, with an image of Ireland on it. On Elvis Presley's birthday he had on a tie with a picture of Elvis wearing blue suede shoes. Today, he had on a grey tie with two vertical stripes, one orange, the other purple.

"This may be a first," said Nadiri. "Both of us have worked with the Inspector."

"True, but you worked with him for years. I had two cases. Still, I learned something."

"Well, Alvin, I need you. Or I need somebody. I'm not getting far with the Marson case."

"I don't know a lot about it. All I know is that a dentist was murdered on Bloor Street."

Nadiri picked up the file she had brought with her and passed it across the desk. "Take a look at this. It will be useful to have fresh eyes on the case. I'm not getting far."

"What do I look for?"

"I don't want to say. Just look and tell me what you

think. Did I miss anything? Is there something I forgot to check? How would you go about trying to solve it? I'm human, Alvin. A few years ago Ted Hoeneker came onto another case we were working on. He opened it up and we solved it."

"Sounds good. I'll get back to you in a few hours or so."

"Right. Now, let me ask, does the tie have a meaning?"

"It's a very obscure one. Today is National No Rhyme (Nor Reason) Day. Something people who like language have fun with. It celebrates words that have no rhyme in the English language. Two of those words are orange and purple. There's also spirit, ninth, and chimney. And others."

"How about lozenge for orange?"

"Good try. It's close but not a perfect rhyme. Purple has a lot of near rhymes. I looked it up. Sometimes poets use turtle or burgle. Again, not perfect."

Alvin left with the file. Nadiri went to the secretary who handled Danny's schedule, Evelyn Homewood. She asked, "Can I have a few minutes with the Inspector sometime today?"

"How important is it?" replied Evelyn.

"No case is involved. It's a personnel matter."

"How about tomorrow morning at ten?"

"I'll be here."

The next morning Nadiri met with Danny. They exchanged some news about their families, as friends do, and quickly got to the matter at hand.

"Sir, I'd like to know what happened with Katie Nelson."

Danny smiled. "I expected you to ask. I think it better if I tell you sometime in the future. There are some delicate issues here and I just want the matter to settle down."

"Did my notes have anything to do with it?"

"Yes. But that was not the tipping point. There were other issues involved. Your notes did give me a sense that what I was doing was correct."

"I'd really like to know."

"I would too, in your position. I'll tell you one thing now, in confidence of course."

"Yes?"

"I wasn't the only person involved. This was a matter which went ultimately to the Chief."

"So, the transfer wasn't just about Katie's incompetence or her prejudice?"

"I'm not going there now, Nadiri. Just get on with your work, with Alvin as your partner. I'm in charge of the administrative side of the squad. Your job is to solve crimes."

"How long is sometime in the future?"

"I don't know. When things settle down. The matter is still alive. I don't want it to be a diversion from our real work."

"OK, sir. You partnered with Alvin. Is he as smart and nice as I think he is?"

"Yes. You can help him to grow and he'll be a partner you can rely on who will help you. I don't think I'm wrong on this."

"Thanks, sir. Whatever happened with Katie, I'm glad not to be with her any longer."

At noon, Alvin and Nadiri got together to discuss the Marson file.

"Did you find anything?" asked Nadiri.

"Nothing glaring at all. But I have a couple of questions." Nadiri indicated with a gesture that he should continue. "First, the receptionist said she unlocked the door on the morning after the killing. Does the outside door lock automatically? If so, then the person who did the killing had a key. That would be a big help."

"I did think about that on the day of the killing, and tested it. It locks automatically. I probably should have put that in my report. But that's good thinking on your part. What's the second concern?"

"Marson stayed late to take some patients after the office officially closed at five. The notes aren't clear about your inquiry into that."

Nadiri leafed through the file. "Again, I should have updated it immediately. I sorted that out only a few days ago. After we speak, I'll add to the file. The last three patients were Ronaldo Guzman, Evora Pinto and Jane Eodine. Guzman and Pinto reported that everything was normal. They were regular patients and accounted for themselves for the rest of the evening. Eodine....Oh, I did notice that the first three letters of her last name spell Doe backwards, a sick joke by someone planning a murder....Eodine was unknown, a new patient. She was scheduled for 7:30. Amy Zhao left a form for her to fill out. Of course, nothing was on it. She is either the murderer or the person who set up the murder. But she doesn't exist and no one saw anything in the neighborhood."

"So," said Alvin, "we have little to go on. What about the guy who runs the gambling house, Ying Chan?"

"We investigated him after the interview. He's a developer as he says. Really, he's a guy who flips real estate, makes investments, and runs a small-time gambling operation. He's been charged twice about the gambling in the past, but both times the case was dropped for lack of evidence. As far as we know, he hasn't had any relations with hired hitmen. Could it be someone else who gambles with Chan? Maybe, but he's shut down the gambling for now. The Wednesday night games may still exist, but not on Robinter Drive."

"The Inspector told me there would be cases like this," said Alvin, "those where you work hard and don't get very far. I'll do some more thinking, but so far I haven't had the aha moment I'd like."

"Me neither. We'll work on this, but we'll also be getting other cases. This one may never be solved, something that really bothers me."

XXVII

On Friday evening Danny was not in the best of spirits when he arrived at the Feldman's home for dinner. There were too many outstanding cases in the squad, Delta was now being called the fourth wave, and Gabriella was away, conducting for a week in Toulouse.

Ruth, who knew Danny's every gesture, posture and mood, noticed his gloom and asked, "What's gotten you down?"

"Life in general. Nothing special. Like most of the world, I'm weary of the pandemic, which is feeling as if it will last forever, and all that goes with it. Work isn't going well. And I miss Gabriella."

"All good reasons to be in a funk," said Ruth. "I'm trying to get ready for Rosh Hashanah next week, but even though we can observe it in a tent outdoors with others this year and have a family meal together, it's hard to look forward to more of the same."

"Let's not give in to the gloomy mood. Who's coming tonight besides Avi and Molly, and Deborah and James?

"Just Evelyn Zuckerberg, our friend down the street. Her husband, Aaron, is out of town, in Montreal, looking after some matters for his parents there. Her two married kids live in Vancouver and Winnipeg, so she would be alone. We've known each other for decades."

"Isn't she at Sick Kids?"

"Yes. She's a hospital administrator. She looks after programs for kids with eating disorders, among other things."

The others arrived soon thereafter and the group gathered in the dining room, welcomed the Sabbath with hymns, and began the ritual meal.

"Evelyn," said Danny, "have you experienced any problems getting into your hospital?"

"I haven't," she answered, "but across the street at Mt. Sinai, and up the street at the General, my colleagues have had problems with demonstrators blocking the entrance."

"How can you justify blocking the entrance to a hospital?" asked Molly. "Whatever your beliefs you don't help your cause by not letting people get into an emergency ward."

"I can't answer you Molly," said Irwin. "I don't understand why."

"There's more," said James. "Now the anti-vaxxers are tailing Trudeau as he travels around the country campaigning."

"They're not only trailing him," said Deborah. "They're publicly cursing him, trying to stop him from speaking, and throwing gravel at him. What has happened to our civil discourse?"

"That's the important question," said James.

"The word I used in a press conference," said Danny, "is coarsening. We have now a coarsening of our civic affairs."

"I blame the Americans," said Evelyn. "They're the model for these people."

"I don't agree," said James. "People are responsible for their own behavior. The nastiness is now a Canadian thing. There is even a small political party, the PPC, which is encouraging the demonstrations and harassment."

"Let's move to something more pleasant," said Ruth. "How do you think next year will be?"

"The most important matter is to get our young people back on track," said Evelyn with some vigor. "They need school, they need to look forward to a full life, they need to play freely, and frankly, they need adults to show they care about climate change and their well-being."

"It's an important moment," said Irwin. "I hope we old folk can make it a better world for the young."

"That's our job, Daddy," said Deborah. "And we haven't been doing it well in the last several decades."

"Then," said Ruth, "as we reflect on the new year soon and in the Days of Awe at its beginning, let's resolve to not only be better individuals, but let's do one thing, everybody should do at least one thing, to make the planet a better place for the next generation."

"Amen," said Danny. "We're in the middle of an election. Maybe we should think about which party will do that best, and vote that way. How we think about voting is important. In Canada, at least, let's make it about 'us' and not about 'me.'"

"Now," said Avi, "September is a big month for baseball. Will the Blue Jays make the playoffs? I say yes. They're several games behind, but they're going to make a move."

That, too, became a spirited discussion, in this case with no consensus. Avi had the last word. "They are not the Maple Leafs, who have the trope of disappointment built into their story. The Jays can do succeed."

XXVIII

On Saturday, Danny received an unusual call while he was practicing on his violin. The assistant to the Chief asked him to meet with the Chief. "Any special reason?" asked Danny. "He wants to discuss something with you," was the evasive reply.

John Kingston had been the Chief of the Toronto Police service for nearly five years. He was approaching retirement, though a number of politicians, journalists and his fellow officers were urging him to stay on. He was not above controversy, for the job had too much politics involved in it to avoid that. But he was regarded as honest, fair, and highly competent, even by those who thought he could do a better job, such as the police union heads and people who wanted the police to be more aggressive in their work. Kingston had risen from the ranks and was the first Black chief in Toronto. He was tall with a strong face and an open manner. Danny and he had developed a very good relationship over the years.

"I could meet with him anytime except Tuesday and Wednesday, which are religious holidays."

"Monday's Labour Day."

"I'm available. I'm also available tomorrow, if that suits him."

"He's in on Labour Day. How about ten in the morning?"

"That's fine. In his office."

Kingston's door was open when Danny went to meet with him on Monday. "Come in, Danny," was the greeting.

"Good morning, John. How goes it?"

"It goes, Danny. Not without some issues, as you know."

"Is that why I'm here?"

"Yes. The Katie Nelson matter isn't going away as quickly as I'd like it to."

"What's the problem?"

"Let me go back. Nelson was transferred to Homicide as the result of the intervention of Superintendent Roscoe Morton, and with the assent and recommendation of the Head of 42 Division, Nathan Laykind. It was, as you know, an unusual appointment. She wasn't interviewed by you or anyone in your command. She was given an excellent recommendation by Laykind, though it turns out her personnel file indicates she is nowhere near his evaluation."

"I was surprised John, as you know. I did ask personnel why I hadn't been informed and why I wasn't involved. Their answer was puzzling. Something like 'this happens sometimes.' I decided to see how it would play out."

"And, as we know, she was unfit for the job."

"So, what's the whole story?"

"Before I get to the story, I'd like to let you know there has been some pushback. You might get pressure as well. Tell anyone who talks with you to talk to me. Don't take the transfer of Katie Nelson on yourself."

"Keep going. I need the whole of the story."

"It turns out that Nelson's grandfather and father are friends of the Premier and the Premier's family. I don't know what went on, but the Premier's office, not the blessed premier himself, got in touch with some others they were friendly with, notably Morton and Laykind. Why, I don't know. Maybe they wanted to do a favor for a friend, maybe they felt they owed something to Nelson's family. That's speculation, and I would never say that in public.

"In any case, you know that in Canada cities are the creatures of the province. They have far less autonomy than many cities in the US or the UK. If you remember, three years ago the cabinet decreed that the Toronto City Council would downsize, from 47 members to 25. The Appeals Court, in a 3-2 decision, upheld the legality of such a change. Maybe the Premier thought that gave him the right to run our police force."

"That's absurd and undemocratic. The whole point is that we uphold the law and that we are not political."

"You're right. And I'll add the mayor not only agrees with you, he called the Premier and threatened to go public if the move was not rescinded."

"I didn't know that. I thought you had done whatever was necessary to nullify Nelson's transfer to Homicide."

"I did. But that meant bringing in the mayor, which by the way wasn't hard at all. He was appalled by the act."

"So the whole transfer became political. And I presume some people are upset."

"That's it. I'm just letting you know, so that if you get any blowback, you can ignore it."

"Thanks, John. What do we do to end this happening in other places in the police service?"

"That's what I also wanted to discuss with you. We have systems in place for promotion, for moving people from one place to another, for handling these matters fairly. How do we ensure these processes are respected and remain apolitical?"

"Off the top of my head, I'll tell you the mayor was correct. Go public. Transparency works. May I add that Rosalie Daniels of the CBC would give a lot for this story. But she would be truthful. I agree the media is sometimes a pain, but it's a necessary one. They keep us honest. Our so called communications people may not like them, but here is a case where their very existence stopped a politician from interfering with the police. Frankly, John, these are not good times for democracy. We need to protect it."

"No argument. Think about it for a bit. If you think we need to put better procedures in place, let me know. I'm asking you and a few others for help here."

"I don't know about better procedures, though that's worth thinking about. What we have to do is insist on those procedures we already have to be followed by people who think they have the power to subvert them."

"Sounds right, Danny. Let me know if you come up with anything. In the meanwhile, don't get involved. Pass any inquiry on to me."

Danny smiled. "Will do. I'll resist the temptation to lecture whoever thinks they can get to me."

"Thanks. Happy New Year to you and yours. Shana Tova."

"And to you, John. Let's hope for a better year. A boring, uninteresting one wouldn't trouble me at all."

XXIX

After two days Danny and Louise met to talk about Jimmy Chester.

"This hasn't happened to us before," said Louise. "We've spent a few weeks getting nowhere."

"It's happened to me," responded Danny. "Twice before. Rarely, but it occurs."

"What do we do? We can't give up."

"We never give up, Louise. Ever. We're missing something. Or we've gone about it in a fashion which reveals nothing. What we do is what we did in a few other cases. We start all over again."

"What if we still get nowhere?"

"I'll answer that question if that happens, not before. In the other two cases we slogged through and found the key. We need to be very persistent. Those people who think you solve cases with some sort of revelation are wrong. Tenacity is ninety-five per cent. Revelation is the other five percent, sometimes less."

"What's the assignment?"

"I'm going to interview the musicians and the people at the Regina. You take the family and friends and the school.

Think of new questions, new ways to think about the case."

Danny first arranged to meet again with the people at the Regina, mainly the day manager, Pauline Hecht. He had seen Hecht and the staff just after the killing. Now the atmosphere was far less tense and he hoped that might help some people to remember an important piece of information.

He tried everything he had learned over the years. He had Hecht close her eyes to perhaps focus her memory. He used words that might evoke something below the level of consciousness. He even had Hecht take the role of the cop and he put himself in her place, so that Hecht could do the questioning. However, only small things emerged: what people were eating and drinking, who sat where, which customers were regulars. But there was nothing that opened up a new avenue of investigation.

Doggedly, Danny then went to the Royal Conservatory, where he played weekly in the Bloor Street group, to see the teacher and leader of the band, Reginald Caruthers.

The conversation started out with Caruthers as puzzled as was Danny about the killing and about why Jimmy Chester was targeted.

"It seems, Mr. Caruthers," said Danny, "that Jimmy was just a good guy."

"That he was, Inspector. I didn't know him well, but he was liked by everyone in the group. He was really cooperative."

"What do you mean that you didn't know him well? Didn't you see him every week?"

"Oh, no. Jimmy wasn't in the class."

Danny got excited, but told himself to calm down. "Wasn't he a member of the band?"

"Not really. Jimmy only played with us if our regular trombonist couldn't make it."

"Are you telling me that someone else is your regular trombonist?"

"Yeah. Henry Brandt. He's in the class and he plays. At least he did. He seems to have disappeared in the last month or two since we came back together. He missed the gig we had a week before Jimmy was killed and he hasn't attended class or shown up to play since. Our guitarist, Antonio, knows him and lives a few blocks away from him, and he told me he hasn't seen him around the neighborhood. He sees his wife, he said, but not Henry. He said he asked his wife about Henry and she said he was fine. Just busy. He's an accountant, and she told Antonio he just got some new clients."

"How long did Henry Brandt play with the band?"

"About three years. He's good. Not great, but better than Jimmy was. Jimmy was fine as a replacement."

"Does your band have a name?"

"The Saturdays. We have our class on Saturdays, so someone suggested that."

"Do you or the Regina advertise? What I'm asking is if I wanted to listen to The Saturdays would I be able to find out in advance?"

"Sure. We have a blog which our drummer, Kent, looks after, and the Regina has a site which gives all the information about who's going to perform and when."

"Do you have Henry Brandt's address? His telephone

number? His email?"

"I have his telephone number and email. He lives somewhere around Leslie, north of the 401. Antonio would know."

Danny was already developing a new theory about the killing. He decided to end the interview now in order to do some thinking and some investigating.

"Mr. Caruthers, this is very useful. I may need to get back to you. Right now, I'd like the contact information you have for Henry Brandt. We may need to have another conversation one of these days."

"Did this help?"

"I think so. We'll see. We're determined to get to the bottom of all this."

"I hope you do, Inspector. Everybody says Jimmy was a good guy."

'That he was' thought Danny. 'And maybe a very unlucky one as well.'

On the way back to the station, Danny was driving automatically. He spoke to himself out loud. "How could you be such a shmuck?" he said. "Wow, are you ever stupid."

At the station he immediately met with Louise and Sara Bellucci.

He recounted the interview with Reginald Caruthers and then asked, "Do you know what this means?"

"I do," said Sara. "A probable breakthrough."

"I'm wondering if I'm right," said Louise. "Have we been investigating the wrong person these last few weeks?"

"Yes," said Danny. "At least almost certainly yes. Seems likely the wrong person was shot. Henry Brandt was targeted. Jimmy played in his place. And the gunman was told to kill the guy playing the trombone."

"What a terrible tragedy for Jimmy and his family and his friends," said Louise.

"Horrific," said Danny. "OK, let's find out if we're right. Time to talk with Henry Brandt."

XXX

Nadiri and Alvin were assigned to another case, though the Marson murder was still active. From time to time, the homicide squad, when there was time for it, also investigated violent crimes. They were now looking into a robbery turned into a home invasion that was nearly a murder.

The home was in the west end, in the wealthy residential Baby Point neighborhood. The house was more isolated than most, in that it was situated on a crescent surrounded by dense trees backing onto the Humber River. The owner and occupant was Riordan Adams, a wealthy hedge fund operator. Adams, sixty years old, was a widower. His one child now lived in Calgary, running an investment office there, so Adams had been alone on the night in question. He spoke to Nadiri and Alvin from his hospital bed.

Normally on a Wednesday evening Adams explained, he would have been at the York Club, where a group of old friends gathered for a weekly dinner and some talk. The ritual had been suspended that week because Sept. 8 was the second day of Rosh Hashanah and two members could not attend.

The two thieves had broken into the home just as darkness was coming, at about eight in the evening. Adams was a stamp collector, known to have several rare and valuable stamps in his collection, including some from British Guiana and Mauritius that were each worth over a million dollars.

When the thieves broke into the home from the back, they encountered Adams. He said he tried to stop them. "I thought I could reason with them," he told Nadiri, "but one of them simply pulled out a gun, a small one, and then the other one started to hit me. Soon I was unconscious."

The next morning, the housekeeper had found Adams on the floor, blood around him. He was taken to the hospital with injuries to his face and the back of his head. At any other time, he would have been in critical care, but the Humber River Hospital had no room, as the critical care ward was fully populated, mainly by Covid cases.

After a day, Adams was no longer listed as critical, and he was expected to recover, though he would be left with some permanent scars on his face.

He described the two men as best he could. "One was about my height, five ten, wearing jeans and a checkered shirt. He was blond, clean-shaven, about forty. He had a slight accent, maybe Irish. He had the gun. The other, the one who hit me, was taller, about six feet one maybe. He looked a few years older than the blond. He had on brown pants, chinos, and a blue shirt. He was dark, black or dark brown hair, a moustache, no beard, and had a deep scar on the left side of his face about six inches long, from near his lip up to his cheek."

When Nadiri and Alvin went to the house, they saw that the study, where the stamp collection was housed, had been ransacked, and much of the stamp collection was gone, ripped out of its cases and drawers. The two men had gotten away with rare stamps worth an estimated twelve million dollars at auction.

The forensics people found a fingerprint in the study which turned out to be that of Robert Casey, who had a history of theft in Toronto and the Greater Toronto area. Adams identified him as the man with the gun.

Identifying the second man posed no problem either. Casey had worked with someone matching his description, including the scar, before. He was Christopher Osborne. He had been in jail for five years a decade ago, for robbery and for assault.

Now, the task for Nadiri and Alvin was to find Casey and Osborne. "We'll get them," said Nadiri. "It's not easy to hide for very long in our connected world."

XXXI

The next day Danny and Louise went to the Leslie and 401 area to see Henry Brandt. Danny decided not to call ahead. His intuition told him it would be better to arrive unannounced.

Brandt lived in a neat house on Clovercrest Road, a quiet street with pleasant homes and well-kept lawns, solidly middle- and upper-class, not far from North York General Hospital. The houses were of a style out of the late 1950's, when the area around the Don Valley was built as a model suburb called Don Mills. From the outside they were unprepossessing, not giving much hint of the spacious rooms inside.

Danny rang the doorbell and heard a female voice from inside. "Who's there?"

"I'm Detective Inspector Daniel Miller from the police department, ma'am. My partner and I would like to talk with Mr. Henry Brandt."

"Henry's not home."

"Can you tell me when he'll be here?"

"I don't know."

"Are you Mrs. Brandt?"

"Yes."

"Mrs. Brandt, we need to speak with your husband about a homicide. He is not accused of anything. He has information which will be useful in catching a killer."

"He's not home."

"Mrs. Brandt, if we don't talk face-to-face I am going to arrange for a police cruiser to be outside your home on a twenty-four hour basis."

The door opened a notch, the safety catch still on. "Show me your identification."

Danny and Louise took out their cards and showed them to Mrs. Brandt. They lowered their masks to give her a chance to see their faces.

She opened the door. "Come in," she said, and took them to a comfortably furnished sunken living room a few steps down from the entrance area.

"Please sit down. I'm Lois Brandt. How can I help you?"

"We need to speak with your husband," said Louise. "We believe he has important information to help us solve a murder."

"I know nothing about that."

"We are asking nothing of you, Mrs. Brandt," said Danny. "We need to see your husband."

"As I said, he's not home."

"Where is he?"

"I don't know."

"Where is his office?"

"He works at home. He has an office in the basement."

"Mrs. Brandt," said Louise, "we think you know where your husband happens to be. It will do you no good to try to protect him in this way. In fact, if you're concealing his whereabouts, you are committing a crime. This is not a threat, not at all. We just need to speak with Mr. Brandt. We're not accusing him of anything. As we said, we need information."

"I can't help you," said Lois Brandt, tears running down her cheeks.

"We must persist, Mrs. Brandt. We're talking about a serious matter, a murder and a murderer."

They sat there quietly, Lois Brandt sitting with a straight back, working to keep her composure.

Then the silent tension broke as a man walked into the room. He sat in the chair next to Lois. He reached over and took her hand and said, "I'm Henry Brandt." He then turned to his wife. "Thanks, Honey. You've been very loyal and brave, but we knew this day would come."

"Do you know why we're here, Mr. Brandt?" said Danny.

"I think so, but I'd rather you told me."

"We're here because of the killing of Jimmy Chester at the Regina a few weeks ago."

"I need more from you."

"What we know is that you were supposed to be the trombonist in the band that played at the Regina that day. However, Jimmy Chester filled in for you because you hadn't attended the class for a while. A man walked in, took out his gun and shot the trombone player. It was, I am certain, a targeted killing."

Danny turned to Louise, who completed the story. "We believe," she said, "that you are the person who was supposed to be killed. We don't know why."

"I don't know that I can help you. I have a wife and two kids. I have parents living not far from here. I have two sisters. I can't help you."

"Are you suggesting," asked Danny, "that your family would be in danger if you helped us?"

"You can figure that out."

"But you are in danger. Certainly, whoever arranged the killing of Jimmy Chester knows the wrong person was murdered. Do you think you can just hide out here and it will all go away?"

"I haven't gotten that far."

By this time, Lois Brandt was clutching some tissues and crying openly. "I can't take this anymore, Henry," she said. "We have to do something."

"I'll think of something."

"You've had weeks and months to think of something. Maybe the police can help."

Brandt just slumped in his chair and threw out his hands in a gesture of desperation.

"I'd like to help, Mr. Brandt," said Danny. "We have resources. We can't help if we don't know what's going on."

"I can't tell you what's going on. I'm terrified."

"I'm letting you know that withholding crucial information in a homicide is an indictable offense. Again, this is not a threat. However, we can't just walk out of here and forget about you."

"So, I'm caught between the cops and the mob."

"We will try to protect you," said Louise. "We will try to protect your family. I agree you are in a bad spot. You can't get out of it by doing nothing."

"I thought at first I could run away. But they told me they'd get my family."

"Do they know you are here?" asked Danny.

"I think so. They're just waiting."

Danny decided on a change of direction. "Can I ask you some questions which you could answer yes or no?"

Henry looked at Lois. She nodded.

"Does this have to do with your accounting practice?"

"Yes."

"Does it have to do with your having cheated one of your accounts?"

"Yes. We needed the money for caring for my parents and for the kid's school fees."

"And you can't pay back the funds?"

"That's right. The house is our only asset and it's mortgaged to the hilt."

"Who are these people?"

"I can't tell you. They said that if I told the police they would act. My family is being held hostage in a way."

"Do you think you are being targeted?"

"Yes. I haven't been out of the house in weeks."

"Do you really think," said Louise, "that you can go on like this forever."

"No, I'm living day-to-day. I do some work from home to make a little money so we can live."

"I'm going to ask a hard question, Mr. Brandt," continued Louise. "How do you think this will end?"

Brandt put his head in his hands. "I don't know. Badly. I don't know."

"I think you should give us a try," said Danny. "Frankly, I don't think you have a better alternative. We could protect you. I can't guarantee anything. But we would be on your side in trying to protect you and your family from harm. That doesn't mean you are innocent. It does mean we will try to protect you from being killed and your family from harm until we catch the person or persons who ordered the killing and the person who fired the gun."

Brandt lifted his head. He was clearly at wit's end. "I don't know what to do."

Lois Brandt spoke for the first time in a while. "Can you give us some time to think? Can we talk privately?"

"Of course," said Danny. "Do so. But we are not leaving. We need to have something of a plan."

"That's fine. Can we go into the kitchen?"

"Yes. But we need to talk afterwards."

The couple left and returned twenty minutes later. When they settled, Brandt said, "We've decided to cooperate. There's no other way to go. Can we rely on you for protection?"

"We'll do our best," said Danny. "And in the meanwhile, we'll have someone here in your house.

"I want a guarantee."

"Mr. Brandt, you got yourself into this terrible situation. We'll help. Can we tell you that we'll have an army here to protect you? Of course not. We have resources. They are limited. Some will focus on you."

"The best thing," said Louise, "is to quickly find who is targeting you and who is the killer. If we do that, you and your family are safe. You made the mess, Mr. Brandt.

We can help you."

Henry and Lois looked at one another. Silently, they agreed to go ahead.

"What do you need from me?" said Henry.

"We need information," said Danny. "Tell us how you wound up in this situation."

"Will I go to jail?"

"I don't know. We're investigating a murder. What happens after that will depend on what you did."

"Can we get witness protection if necessary?"

"Witness protection is administered by the RCMP. The program doesn't negate your responsibility for your past actions or past illegal activities. This is something that may occur after a long process. If at all."

After some more silence, Brandt said, "You are the only choice. As you said, we can't live like this forever."

"Tell us what happened."

"I will. The people who are after me are illegal drug dealers. They have their main activities in BC, in Vancouver, and they decided to move into Ontario a few years ago, just before Covid."

"What do you have to do with them?"

"I'll get there. Let me tell it. They need to launder the money they are making. And they need some creative accounting, which I supplied."

"How did they find you?" asked Louise.

"I don't want to answer that."

"All right," replied Louise. "Go on with your story."

"So how do you launder the money, which is mainly cash? What you do is buy a business which is already legal and you fold the illegal cash into the money you deposit each day in the bank. Not too much. Maybe seven or eight thousand extra. You do it every day, so the bank sees a regular pattern and doesn't flag the deposits to the authorities. These guys are smart and they have some discipline."

"What's the business?"

"Three years ago, these guys bought Cornucopia, the high-end retail produce business which has expanded to include prepared foods. They did it quietly. And they hired the former owner to manage it, so nothing seems changed. Slowly, they expanded and increased their take and their deposits. Cornucopia is a successful business, well-respected. Now there are three stores, big ones, one in Rosedale, one on Eglinton near Avenue Road, and one in the fancy shopping mall not far from here in Don Mills. They launder about twenty thousand each day. Add it up. That's about half a million a month. All from drugs." He laughed. "And they do make a good profit from the legal business as well."

"Clever," said Danny. "And who are the people you work for?"

"It's a numbered company. The three main people are John Gagliano from Vancouver, and Soo Kim and Albert Feldstein from Toronto. They have an office and all that. They behave not much differently than any legal company. They sell fruit, vegetables, olive oil, prepared foods such as salmon, salads and beef, and heroin, fentanyl, and other drugs."

"What did you do?"

"I siphoned some money into my account. Not a lot. Five thousand here, five thousand there. I thought it wouldn't be noticed. I didn't know that they had a small office in Vancouver that audits all their stuff. I got caught."

"Mr. Brandt, this is going to take a bit of time to sort through."

Lois spoke, "Can't you just arrest them and get it over with?"

"We can't arrest anyone on the word of anyone else," said Louise. "We need proof. We need evidence."

"What happens now?" asked Brandt.

"What happens is that we will have an officer here in your house for the next few days, maybe longer. What happens, Mr. Brandt, is that we're going to supply you with a Kevlar vest, which you will wear even at home. And we go to work."

"When will this nightmare end?" asked Lois.

"As fast as we can end it," said Danny. "No promises. We'll wait here until an officer arrives. We called for one while you were in the kitchen."

In the car, as they turned onto Don Mills Road, Louise asked, "What do we do now, sir?"

"We talk to Sydney McIntyre. This isn't just a homicide any longer."

XXXII

Inspector Sydney McIntyre was the head of Major Crimes for the Toronto Police Force. She had been head of Homicide and Danny's boss for some years before a parallel move to the Crimes unit. Then, Danny moved up from Sergeant to Inspector and to Head of Homicide. Ten years older than Danny, she was one of the few people talked about as a possible future chief of police, especially if the Mayor and the Toronto Police Services Board decided to appoint the first woman chief in the city when John Kingston retired.

Sydney and Danny had developed a close professional relationship over the years, one based on great mutual confidence and respect. They regularly had lunch to discuss their work, and Danny had helped with several crime cases in the last few years at Sydney's request.

They met in Sydney's office the following Monday. When Danny and Louise arrived, Sydney introduced them to Sergeant Patrick Wu. They bumped elbows. Wu was about five feet nine inches, very neat, with a short haircut. Danny estimated his age at about forty. His eyes were deep and interesting and he seemed open and intelligent. "Patrick will work on the case from our office," Sydney said. "Now tell us what's happening."

Danny and Louise related the story of Jimmy Chester and Henry Brandt as Sydney and Patrick listened quietly.

When they had finished Sydney turned to Patrick. "From the information you gave us on the phone," he said, "I did some research. We know about the Vancouver people moving into Toronto. We know that John Gagliano, Soo Kim, and Albert Feldstein are involved. What we didn't know was that they were laundering the money through Cornucopia. Not even that they now owned the business."

Louise spoke. "Does that give us an opening?"

"Absolutely," said Sydney. "Money laundering is often associated with terrorism. In fact, the law in Canada is called the *Proceeds of Crime and Terrorist Financing Act*. But it's also associated with using money gained from illegal activities for any purpose."

"Well," said Danny. "We want to solve a murder and you people deal with the illegality of drug dealing and money laundering. How do we proceed? Let me note I'd like to move fast because Henry Brandt is in danger. Perhaps his family is in danger as well."

"We'll work together," said Patrick.

"Of course," said Louise. "But how? I think two of us should take on the whole case." Sydney and Danny looked at one another and nodded.

"Once we get as much information from Brandt as we can," said Danny, "you can probably move to get business records to audit and all that stuff, and then minimally get the three owners of Cornucopia to court and probably jail. But I don't know yet how we get them for murder, unless we find someone to confess or someone with knowledge to testify."

"Yes," said Sydney. "You're right. Proving the murder, making a tight case, is harder than taking them down for money laundering."

"I've done one thing which may help," said Danny. "I've been in touch with the people in Vancouver. They have some idea who the gang hires to deal with people who've cheated them or for some other reason. They're now gathering information on three suspects, especially information on flights from Vancouver to Toronto and back. We'll see if that yields anything. We do have a witness to the killing, but I really don't know how much good that will do. The murderer wore a mask, like so many of us. Covid helped him."

"That sounds right," said Sydney. "Let's get Henry Brandt's full information. Then we'll get a court order to deal with the accounting for Cornucopia. Who knows? With luck, we'll find an email with information about the murder, but I doubt it. These people are smart and don't leave evidence lying around. We'll have to see."

"Louise and Patrick," said Danny. "You talk to Brandt. We'll go from there."

XXXIII

On Tuesday Joe Grace went to Mt. Sinai Hospital for his weekly meeting with his therapist, Patricia Morrison. They had met on Zoom from March 2020 until several weeks ago, when Ontario moved to Stage Three of its opening. Now they could again meet in Morrison's office. They sat distanced, so that masks were not necessary.

"How are you doing Joe?" asked Patricia.

"I'm just doing what I do, Patricia. I like doing most of it—the truck, teaching literacy and art at Tessa's—but I also have this pull in me."

"What do you mean by pull?"

"I have this desire to just give it all up. I feel pulled by the nothingness I created for myself years ago after Vicky and the children were killed. It swamps me at times. I just want to stop trying to help people and go into a shell."

"You're not alone in that feeling, Joe. A lot of people are tired, weary. They too just want to stay in bed all day. Here, in the hospital, nurses especially are totally worn out. They just want the constant sense of being over-whelmed to end. Some, good ones, good people, have quit. Others have gone into private practice where they have more control."

"You don't get it. I'm not worn out with work. I'm worn out with having commitments that put me with other people a lot. "

"I think these nurses are also worn out like that. Their responsibilities are too much. Half the time, they tell me they just shut down and work by rote."

"Me, I just sometimes want to give it all up and be the Joe Grace who didn't talk to anyone for years. Being in the world isn't as uplifting as everyone pretends it is."

"Joe, we all feel that way sometimes. What you are feeling is what others feel—people like parents, teachers, doctors, caregivers. Everybody is pushed. And during Covid, a lot of people are just overwhelmed by not knowing what will happen to them next month.

"I never told you it would be a constant high. Life brings setbacks, doubts, guilt, even fears. That's part of it. Especially for people who are self-reflective. That's ordinary. All those feelings go with the territory."

"Well, I'm feeling all of that. I wonder if it's worth it."

"Do you think you could just give up all your commitments and new friends and be content?"

"No. That's the problem. But I still have doubts."

"That's understandable. Joe, maybe it's time to fully give up the old Joe Grace act."

"What do you mean? It wasn't an act."

"Maybe the Joe Grace who can't relate to the world and who doesn't want any commitments or responsibilities is gone. That you sometimes feel that way isn't strange. Lots of people sometimes feel that way. Life can be very tiresome.

But we persist because it also gives us some meaning."

"Do I sometimes talk that way?"

"More than sometimes. When was the last time you told someone you didn't like to be responsible?"

Joe smiled, something the old Joe didn't do as a matter of principle. "It was with Anna, a week or two ago. In the art class."

"And what did Anna say?"

"I was good at teaching. That's what mattered."

"Was she correct?"

"Yeah."

"Think about this. Anna values you. The women you teach value you. The truck helps some people. I'm not telling you to go and do more. Don't get manic about doing some good. You have the truck and you have your teaching. Keep a balance. And take a timeout occasionally."

"I guess I'm fully back. What do you think?"

"You're back, but you're not back as the person you were before. You've changed. We all change."

There was a silence, a quiet which was not uncomfortable for either of them.

"I'd like to raise one more matter," said Patricia.

"What's that?"

"I want to suggest that we meet every other week or two weeks out of every three."

"Patricia, this has been the only steady thing in my life since Vicky and the kids died. I can't let it go. Don't fire me."

"I'm not doing that. We used to meet twice a week. Then once. There are two reasons I'm suggesting this, which you'll understand."

Joe indicated with a gesture that Patricia should continue.

"First, I'll always be available, and we no longer need a weekly meeting. Second, not only are you and others feeling overwhelmed. The system is overwhelmed. The demand for support for mental illness and concerns has grown much larger during Covid. I have a friend who is a therapist, a psychologist, in private practice. She is kind and works long hours. She just posted on her Web page the statement that she can't take any new patients until at least six months from now. People wait a long time for help. Too long."

"I didn't know that. I know that Molly is going crazy at Tessa's and can't help all the people who need her support. She tells me she says no so often that she wants to beat herself up."

"She's not alone. Kids are suffering, parents are suffering, the elderly are isolated with no help. Covid has stretched us to bursting."

"So, you need to triage and Joe Grace isn't as needy."

"I could use the hour for someone else. All my colleagues are doing the same. We met and talked about the problem. Doing so hurts, but it has to be done.

"Can we do two out of three to start?"

"Sure. And if you need more, get in touch."

XXXIV

That evening Danny went to the airport to pick up Gabriella, who was returning at 7:00 from conducting the *Orchestre Capiltole National de Toulouse*. Shockingly, and happily, the plane from Paris was virtually on time, only ten minutes late. As had become their custom, they didn't discuss anything about Gabriella's conducting in the car on the way home. They talked about family, French responses to Covid, and the coming federal election, scheduled for next Monday. "We should vote in the advance poll on Saturday or Sunday," said Gabriella. "There are fewer polling stations because of Covid and there will be big line-ups on Monday."

When they got to Gabriella's apartment, they opened a bottle of Pinot Grigio and sat in the living room.

"Now, tell me what happened," asked Danny.

"It was good. They're very good, not as good as the Toronto Symphony, but close. And they are professional, but they were rough. I'm grateful for having had the experience of starting up Bloor Street. I tried at first to calm things and let them know that every other orchestra was facing the same problem. I even talked about Bloor Street and let them know that we had made progress fast. I told them how I was disappointed with my own playing of the flute, but it was getting better. That helped."

"It helped because you made yourself one of them. That's one thing you do well. You're a colleague, not a boss. How was your French?"

"It was acceptable. We worked mostly in English, which most knew. And two of their number, a violinist and an oboist, are Italian, so when I spoke fluent Italian that got some eyebrows raised. Between the three languages we got along."

"I envy you. My French is, as you know, the kind that can listen but not really make deep conversation. The lack of fluency always bothers me."

"That's your Canadian conscience, Danny. You can still do something about it by taking courses. And you do have a second language in Hebrew. There was at least one Hebrew-speaking person in group."

"When do you go to Boston?"

"Near the end of the month."

"How do you feel about going to the States?"

"I don't think Boston will be a problem. Their rate of vaccination parallels that of France. If you asked me about going to Florida, which I am doing in a few months, I'd be wondering."

"Which piece did you like best?"

"Torelli's trumpet concerto. For some reason it was the most vibrant and joyous. Probably because the trumpeter was among their best musicians. The concerto is short, but it rightly got the most attention from the audience. We should include it at Bloor Street. Enough of me, Danny. Tell me about you and the family."

"There's little to tell. Everyone's fine. Avi's enjoying McGill. And I missed you and worked a lot. I'll tell you about one of the dumbest things I've ever done. As a detective, that is. I've certainly done a lot of other dumb things."

Gabriella laughed. "If you're looking for a compliment, forget it. Now tell me."

Danny related the latest news in the Jimmy Chester case. He concluded, "and so, with Yom Kippur starting tomorrow night, I'm reminded how easily bad things can happen to good people. Not only Jimmy, but his family and friends who loved him."

"I don't have to remind you that life is often not fair."

"You don't. But this goes beyond that. Life is often harsh and unjust. We'd all like to be protected from that."

"What are you doing on Yom Kippur?"

"What I've done for the last several years. I'll go to Lake Ontario and take a walk along the water and think about the year past and my hopes for the coming year. That's what I think Yom Kippur is really about."

"Are Ruth and Irwin able to go to synagogue?"

"Yes. They'll do Yom Kippur their way and, as usual, the rebel in the family will do it his way."

"Some rebel. It probably does you good to think of yourself that way, but you are rock solid my love."

"Well, I've fooled you and that counts for a lot."

"Time to go home, Danny. You have a day ahead of you before the solemn holiday."

On Yom Kippur, the Day of Atonement, the holiest day in the Jewish year, the weather was good, sunny and cooler than the summer heat. Danny drove to Ashbridge's Bay, to the very wide beach on Lake Ontario connected to a lovely park.

There were people there on this Thursday in mid-September, but not many. Several parents and young children were in the playground, some retirees were on benches and occupying picnic tables, and a few hardy souls were on the beach. This particular stretch of sand was a center for beach volleyball for the city with many playing fields, but only one group of four was playing and/or practicing. Fall was in the air and on the ground.

Danny decided to walk along the boardwalk as he reflected. He first went west and then a bit south, to the end of the boardwalk at Ashbridge's Bay, where there was a lovely view of the wide beach amid large rocks, some on top of one another. He sat for a bit and just let his gaze wander, admiring yet another fine place in his beloved city.

Then, he retraced his steps in order to traverse the entire boardwalk, all the way to the end of the beach.

In his mind, he thought about Covid as a metaphor: for our inability to control our own destinies; for the power of nature in the taming of civilization; for the need for healing that we all share on this planet of ours; for a single germ changing our fears and our hopes.

He pondered what he had come to believe long before Covid, the fragility of civilization. Fragile not only because of a pandemic, but because we ourselves have in us the possibility of destroying our own lives. How, he asked himself, have I contributed to decency and kindness? How can I do better?

He wondered about the world being left to the next generations. Covid was terrible, he thought, but it will be conquered, sometimes in spite of our behavior. But climate change is the great unknown. Not that it wasn't happening already. But what might it yet become and what do we do about our own contributions to making the planet unsafe, possibly even demonic?

'Enough big questions,' he said to himself. 'On this day of atonement, I am supposed to ask for forgiveness from god and humans. I don't know about god, but there are matters in my relations with other people in the last year in which I could have behaved a lot better.' And he thought about his behavior and his choices.

He reached the end of the boardwalk and sat for a bit, looking at the water, which for him was full of life, beauty, and both serenity and danger. Then he stood up and began the trek back, back into his world. 'I have to keep going,' he thought. 'But I have to do it better. Jimmy Chester things happen, and that is hard to comprehend. All we can do is what his family is doing. Keep going, if only for the sake of those to come after us.'

He found it hard to judge himself satisfactorily. 'I'll try to be a better person this year. That's all I think I can do. That's all I think we can do.'

He drove home in a kind of fog, enveloped in his thoughts. When he got to his house, before he left the car, he said out loud, "OK, Mom and Dad, it's not exactly what you did on Yom Kippur, yet I think this is what you did in your own way."

He waited until some minutes after sunset, and he then served himself a rare shot of schnapps to end the day.

XXXV

Danny, Sydney, Louise and Patrick worked quickly on the Jimmy Chester/Henry Brandt case, one which combined drug peddling, money laundering and murder, along with related matters in both Toronto and Vancouver.

Brandt became their source of information and the main witness. Louise and Patrick quietly went to the Brandt home, sometimes separately, to do the interviews, not wanting to take Brandt to the station and telegraph what was happening.

On the basis of Brandt's testimony, they obtained a court order to examine the books at Cornucopia. As careful as the drug consortium was, it was clear that the three Toronto stores were being used to launder money. On that basis the three officers of the company, John Gagliano, Soo Kim, and Albert Feldstein, were charged, along with several others.

They had expensive and prominent lawyers defending them and there was a lot of posturing about due process, evidence and rights. Sydney and Patrick were dealing with them because this case came under Major Crimes. Sydney strongly defended what was done and demonstrated that they had been careful to follow all the rules. In addition, at one meeting with the defendants and the lawyers, Sydney slipped in a warning. "I want you to know that if anything happens to a person named Henry Brandt, we will know where to look."

The lead lawyer, Ralph Mostyn, from the firm of Andrews, Mostyn LLP, looked puzzled when Sydney raised this point, seemingly out of the blue. "I don't know what you mean, Inspector," he said.

"I think," answered Sydney, "you may need a further conversation with your clients. This case is very complicated, as you know. It involves more than money laundering."

"Here, we are dealing with what has been charged," said Mostyn, "and that only involves money laundering."

"So far, counsellor," said Sydney somewhat enigmatically. "Let's get back on track."

Danny followed the murder investigation to Vancouver. The police there had three names of individuals possibly hired by the drug organization to kill Henry Brandt. Luckily, one of them, Charlie Foster, a person who had recently finished serving a ten year term for manslaughter, came up on the computer as having flown to Toronto the day before the murder, and then flown back to Vancouver from Montreal a week later.

He was questioned by the Vancouver police who hadn't come up with anything definite. Still, Foster couldn't account for what he had been doing in Toronto. He refused to say where he had stayed or even to say how long he had been in the city. He said he had business in Toronto and Montreal. On a long shot, Danny got in touch with the

Montreal police, but there were no outstanding cases of anyone being shot in that city at that time.

The Vancouver police sent a picture of Foster to Toronto. Danny made a strange request for a second photo. "Could you," he asked, "get a photo from Foster's back? He should be wearing a light suit jacket. No hat." They did so.

Danny and Nadiri showed the two photos to Shawn Dennis, the law student who had chased Jimmy Chester's killer.

"Could be," said Shawn. "I can't be certain. It looks like the guy, but I don't know that I can swear this is the person on the basis of these photos. How tall is this guy?"

Nadiri consulted the file. "Five feet, ten inches."

"What does he weigh?"

"Seventy-seven kilos. About one hundred and seventy pounds."

"Could be. The guy I saw was normal height, normal weight."

On that basis, Danny went to Vancouver, accompanied by Shawn Dennis, to be part of the second interview with Foster. It was, Danny believed, a very long shot that anything would result from the trip, but it was the only chance he had in the case. His liaison was Detective Sergeant James McGrath of Vancouver's Homicide Squad.

"The evidence is circumstantial," said McGrath. "The drug organization knows we're looking into it, and this has resulted in their scaling back some of their operations, especially in the suburbs."

"More circumstantial stuff," said Danny. "We can't

move on the basis of people being scared. I think we keep going and then see where our investigation lands. As I briefed you, I not only want to find the killer of the unlucky Jimmy Chester, who was in the wrong place at the wrong time, I want to prevent further violence."

"Well," said McGrath, "we have two things to do. First the line-up for your witness, then the interview."

"Maybe a third," said Danny. "But we can get to that later."

Line-ups look good in media depictions of police activity. They are dramatic and suspenseful. However, in real life, in Canadian courts, the evidence of eyewitnesses has often been found unreliable. The courts are leery of making wrongful convictions only on the basis of an eyewitness, even multiple eyewitnesses. Today, judges issue cautions to juries when only eyewitness evidence is used for identification.

In addition, the rules for organizing a line-up and presenting the line-up to a witness are very strict. Consequently, neither Danny nor McGrath was involved in the exercise. It was organized by an officer not known to Shawn Dennis. Danny also noted that Shawn had been informed about the height and weight of the suspect, and requested that all the men in the line-up be roughly five feet ten inches and one hundred and seventy pounds. As well, the killer had worn dark pants and a blue jacket, and all the men on parade were furnished with those clothes.

On top of all the concerns about line-ups Covid intervened. The killer had worn a black mask. Hence, all the people in the line-up were supplied with a similar face covering.

Danny and McGrath watched the event from behind a one way glass. There were six men in the line-up. Charlie Foster was number three. Shawn was instructed by the officer to take his time. "We have all the time in the world," he said, and then he moved to the back of the room.

Shawn didn't identify anyone immediately. Danny learned later that he had researched line-ups and their use in the law library, and was aware of how much error there might be. He was composed and took his time. He also asked to see them from the rear.

Then Shawn asked, "Can I eliminate some people, rather than just choosing one?"

"Yes," came the answer from the officer.

"I eliminate number one and number four."

The officer instructed those two to leave the room.

Shawn again took his time. After a few minutes, he said, "I eliminate number two."

Numbers three, five, and six remained. There were certainly affinities in addition to height and weight. Their hair color was similar. What could be seen of their faces had a shape that was alike.

"Can I still take my time?" asked Shawn.

"Yes, sir," said the officer.

Finally, after a few more minutes, Shawn said. "I'm sorry. I can't eliminate any of the three. But I'm fairly certain one of these men was the one who shot the person in the Regina."

"Is there anything else?"

"No. That's it."

"OK, gentlemen. Please leave the room."

Danny and McGrath greeted Shawn when he too left the room. "I'm sorry," said Shawn. "That's the best I can do."

"Don't be sorry," said McGrath. "You did the best you could. I think you were very credible. It's the most difficult line-up I've ever witnessed."

"We'll talk later," said Danny. "On the plane when we return to Toronto. You did fine. You were very straight and honest."

The next piece of Danny's day was to sit in and participate in the interview with Foster.

McGrath and his partner, Jeanne Raveline, were doing the interview. Charlie Foster had a lawyer present, Maryanne Greene. Danny had been informed that Greene was one of the most prominent criminal lawyers in the province. "Clearly," said McGrath, "she's been hired by the organization. Foster couldn't afford her fees."

After the preliminaries of noting identification and time, McGrath began. He addressed Foster. "We're interested in your trip to Toronto several weeks ago. Could you tell us what you did on your visit?"

Foster was silent as Greene answered for him. "Is there any reason a citizen has to answer for taking a holiday, doing some business, and visiting friends?"

"We believe," answered McGrath, "That your client may have been involved in criminal activity. We'd like to know what he was doing in order to further our investigation of a murder."

"My client was visiting friends on a holiday. As far as I know, unless there are compelling reasons to deny their rights, citizens in Canada, even now in Covid, have the right to travel and associate with others. They certainly don't have to answer for those activities."

"We suspect Mr. Foster of killing one James Chester in Toronto while he was in the city. We'd like to know if he has an alibi."

"On what grounds do you suspect him? That he was in Toronto? There were millions of others in the city at that time."

"Mr. Foster has a history."

"Mr. Foster served his time in jail. You know you can't use his history to claim he now is again committing crimes."

McGrath directed the next question to Foster. "Where did you stay when you were in the city of Toronto?"

Greene answered. "My client stayed at the Holiday Inn on Carlton Street."

McGrath again looked at Foster. "Where were you on the afternoon of August 17th?"

"My client was in his hotel room, working and reading."

"Did you speak with anyone, in person or on the phone?"

"My client was not in contact with anyone at that time."

"So, you don't have a witness to substantiate your alibi?"

"Nor do about a million other people in the Greater Toronto area, Sergeant," answered Greene.

"In the earlier line-up, a witness to the murder identified Mr. Foster as one of three possible people out of six men in the line-up."

Greene smiled ruefully. "Come off it, Sergeant. You're telling me that the courts are going to find Mr. Foster guilty of murder on the basis of that? You know better. Line-ups and identification are suspect anyway. Three of six? All masked? Ridiculous. If you want, we could ask your witness how he saw the murderer. How many seconds transpired? Did he see the person full frontal? You need a lot more than that."

Danny intervened. "Mr. Foster, do you own a gun?"

"My client at this time does not own a gun."

"Did you own a gun?"

"You know the answer to that. Mr. Foster owned a gun ten years ago."

Danny was scrambling in his mind. He knew the interview this was going badly and searched for some way to rescue it. He decided to put the question directly. "Did you kill the trombone player at the Regina Hotel several weeks ago?"

"Are you accusing my client of that act? What evidence do you have? That he was in Toronto at the time? That he has a history? That in a line-up he may be one of three masked people? As far as we are concerned, we have co-operated with you in this flimsy matter. We're leaving. Either give us better evidence or we're gone."

McGrath and Raveline and Danny were silent. Greene put her file into her briefcase and she and Foster stood up. "Good day," she said, and they left.

There was some frustrated silence for a time. "There's one more way to go," said Danny.

"What's that?" asked Raveline.

"We have the bullets that killed Jimmy Chester. They came from a Smith and Wesson .357 revolver. Will the court give us permission to search his apartment?"

"I doubt it, Danny," said McGrath. "We don't have a strong enough case to make. Besides, the gun may be at the bottom of Lake Ontario or one of the rivers near Montreal."

"Can we try?" said Danny.

"I'll make as strong a case as possible. It's a long shot."

"At the moment, James," said Danny, "it's all we have."

When he returned to Toronto Danny immediately met with the other members of the team, Sydney, Louise, and Patrick.

"What do we have?" he asked. "And where are we going to go?"

"There are still three issues," said Sydney. "A murder, drug dealing and money laundering. I'd like to start with the money laundering."

"That's well in hand," said Patrick. "We have enough evidence to make charges against the three owners of Cornucopia and others. The laundering has stopped, of course, and the business is in trouble. The charges have been laid and the case is in the hands of the Crown."

Patrick continued. "The drug dealing is being investigated, and it's not as rampant as it was before. We've decided to go with what we have. We're going to charge some of the lower level dealers and players, those for whom we have evidence. We don't think we can get the top people this time around. But the dealing has effectively slowed down almost to a stop. So we've broken up the drug ring. At least for the group here in Toronto."

Sydney looked at Louise. "And the murder?"

"It's very frustrating, ma'am," said Louise. "We think we know who ordered it and who did it. But there isn't enough evidence to do anything about it. It reminds me of a case we had a few years ago when we knew who killed the victim, but couldn't charge the person for lack of evidence. We did get the person on other charges, but the murder was never solved. Here, we are fairly certain Charlie Foster did the killing, and that the orders came from the top of the organization in Vancouver on the recommendation of one or all of Albert Feldstein, Soo Kim and John Gagliano. But we have no evidence. It's all circumstantial and, frankly, very soft."

"What about your trip to Vancouver?" asked Sydney of Danny.

"It only adds to the frustration. Our witness, Shawn Dennis, did well, but couldn't make a positive identification. He narrowed the line-up down to three, but even a law student in first year could laugh that out of court. We have Charlie Foster in Toronto and Montreal at the time. We don't have a weapon, one which was likely thrown away after the killing. We tried to get a warrant to search Foster's apartment. The judge wouldn't issue it with such flimsy evidence. Nadiri is correct. We probably won't get the satisfaction of a solution."

"Do we close the case?"

"No. We keep looking. Especially if we can find more witnesses. I doubt that will happen, but we'll survey people again. I expect that this one won't have a satisfactory result."

They talked some more, clinging to the meeting in the hope that something useful would arise. Nothing did. Finally, they decided to end it.

Danny felt he had two more things he needed to do before putting the case on the side. First, he had a conversation with Lois and Henry Brandt the next day. He summarized what was happening and then said, "Mr. Brandt, we think you are safe. There is enough heat on these people that they could not take action against you without severe consequences. I also think that by this time you are a tiny matter relative to their troubles. So, we believe you are no longer on their radar and, moreover, you will not be back on it."

"Can Henry leave the house safely?" asked Lois.

"We believe so. Here's my advice. Wear the vest when you are out for the next while. You'll feel safer. Then, after a time, you won't need it. We'll also send a police car around to the house several times a day. Just to pass by and show a presence. After a time that also will not be necessary."

"What happens to me now?" asked Henry.

"That depends on you, Mr. Brandt. I'll be blunt. You got yourself into this mess and you will have to figure out how to get back into life again. Some things are clear. As you know, the Crown has made an arrangement with you via your lawyer. You will be charged with money laundering. Because of your co-operation and the small magnitude of the fraud, you will be found guilty and likely be given a suspended sentence. No jail. So you can start again."

"I'd like to go back a few years and do it all over again," said Lois.

"Unfortunately, you can't. You two will have to decide

with your children how to move on as a family. I don't have any special advice for you. It won't be easy. The next few years will be tough. I personally don't think you are bad people in the way I think people who profit from selling drugs on the street are bad people. You are probably good people who wound up because of circumstances doing some bad things. You'll have to figure out the next steps."

"I guess there are people worse off," said Lois.

"I agree," responded Danny.

"What do you mean?" asked Henry.

Danny looked at Lois. "You tell him," he said.

"Henry, we have each other and the children. The Chester family have suffered has a loss that is terrible and can't be fixed. They did nothing wrong and look what happened. We're going to have to live with that whatever occurs."

Danny's second matter was to speak with the Chester family the next day, Jimmy's widow Susan and Susan's brother and sister-in-law, John and Faye Bomart. He went to Susan's home and over a cup of coffee Danny summarized what had happened so far in the investigation.

"Do you think you will eventually be able to charge people for the murder?" asked Susan.

Danny visibly squirmed. "I doubt it. We'll keep trying. I'm not giving up. But we need clear evidence."

"I think I get it, Inspector," said John. "Can't you arrest Foster and maybe that will make him talk?"

"Sorry, John. What we have isn't close. I can't offer you the closure of a trial and a sentence. I wish I could."

"We appreciate your coming here and your honesty," said Lois, "but we do feel let down."

"I won't argue with you, Mrs. Chester. I sometimes feel as if I'm letting you down. But we live in a certain kind of society. We're not in Russia or China or Saudi Arabia. Democracy is imperfect, but it's all we have."

"Nice words, Inspector," said Faye. "They don't help. This is the shittiest thing that could happen to a good person and a good family. And nothing is being done."

Lois reached across the table and put her hand on Faye's. "I agree, Faye, if it weren't for the kids, I'd give up. I really would. But I can't. We have to move on."

"I'll keep in touch," said Danny as he stood, getting ready to leave. "I only wish you well in the future."

Faye spoke, "Do you have a wife and kids?"

"I have a wife and a son."

"What would you do if this had happened to you and one of them was killed stupidly?"

"I don't know, Faye. I really don't know."

XXXVI

Nadiri and Alvin had searched in vain for Robert Casey and Christopher Osborne over the last several weeks. They issued a provincial bulletin and spent time talking with Casey's and Osborne's families and known associates. They did a search of Casey's apartment in Etobicoke and Osborne's apartment in East York. They monitored their credit cards and their hangouts. They spoke with all the known stamp dealers in Toronto and the greater metropolitan area. They surveyed the pawn shops which might deal in stamps. They even got in touch with prominent stamp collectors to ask if they had any information, because they believed that the robbery was likely sponsored by someone who coveted the rare stamps, in much the same way as some art thefts are initiated by individual collectors.

Finally, they met with Danny to ask if they were missing anything.

"How, sir," asked Nadiri, "do you disappear in this world? They have to eat. They need a place to stay."

"I think they're being protected, hidden and provided for by someone. It could be a relative, a friend, or even the person who might have hired them to do the theft."

"We also thought that the timing of the theft was important," said Alvin. "Someone knew that Riordon Adams had a regular Wednesday evening dinner at his club. We spoke to all the participants. Of course, they all denied they had anything to do with the robbery. And the point is that they would have known Adams would be at home that Wednesday, which gives them a kind of alibi."

"Unless they have a better alibi, it doesn't rule them out," said Danny.

"We know that," responded Nadiri. "One of them could have used the obvious logic to mask their involvement. Two of the ten regular dinner members don't have clear alibis. They are Marshall Combrian and Stephen Entender."

"What do they do?" asked Danny. "What do we know about them?"

"Combrian is the owner of a business that makes boxes," said Alvin. "All kinds. From cereal boxes to large ones for all kinds of businesses. Entender is a major hospital administrator with the University Health Network. As far as we know, they are not stamp collectors."

The three of them spent more time trying to find a way to solve the dilemma, but came up with nothing. Danny summed up. "Keep going. I think you should start again. Keep talking to relatives, friends and associates. We'll get there somehow. It's not yet time to throw in the towel. Let's just hope something turns up."

The answer did turn up in an unlikely manner. Nadiri and Alvin split the task of going back to talk with all those they had interviewed. The next Monday afternoon, Alvin, who had already seen a relative and two friends of Robert Casey, found himself near an Irish bar and grill in Etobicoke often frequented by Casey. They had seen the owner once, but since he was only a few blocks away after yet another frustrating interview, he went again to The Bog Pub.

The lunch crowd had finished and it was quiet at a little before three in the afternoon. Alvin reintroduced himself to the owner-manager, Ed Connor, a man in his fifties, something of a neighborhood institution by now. Connor offered Alvin a drink, which he turned down in favor of a glass of water. Connor pulled a beer for himself and the two went to a quiet table.

"We're reviewing the case," said Alvin. "and we just wanted to check in again with people who knew Robert Casey. Have you thought of anything that might help us locate him?"

"Bob's disappeared," replied Conner, taking a long drink from his glass. "He's nowhere around. I did ask a few people about him."

"Thanks for doing that," said Alvin. "He's not turned up. Can you think of anything you can tell me that might help?"

"Bob's a nice guy. Very sociable. But he's also firm in his opinions."

"What do you mean by firm?"

"Things like politics. He hates the Liberal Party. The NDP drives him up the wall. So people stay away from that when chatting with him. He loves rugby and roots for Ireland, of course. Even when they play Canada. He likes eating seafood—he usually orders shrimp or sole—but he thinks people who eat oysters have no taste. He was anti-shutdowns and blames the Liberals, especially the prime minister, and was an anti-vaxxer. He joined some demonstrations."

"What do you mean he *was* anti-shutdowns and anti-vaxxing."

"He was. Until two of his cousins—he has a lot of them—got Covid and wound up in critical care and on ventilators. One died. So about six weeks ago he told me he was now convinced that vaccines were necessary. He turned around, got a shot, and annoyed everyone then with his firm insistence that vaccines were necessary."

"People who are certain sometimes move from one certainty to another."

"I don't know about that," said Connor. "He got his first shot then and he was loud about it."

They conversed some more and then Alvin thanked Connor and went to his car. He immediately called Nadiri and told her about the conversation.

"Do you think," asked Nadiri, "that he'll get a second shot?"

"I don't know," replied Alvin. "Maybe he already got the second shot. Maybe he'll not get a second shot now that he's hiding. But…."

Nadiri interrupted. "I'll get on it right away. I'll see you when you get here."

Nadiri made several calls before finally contacting the right person and securing permission to check the vaccination reservations. It took time because several people asked to call her back to make certain she was indeed from the Toronto police. Nadiri knew they were correct in doing this, but she was also impatient. Still, she told herself to calm down. 'I'd do the same thing if I were in their position,' she thought.

The information she got excited her. Robert Casey had an appointment to receive his second Pfizer shot the following Thursday, September 30, at 11:20, at a vaccine clinic located at 7120 Hurontario Street in Mississauga.

Nadiri immediately called the Homicide squad in Mississauga. She spoke to Detective Sergeant Philomena Conforni and they agreed to have a Zoom meeting in order to make arrangements. By the time the meeting was held in the late afternoon, Alvin was also present.

"I know the site," said Conforni. "My husband and I got our shots there. It's large. The good part is that the person getting the shot sits down and the staff and nurses come to them. So if Casey shows up, we'll know where he'll be. As you probably know, there's a waiting period after you get the shot to check that there are no reactions. We can arrest him while he's waiting. We'll have four people there, including me."

"We'd like to be there also," said Nadiri.

"Of course. Let me make my arrangements and I'll speak with you no later than Wednesday to sort it out."

"Sergeant," said Alvin. "Remember that his partner had a gun. He might have one also."

"Thanks for the reminder. I'm counting on the fact that we will not be expected."

"I agree," said Nadiri. "But let's also remember that they nearly killed Riordon Adams, the person who they robbed."

On Thursday, Nadiri and Alvin drove to Mississauga to meet with Philomena Conforni and her colleagues, all in plain clothes. Precautions were taken. Once Casey appeared—if he appeared—a constable would be behind him, seeming to be getting his second shot. As well, Casey would be escorted to a place at the end of a closed corridor to get his shot and to wait. Yet another constable would be 'waiting' nearby. The arrest would be made by Conforni and the third constable on the assumption that Casey may have heard about Nadiri and/or Alvin from one or more of the people they interviewed.

Casey arrived alone at a few minutes after eleven and. parked near the entrance. He donned the required mask, put up the hood of his jacket, and then went in. Still, he was spotted by both Alvin and one of the constables who then entered the site with a 'reservation' just after Casey.

All seemed normal. Casey's reservation was checked by a young worker. He was directed to a short line, and waited, distanced from others, keeping his hood on. When his turn came, he was shown a place to sit and the nursing aide brought the vaccine to him. "This is your second shot, is that right?" asked the aide.

"Yeah."

The aide picked up a needle and cleaned the spot on Casey's arm." I'll bet your glad to get this," he said, trying to make small talk.

"Yeah."

The vaccine was administered. "You need to stay here for fifteen minutes" said the aide. He gave Casey a form indicating the time he could leave. "When you can leave, go to one of those tables at the other end of the hall and you'll get your proof of vaccination slip."

Casey looked at his watch. He said nothing. The aide moved on to his next appointment.

Conforni let five minutes pass. She then signalled. She and one constable went directly to Casey. The other two constables were close, back and front. She had her badge out. In front of Casey, she said, "Mr. Robert Casey, we are arresting you for robbery and assault. You have…." Casey jumped up, pushed Conforni away and tried to leave. He was subdued by the three constables and handcuffed. Conforni then informed Casey of his rights. He was escorted to a waiting police car with three other officers, where he would be taken to Toronto to be formally charged and held. Conforni then joined Nadiri and Alvin and they followed the police vehicle.

Alvin drove and Nadiri immediately got on the phone to find who owned the car Robert Casey used. It turned out to be someone Alvin had interviewed, Donald Casey, a first cousin of Robert, who lived with his wife and child in a small home in Etobicoke, on Sandcliff Road, not far from Robert's apartment. Alvin had been there, he had spoken with Donald and his wife Melissa, and had found no reason to suspect they might be hiding Robert or had been in contact with him.

First, they went to the station to charge Robert Casey. They did put him in an interview room, but Casey refused to speak without his lawyer present. As a result, arrangements were made to meet with Casey and his lawyer on the next day. While all this was happening, Alvin managed to get a warrant to search Donald Casey's home.

"Do you think we'll find anything there?" asked Alvin.

"I don't know. If nothing's there we still have the fact that Robert borrowed his cousin's car. The family aided a known felon. But I'd like to find something there. This case is tough."

They arrived at six-thirty in the evening and knocked on the door. Melissa answered. She recognized Alvin who had the warrant in his hand. "We intend to do a search of your house, Ms. Casey," he said. "We have a warrant and we have Robert Casey in jail at the moment."

"Wait here," she replied. She tried to fully shut the door but Nadiri managed to stop it. "It's my home," Melissa said. "The court has given us the right to search it," replied Nadiri.

Melissa disappeared inside and came back two minutes later trailing her husband. "You can't just walk into people's houses" he said in a loud tone. "We have rights."

Alvin handed him the warrant. "We suspect you of hiding a known felon. Your cousin is now in jail and we will be interviewing him with his lawyer tomorrow morning."

"We were just helping a family member," said Donald.

"Sorry, Mr. Casey. You knew from the time I interviewed you, maybe before then, that we were looking for your cousin on charges of breaking and entering, robbery and assault. He used your car to get to the vaccine center. The car is now being examined by our forensics people."

Donald looked angry for a few seconds, then his face turned blank. He stepped aside. "Do what you do," he said.

The search found that Robert Casey had hidden in the basement of the house. He had a bed, reading material including some pornography, a television set and a bathroom. His clothes were folded on a bench. In the back of a cupboard they found both a gun and a bag of cash with some coins on the bottom. They also found a notebook, but no stamps—and no indication of where Christopher Osborne might be or even if Casey had communicated with him.

After finished, Nadiri and Alvin sat in the kitchen with Donald and Melissa.

"How long was he here?" asked Nadiri.

"We're not answering any questions until we talk to our lawyer," was the reply from Donald.

"Actually," said Alvin, "you might well be guilty of obstruction of justice, a crime punishable by a jail term." Alvin made a gesture by putting up his open hands. "This is not a threat. But it is a fact."

"We need to talk to our lawyer," said Donald. "We're not answering anything until we do."

"That's your right, Mr. Casey," said Nadiri. "I think you should talk to your lawyer soon, because this investigation isn't over. We'll leave now, but we'll be back. And the forensics team might decide to examine your basement."

In the car, Nadiri said, "We've finally made progress. Forensics will examine Robert Casey's computer and the phone found on him when he was arrested."

"Yes," said Alvin. "In this connected world it's hard to keep a secret."

Once back at the station, they logged the gun as a Dan Wesson M191 ACP pistol, made in the United States. The money found counted out to $23,455.65.

XXXVII

The art show at Tessa's Place, which Nadiri had hoped to attend with Debra, had its opening on the late afternoon and evening of that last day in September. Over the last several years, it had grown into something more than just a presentation of the work of the art classes. Molly and the board were using it as a kind of showcase, and they had invited a number of donors, potential donors, and some civic personalities to the event. A jazz quartet which donated its time greeted people in the open space on the first floor when they entered.

The art was hung in all the public spaces of the house. Anna was assisted in mounting the show by Debra and Joe, as well as some of the people still using the house as a shelter. She treated the event in the same manner she would any exhibition. Each piece had a title and identified the artist. When it was possible, she put pieces with similar themes in the same space. Hence, several pieces referring to body and body image were together. Several colourful abstractions were in the small library.

The collaborative painting, *Broadview and Queen*, was hung in the ground floor lounge as the star of the show. A number of visitors were lingering by it because of its strength and colors.

Anna invited her boss, Tom Pendleton, who owned a major gallery on Hazelton Avenue and part of another, the place where Anna worked, in the Distillery District.

At the start, Molly and several board members took visitors around, showed them the art and answered questions about Tessa's, its mission, and how it worked. In some cases, the donors were long-standing friends, some from corporations, some from banks, others who were introduced to Tessa's because of what had occurred in their own lives or the lives of relatives and friends. This group was led by Anna. They were very relaxed and enjoyed talking with some of the women artists and Molly.

In other cases, there were potential donors, either individuals or those representing a foundation, sometimes a family foundation, or a corporation. Molly and some veteran volunteers stayed with this group, never asking for money, which was implicit, but trying to tell them about the importance of Tessa's in the life of the city.

Debra and Tom Pendleton, belonging to neither group, found one another, and went around the house together.

"Are you the Debra Castle who wrote for the *Globe* and was on the recent library task force?" asked Tom.

"I am," Debra answered. "But I don't like the notoriety. I'm just a librarian who loves good books and the kind of work that Tessa's does. I'm also a friend of Anna's."

"I know that," said Tom. "I also know you took care of Anna after her ordeal. I want to thank you for that."

"No need. That's what we do. You also helped Anna, as

she told me."

"Well," said Tom with a smile, "Anna never formally introduced us but she has told each of us about the other."

"The ordeal, as you call it, changed her. It made her stronger. It was what gave her the motivation to help at Tessa's."

"You're right. She's grown professionally as well. She'll be ready to curate on her own soon."

"Let's stop talking about ourselves," said Debra, "and look at the art."

"One question first. Anna told me you write about rare books and things of that sort. Also, that you helped with the restoration of the stolen paintings to the Gelernter family."

"I do some book scholarship. Some of it is similar to what people research in art. Provenance, history, originality. All that stuff."

"I've never gone around a place with a book person."

"I've never gone around an art gallery with the owner of a major one. Let's do it."

They were in the main lounge and Tom turned to look at *Broadview and Queen*. "What do you think?" he said.

"First, unless you know it, I'll tell you the story about how it came to be."

Tom nodded and Debra told him about Joe and the women who created the work. "Joe is around. I'll introduce you if we bump into him."

"Remarkable," said Tom. "The image has a coherence and singular strength which would have fooled me into thinking it was made by one artist."

"Maybe Joe as the teacher helped to give it its shape

and meaning."

"He must be a good teacher."

"That he is, says Anna."

"It has depth, the color relations are excellent. Even the white spaces work. This is a real work of art."

They then went up the stairs, where on the wall hung several paintings related to fantasy worlds. "These are good," said Debra, "especially the one titled *Mary's Dream*, but nowhere near the *Broadview and Queen* image."

"I agree," said Tom. "Some of these women have potential, Mary foremost, but they are not really finished works."

On the second floor the library contained images of children and animals. Debra asked, "What did you mean when you said that the image made with Joe's guidance was a real work of art and that the paintings on the stairs, presumably these as well, are not really finished works?"

"There's a critical issue," answered Tom, "that I've never fully sorted out in my mind."

"And that is?"

"If a work comes out of a therapeutic situation, is it a work of art therapy particular to the psyche of an individual or is it a work of art?"

"Give me an example. I'm not certain I'm following you."

"Do you know the essays of the psychiatrist Oliver Sachs?"

Debra nodded. "Terrific stuff."

"Well, in one of them he is dealing with a musician who

orients himself to the world as much by sound as by sight, because he developed a severe case of agnosia. The musician was a very good amateur painter for much of his adult life. In his home some of his paintings were hung chronologically. He moved, said his wife, from representation to abstraction. Sachs saw it differently. Sachs saw the paintings as moving from a coherent world to an incoherent one. For him the recent images weren't abstraction, they were evidence of a pathology."

Debra did some thinking. "Can't an image be both?" she asked.

"Yes, that's where I'm landing. But I'm not certain I'm not fudging the matter. Which are works of art and which are personal statements about one's psyche? You see, I would put the *Broadview and Queen* painting in the work of art category, but I'm not certain I'd put these others there. Maybe in a grey territory between art and art therapy. Maybe just in art therapy."

"Can I try something on you that relates?" asked Debra.

"Sure."

"Do you know Van Gogh's last painting? At least the painting commonly regarded as his last painting?"

"*Wheatfield with Crows*, July 1890."

"That's it. When I first saw it—and I love Van Gogh—I didn't think it was a work of art. I still don't. I only think it matters because Van Gogh painted it, not because it's a great work. To me it's clearly the work of a deranged mind. Not that that matters. But it conveys incoherence and personal suffering, not tragedy or beauty. If you or I had painted it, it would be forgotten in an instant. Even now, it matters biographically, not artistically."

"You're right. If someone came in with it to my gallery, I'd instantly tell him it's not a good work of art."

"Yet, of course, others of Van Gogh's works, *Starry Night* for example, are both magical and wonderful, painted also by an unusual mind."

"You're helping me sort out something that's been on my mind for a long time. Still, I know there are some images which are evidence of pathology or just a personal statement, and I know there are some that are works of art. But there is still the grey area."

"Life is often grey, Tom. I don't like people who are so certain of everything that every response to the world is black or white. We human beings are complex characters. Maybe the literary equivalent of Van Gogh is Virginia Woolf. And you know that both of them took their own lives."

The two then quietly worked their way through the rest of the show, reflecting.

When they got back down to the ground floor, they found Anna, Irina from the art class, and Joe Grace with one of the board members, all standing near *Broadview and Queen*.

The board member, a well-dressed woman of about fifty, and Anna were in the middle of a conversation.

"I'd still like to buy it," they heard the woman say.

"We need to check with Molly," countered Anna. "And with some of the people who created it. And then we'll see if it's for sale."

Anna looked around. "Could someone find Molly?"

"I'll do it," answered Debra.

"What would it cost, if it were for sale?" asked the woman.

"Ms. Lundell, I'm not certain," answered Anna. "I have a figure in mind, but I'll deal with that if it goes on sale."

Meanwhile, several others, people associated with Tessa's as well as some visitors, were gathering around, joining Tom in listening to the interesting exchange.

While waiting for Molly, Anna remarked, "It is certainly a very good work of art."

Anna looked at Tom after she spoke. He nodded slightly.

"I think so," said Margaret Lundell. "I want it for my dining area."

After a few more minutes, Molly appeared.

Anna explained that Margaret Lundell, who Molly knew as a member of the board and a major donor, wanted to purchase the work.

"I can't tell you if it's for sale," said Molly, "until we talk to the artists."

Irina then spoke softly. "It can be for sale, Molly. We all spoke about it. We agreed the money should go to Tessa's."

"We'll worry about who gets the money later," said Molly. "You're telling me that the group agreed it can be sold?"

"Yes, all of us agreed."

Molly looked at Joe. "What do you think, Joe?"

"If the artists are OK, then I'm OK."

Then Molly turned to Anna, who said, "I'm fine with it."

There were now ten other people in the room listening in to the exchange, in addition to those involved.

"What are you asking for it?" said Margaret Lundell. But she wasn't finished. She then said, "Who are you to put a value on it?"

Molly gave her a hard look. "She's Anna Crowe. She teaches our art group and she runs a gallery in Toronto. Her credentials are as good as mine are in terms of working with battered women."

"All right," said Lundell. "What's it going for?"

"Four thousand dollars," said Anna firmly. Tom and Debra, standing in different parts of the room, both smiled.

Lundell hesitated. Then she said, "I'll give you three thousand."

Anna was about to decline the offer but she never got the words out. From the audience of ten, a man said, "I'll give you the four thousand." It was Sam Parkel, another member of the Board, who taught psychology at York.

"Sam," said Lundell. "Don't interfere."

"I'm not interfering. I'm offering a price. You want the painting, try to beat my price."

"Forty-five hundred," said Lundell.

Everyone looked at Parkel. "Forty-seven," he said.

An angry Lundell immediately responded. "Five thousand."

Parkel looked as if he was giving this some thought. Finally, "It's yours."

Tom broke the tension. "You can use my van to deliver it."

"Thanks, Tom," said Anna. She turned to Lundell.

"That's the owner of the Pendelton Gallery on Hazelton. He too knows something about art."

They broke up with Lundell unhappy and angrily talking with Parkel. The latter just listened and remained very calm.

Molly continued with the scheduled event. She spoke to all about the importance of doing art as part of healing and the work done by Tessa's. She thanked everyone for coming and invited all to visit the house again. "Hang around as long as you like," she said as she ended the formal part of the evening. "The music will continue."

XXXVIII

Nadiri scheduled the interview with Robert Casey and his lawyer for noon the next day, expecting by then to have some of the information available on his phone and computer.

She got a call at 11:00 from Bill Flaherty, a technician from the lab. "We got into both of them," he said, and I have some information for you now. We'll try to get more. I know you wanted something by noon."

"Thanks. First, anything about Christopher Osborne?"

"Casey and he communicated both by phone and text. Osborne turned off the Google tracking so that doesn't help. The phone number is a Toronto one, but that means nothing because he could use it anywhere on the planet. But Osborne said he's also staying with a relative and in an aside noted that he had eaten a peameal bacon sandwich, so that very likely means Canada."

"He comes from Stoney Creek, just outside Hamilton," said Nadiri. "He has relatives there. His mother, an aunt and two cousins. The local police questioned them and they denied any knowledge of the robbery or the whereabouts of Osborne. But Casey was protected initially by his cousin. Maybe it's the same with Osborne. We'll get on it. Anything on who hired them to do the robbery? Anything on the stamps?"

"Only that they got paid on delivery. We'll look again and we'll send everything to you."

"Sounds good."

Nadiri briefed Alvin on the findings as they talked about their strategy for the interview. "I'd like to have the information on the person who got the stamps," he said. "That would tie it up."

"I agree. But we'll work with what we have." Nadiri looked up. "What's with today's tie? You've had neutral ones for a while."

Alvin's tie had three single dose vials on a blue background. "I thought I'd call attention to the need for boosters. I'm also a big supporter of getting the vaccine. We still have too many people refusing."

"There was an article on the CBC site this morning saying that mandates are moving up the numbers."

"A good thing. Covid is not just something about oneself. The more people who get vaccinated, the more we are all protected."

"Agreed. Now let's put on our masks and see Casey and his lawyer."

They went to the interview room, where Casey and his lawyer, Daniel Walsh, were waiting. Walsh was not known to either Nadiri or Alvin. He was in his forties, dressed conservatively in a suit and tie. The mask hid many of his features, but Nadiri noted his hair was just greying and his eyes were blue beneath a creased forehead. Introductions were made and then Nadiri opened the questioning.

"Mr. Casey, we have evidence that you were in the house of Mr. Riordon Adams, and he can identify you. We also know that you were hiding from the police in your cousin's basement and that you had in your possession a sum of money close to twenty-five thousand dollars. How did you receive that sum of money?"

"It's my money," Casey replied. "How I keep my money is my business."

"Did you earn the money? Did you receive from it someone for services rendered?"

"It's my money," repeated Casey.

Walsh entered the conversation. "My client has given you his answer, Sergeant. There will be no further information on this matter."

'Damn it,' thought Nadiri. 'We're probably not going to get very much more.' "Do you know Christopher Osborne?"

"He's a friend. We sometimes have a drink together at The Bog."

"Did he accompany you in the robbery of Mr. Riordon Adams?"

"My client," said Walsh, "has not admitted to any robbery."

"All right," said Alvin. "Mr. Casey, did you on the evening of September 8th enter the home of Mr. Riordon Adams, and assault him and rob some of his stamp collection?"

"My client has no comment," said Walsh.

"Counsellor," said Nadiri, "we have enough evidence to charge Mr. Casey with breaking and entering, assault and robbery. Keeping silent is not going to help anyone."

"I've have no comment on that, Sergeant. Nor does my client."

Nadiri reached down into a case she had brought with her and took out a gun in a plastic covering. "Mr. Casey, is this your gun?"

"No comment," said Casey.

"Do you have a permit to own a firearm?"

"No comment."

"Mr. Casey, we are now formally charging you." Nadiri went through the charge and the notification to Casey of his rights.

When Nadiri and Alvin were alone, Alvin asked, "Does this happen a lot? Do people who are going to go to jail simply clam up?"

"Not a lot," answered Nadiri, "but enough. It happens."

"Is it about the code? Does he think he must keep silent to defend his friend? Why is he protecting the person who hired and paid him?"

"I don't have a clear answer, Alvin. It may be about the code. It may be some perverted form of what he thinks is the manly thing to do. It certainly is not about mitigating his sentence. I think you need a psychiatrist to deal with your questions because saying that people always act in their best interest doesn't answer them."

Part Three

XXXIX

The next Monday morning Danny received an unusual call. It was from a person who identified herself as Sandra Kovolechov, the administrative assistant to the Premier of Ontario. It was the first time in his career that he had had any communication with Queen's Park, as the provincial government is often called.

He took the call and he and Kovolechov exchanged pleasantries, both dancing around the reason for Queen's Park initiating the conversation. Finally, Danny asked directly, "What might you be calling about, Ms. Kovolechov?"

"Call me Sandy, Daniel. I wanted to ask you whether you might reconsider the decision to transfer Constable Katie Nelson from your squad. Our understanding is that she has been sent back to her former position."

"That's correct. But I can't give you an answer one way or the other. The matter is on the desk of the Chief. If you have a formal request, you should get in touch with him."

"We're not making a formal request. This is just an inquiry. We think she's really good at her job and were wondering why she wasn't continued."

"Again, you'll have to talk to the Chief to get an answer."

"Didn't you hire her?"

"No, she was assigned by the force to my squad. Which, may I add, is unusual."

"How did she do?"

"I'm not at liberty to discuss performance evaluations with anyone outside the people to whom I'm responsible. Again, call the Chief if you want to discuss this matter."

"Katie was under your supervision for about two months. Are you willing to support her return to the Homicide squad?"

"I'll answer that question when I'm asked by a superior in the police force."

"We would be grateful for your support."

"May I ask who the we happen to be?"

"You understand what I'm saying."

"Is there anything else you would like to discuss?"

"No. Thank you, Daniel."

Danny hung up thinking, 'The only people who call me Daniel are those who want me to think they're my friend.' He immediately sent an email to John Kingston, informing him of the conversation.

In reflecting on the timing of the call, Danny remembered that on the previous Friday Canada's Supreme Court upheld the law that slashed the size of Toronto's City Council during the last municipal election. It was, he noted to himself, a split 5-4 decision in which the court found the change imposed by the Premier did not violate the free-expression rights of candidates or voters. He wondered if the bold intervention had anything to do with the Premier's office thinking it could now interfere in any city matter.

Later that afternoon, Danny got a thank you email from the Chief. Then, he received a communication from the assistant who kept his schedule that a Zoom meeting had been arranged between the mayor, John Kingston and Danny for 8:30 the next morning. Danny had met the mayor several times, but had never had a conversation with him. He wondered what was happening that occasioned the need for a three-way meeting.

When the meeting began, the Mayor took charge and got right to the point. "As you both know, we have had calls from Queen's Park about the career of Katie Nelson. Inspector Miller, I've spoken with John about this and I think some important principles are at stake. Most especially, the integrity and independence of the police force, and the fact that police personnel decisions are not made for any political purpose. I want to make certain we're all on the same page here. John, let me have your sense of what's going on."

"I agree entirely," said John Kingston. "You and I have talked. I've asked Danny to send all queries to me and he did so with the request from the Premier's office on Monday. It can't be. We're not responsible to the Premier. Moreover, no police force could do its work with this kind of interference."

"Danny?" asked the mayor.

"This is serious, Mr. Mayor. I won't give you a long speech. You know what I'm going to say. This kind of interference only happens in countries that toy with democratic values. It's not only interference, it's playing with the law, and I agree with the Deputy Prime Minister that we are a nation of laws and place deep importance on the rule of law. Enough high theory. I think, frankly, that if this pressure continues, we go public. And if it succeeds, I'm prepared to resign in protest. My guess is that other colleagues will do so as well.

"I agree," added John. "I can't continue if this is the way things are run. I'll join you, Danny."

"So might I," added the Mayor. "Thanks. I needed to know that I have the support of the force. I'm sorry this has arisen. I'll either put a stop to it, or we'll have a very public fight. I wonder if Queen's Park thinks the Supreme Court gave them leave to do whatever they wanted to the city. That's not what the ruling said."

"I also thought about that," said Danny. "If that's the case the government is not only politicizing the police, they're politicizing the courts.

"Absolutely," added the Mayor. "I'll look after it. While I have you both, clue me in on homicide in the city. What's happening these days?"

They had another fifteen minutes of briefing the mayor and of general conversation. All three were relieved that a consensus had been reached so quickly on the major matter.

XL

Stoney Creek retained its name and identity, although in 2001 it had become part of the reorganized City of Hamilton. Nadiri liaised with the Hamilton Police Service to initiate a deeper search for Christopher Osborne. As in the case of Casey, Osborne was found in a relative's house, in an attic. He, too, had lots of cash among his possessions, $24,200.

Osborne was brought to Toronto, charged, and detained. Now, having gotten himself a lawyer from legal-aid, he would be interviewed.

Nadiri and Alvin greeted Osborne and his lawyer, Brenda Patel. Patel was in her mid-thirties, had black hair and brown eyes and was dressed in a blue pants suit. Alvin had noted to Nadiri that he had met Patel on a previous case and that she seemed highly competent and very professional. The two nodded to one another when Patel came into the room.

Nadiri went through the formalities and then opened the interview with a direct question. "Mr. Osborne, we have spoken with Robert Casey. As well, we have a person who can identify you as having been in Riordon Adams' home on September 8th. We know you assaulted him and robbed him of much of his stamp collection. Is this true?"

Brenda Patel answered. "We are willing to cooperate, Sergeant. We would like to know if Mr. Osborne's cooperation will be taken into consideration by the court."

"As you know, counsellor," answered Nadiri, "the charges will formally be made by the Crown. The police have no hand in determining how the Crown and the Court will act. That's just reality. On the other hand, it's my experience that your cooperation will be taken into account. That's the best I can offer. If this case goes to trial and you cooperate, I would testify to that. If you cooperate, I would put in the file that you did so."

"I need a guarantee," said Osborne.

"I can't give you that," said Nadiri. "Ms. Patel knows this. I can tell you we will acknowledge cooperation."

"It is my experience," said Patel, "that other members of the force have sometimes given assurances."

"That may be," said Nadiri. "You know they may have gone too far. I'm telling you what we *can* do."

"OK," answered Patel. "We understand. Let's move on."

Osborne indicated to Patel he'd like to speak. He turned to Nadiri, "Can I speak privately with my lawyer? I'm not sure I get all this."

"Of course." Nadiri put off the tape, indicating a pause in the interview. She said, "We'll be outside. Just knock on the door after you talk and we'll return."

Outside, Alvin asked Nadiri. "What's happening?"

"I think he wants to do a deal, but it's not in our power

to offer guarantees. They'll decide how far they'll go now."

The interview resumed after ten minutes.

After getting settled again, Nadiri asked, "Mr. Osborne, along with Robert Casey were you involved in the robbery of Mr. Adams on September 8th?"

"Yes."

"Did you strike Mr. Riordon Adams in the course of the robbery?"

"I hit the person who was there. We were told no one would be home. I didn't mean to hurt him badly."

"Who told you no one would be home?"

"The person who hired us to do the robbery."

"Who is that person?"

Osborne looked down, wriggled in his chair, and seemed to be making a decision. Nadiri let the silence do its own work.

"Do I have to tell that?" asked Osborne.

Patel answered. "You can keep silent. It's up to you to decide how much cooperation you give."

"I don't want to be locked up again for a long time."

Nadiri asked, "Do you want to have another conversation?" This was unusual, but Nadiri thought it important to show that, however far Osborne cooperated, and whatever information he gave, it was his choice.

"Maybe," said Osborne.

"Do so," said Nadiri. "We'll be outside."

After another ten minutes, Nadiri and Alvin returned to the room.

"Let's continue," said Nadiri. "Who was the person who told you no one would be home?"

"Eddie Hagan. He hired Bob, Bob took me on, and we split the $50,000."

"Who's Eddie Hagan?"

"He hangs around The Bog. He's part of a gang that runs businesses."

"What kind of businesses?" asked Alvin.

"I don't know. I'm just a guy they hire. I know some of their businesses are legit."

"What about the illegal ones?" said Alvin.

"I don't know. I'm not a big guy in this. I'm a hired hand."

They learned little else. Osborne had admitted his guilt, said he'd accompanied Casey, and identified Hagan. That was progress. As Nadiri put it to Alvin, "Now to find Hagan and see if we can move up the line."

XLI

The interference of the Premier's office both saddened Danny and made him even more determined to not get involved in the politics of policing. He signalled to Sara that he would welcome getting back on the street, for solving crime was what he believed the job was about.

An opportunity came up quickly. "There's a murder in a house around Yonge and Eglinton," said Sara as she walked into Danny's office the next day. "On Helendale Avenue. Why don't you take it? Your impatience is showing."

"Thanks. Find Louise and send her along."

Danny drove the short distance up Avenue Road, onto Oriole Parkway, took a right on Eglinton and a left onto Helendale, just past Eglinton Park.

He found the street closed temporarily with a squad car and yellow tape in front of #131. There was another squad car with a woman sitting in the rear. Two officers were inside the small home.

Danny showed his identification, looked at the name tag of one of the officers and asked, "What happened, Lowmayer?"

"There's a body in the kitchen, a male with a knife still in his back. Lots of blood. He was found by his friend, the woman who is waiting in the car. We didn't disturb anything. We just made sure he was dead. Forensics is coming."

"Good work. Tell the woman we'll talk to her shortly. I'm going in. My partner should be along in a few minutes."

Inside the small home, which Danny estimated was only about twelve feet wide, the body was lying on its side in the kitchen, at the rear of the first floor. In looking around, Danny found nothing odd. There were two mugs on the kitchen counter, each holding a small amount of tea. Danny couldn't discern footprints on the floor, but he knew the forensics people would look after that.

He reached into the pocket of the dead man and took out his wallet. He learned that the man was Gary Gerrity. The wallet contained some money and the usual array of cards, from Mastercard to Starbucks to Presto to the ever-present driver's license and Gerrity's Ontario Health Card.

Louise and the pathologist, Hugh O'Brien, arrived at the same time. "It's all yours, Hugh," said Danny. "Let me know when I can return."

Danny and Louise took the time to walk around the rest of the house. The living room had simple and decent furniture, some newspapers and magazines on a coffee table and a large television screen. There was a small bookcase with some paperbacks and magazines. Upstairs, there were two bedrooms and a bathroom. The closets told them that Gerrity lived alone, though in one of them there were some female clothes.

They went outside and entered the squad car to speak with the person who had found him. She identified herself as Amanda Salderson. She indicated that she lived with her daughter in an apartment nearby and had a relationship with Gerrity. She was distraught but indicated she could talk. "I have a key," she said, "and I was coming to meet him. We talked the day before and we were going to go to an early movie at the Cineplex nearby. I knocked and rang the bell and no one answered. That was odd. So I entered and there he was, on the floor, dead, with a knife in his back. I called 911. That's all I can tell you."

"Thanks, Ms. Salderson," said Louise. "Can you tell us what Mr. Gerrity did for work?"

"He's fifty-five. He's kind of retired. He has some family money and an income from some property he inherited. The house belonged to his parents before him."

"And you? Are you employed?"

"I work in the local Metro supermarket in the mall nearby. I'm a kind of bookkeeper and I sometimes fill in on the cash register. It's not full-time. Twenty-five hours a week."

"Is there anything else you want to tell us now? We'll have a longer interview soon."

"No," she answered, wiping her eyes with a tissue. "Gary was good to me and my daughter. He was a nice guy."

By now, Hugh O'Brien was waiting for Danny and Louise at the front of the house. "Not much to tell yet," he said. "The knife, which is an ordinary long kitchen knife, killed him. There is more than one blow. My guess is that the first blow had him on the floor and then the killer made certain he would die with one or two more blows. The team will be searching for fingerprints, footprints and other evidence. The scene looks like it was cleaned after he died, but I can't be certain. We'll see."

"We know something, Hugh," said Danny.

"And that is?"

"There's no evidence of anyone breaking in. Gerrity let the person in and they had tea together. I'll check again once your people are finished just to make certain this is so."

"Before you ask, I'll tell you," said O'Brien. He looked at his watch. "It's now eleven or so. He was killed last night. I'll get a clearer estimate when I do the autopsy. Do you want to be there?"

"One or both of us will attend," said Danny.

"Sounds good, Danny. I'll see you then."

They surveyed the neighbouring houses to ask if anyone had seen anything unusual the night before. Two of the neighbors told them to check with the person who lived across the street in #134. She was identified as Marcia Macintosh. "She's a retired Social Studies teacher," said one, "and she loves finding out what's going on with other peoples' lives on this street."

Macintosh was about sixty, white-haired, slim, with something of a squint. They asked her if she had seen anything suspicious. "Nothing odd occurred," she said. "It was a dull evening."

While waiting for the forensics people to finish their work, Danny said, "What do we have?"

"Not much," answered Louise. "A murder. A house that has little personality and hardly any information yet about the victim. We have, sir, a lot of digging to do."

"That's where I am also, Louise."

"No revelation like the Baldwin Street murder?"

"None at all. This is different. This requires both patience and tenacity, unless I'm wrong. Let's get to work on it."

XLII

By Friday, Danny was welcoming the long Thanksgiving weekend. It would start normally with Shabbat dinner at the Feldmans, though the rest of the weekend he would be on his own. Gabriella and Avi would be present on Friday evening. However, Gabriella, with whom he now always celebrated Thanksgiving, was leaving on Saturday afternoon for London, in order to conduct the English Chamber Orchestra that week. And Avi always spent Thanksgiving with his mother and her new family.

When Danny got to the Feldman home, he had his nosh with Ruth and Gabriella in the kitchen and, as was happening regularly, he went up to Irwin's study to have a conversation with his brother-in-law.

Irwin greeted him with a smile and asked, "How are you doing?"

"I'm annoyed these days, Irwin. Politics has intruded into my professional life which I'll tell you about when the problem is settled. Also, we have too many outstanding cases. I did manage to get out onto the street a few days ago and that has helped my mood, though it looks like a difficult case to crack."

Danny continued, changing the subject. "What's happening with your firm since we talked about possible changes due to Covid?"

"The answer, I'm sorry to say, is nothing, or next to nothing. I supported a review because of all the needs we learned about during Covid, but I'm in the minority on this one. Most just want to return to what they call 'back to normal.'"

"Are your colleagues reluctant to accept the need for change?"

"I don't know. I, and some others, put forth what we learned during Covid about the need for people to have access to good legal representation." Irwin smiled. "As you intimated some weeks ago, I've been influenced by what Deborah and her firm are doing pro bono. Really about what Covid revealed about what social needs happen to be. Just as Covid opened up the great need for food banks, for changes in elder care, and so many other things. That we should think about who we represent and how we can be better corporate citizens."

"Is the opposition about money?"

"No one says it's about money. No one can say the words 'social responsibility' at a large legal firm without some partners envisioning a financial hit of some sort."

"With respect, the senior partners at your firm do very well."

"We do. There's no senior person taking home less than a quarter of a million a year. Many do much better. But when I raise that fact, some compare us to the States, where lawyers make twice as much."

"The US is hardly a model for people with a social conscience. That society has the biggest gap in the developed world between rich and poor. Biden can't get his bills through Congress because some of his own people oppose him, in addition to all Republicans."

"I pointed that out. In a less confrontational manner, asking instead to judge ourselves against some Scandinavian countries. My argument didn't get far."

"I imagine your main income comes from corporate clients, not individuals."

"Yes."

"I don't know what to tell you. Covid is a good time to re-evaluate how we look after everyone in society. The recent Black Lives Matter and the revelations about Indigenous people's history should at least cause reflection. My guess is that people who are privileged don't want to open the box for fear social responsibility would affect them adversely, which it might."

"You may be correct. I don't know. I do know the legal profession needs someone to do a study about what its future might be."

At that moment Avi was at the door. "Aunt Ruth said our guests are here," he reported.

Irwin and Danny rose. "Let's continue this, Danny," said Irwin. "I don't want to let the issue go just yet."

On the way home with Gabriella, Danny summed up his exchange with Irwin.

"He makes an important point," said Gabriella. "Maybe the partners need to take their obligations as seriously as they take their privileges. I think everyone should spend a day shadowing some nurses and grade-school teachers. That might be a good dose of reality. And maybe we should pay lawyers what we pay nurses."

"Let's see what happens," said Danny. "Clearly, we Canadians shouldn't be so smug about our decency that we get blinded about the need to reform parts of our society. Now, tell me what you're conducting."

"The music is part of the repertoire I'm familiar with. Some Vivaldi, some Locatelli, some Haydn, and a piece I adore, Mozart's Concerto for Flute and Harp."

"You didn't mention you were playing as well."

"I'm not. Their main flautist is the soloist. In a way, I'm glad because I don't think my playing is yet as good as it was BC, before Covid. In any case the harp gets the most attention because there are so few pieces written for it in the canon. I'm looking forward to this engagement. They're a fine group."

Danny pulled over as he got to the entrance of Gabriella's condo. "I'll pick you up tomorrow afternoon to take you to the airport," he said after they hugged. "And next week when you return."

Danny waited for Gabriella to enter the building. She turned and they both waved. Then he drove the short distance home, feeling better than he had for several days.

XLIII

On Sunday, Danny spent the morning delighting in his old, pre-Covid, ritual. He went to the Y on Bloor and Spadina, and first had a squash match with one of the group, Andrew Quilt, which he won in four sets. Then, the nine men attending this week went to the sauna for a shvitz and a shower. At about eleven-thirty, they went to the cafeteria, took a large table and had a bagel and coffee.

They had several conversations going, everything from inquiries about family and tales of children and grandchildren, to who might be in the next federal cabinet and worries about climate change.

As they were finishing their bagels and topping up their coffee, Danny decided to ask a question which he had been pondering ever since his talk with Irwin two days earlier. He got the attention of the table, and then said, "I'm bothered by something. Can I ask how Covid has changed the way you work, how your job or profession has responded to the new reality?"

"Why are you asking?" said Lenny Donnerstein, who was the Head of Psychiatry at Toronto General Hospital.

"Is that a Jewish answer or a psychiatrist's answer?"

said Danny.

"Both. There's something on your mind."

"Yes," said Danny. "Covid has made us realize there are problems we didn't see. How nurses are treated. In your case, Lenny, how mental health needs have grown. How food banks are growing. All kinds of things. Do we now just ignore the two years and go back to what we thought was normal? I'm hearing that and I don't like it."

"OK, I'll start," said Jack Handler. "You know my store. Near here, at Bathurst and Bloor. It's grown into a neighborhood grocery and more. We now give any food that might be too old to put on the counter to the food bank. We donate two per cent of our receipts to CAMH. Our supply chains are nuts and I scramble to fill the shelves. There's more."

"I teach both on-line and in person," said Joe Maguire, a high school head of English. "We have to be ready for anything. Most people in my department are worn out from trying to do what we're supposed to do. Some call students who don't show up and seem to be lost. What has happened in Covid stinks. We feel we're not doing right by the kids. We adjust. And we make believe sometimes that everything is going to be all right. Covid has given Lenny lots of business."

"Too much business, Joe," said Lenny. "We can't keep up. The demand is too great. What about you, Danny?"

"We are probably one of the few workers who do more or less what we did before. We catch thieves and murderers, we uphold the law, and all that. Still, I probably have to leave a murder unsolved because the murderer wore a mask."

Danny turned to his friend from his boyhood, Mike Ryan. "What about you, counsellor? My brother-in-law, who you know, is a member of your noble profession. He tells me people are resisting change."

Ryan, who was a major partner in a prominent 'Catholic' law firm and who also did a lot of legal work pro bono for the Toronto Catholic community, thought for a few moments. Then, "My answer has at least two parts, so bear with me. First, the bad part. Major firms that I know about acknowledge greater needs because of Covid, but few, if any, are doing anything about it other than saying they do pro bono work. Little has changed. Now the good part. Two things. Some small firms, for example Clark LLP on Huron Street, have become major players for those who need legal help because of Covid. Also, a lot of individual lawyers in big firms are doing more volunteering, at least in the area of Catholic social services. I imagine this is also happening in other communities. What it means is that young lawyers who are expected to work twenty-five hours a day for their firm are somehow finding time outside the firm to contribute."

"Why can't that happen inside the firm?" asked Jeremy Gelernter, who was a curator at the ROM.

"I'll give you the worst answer," said Mike. "Because of money. Because the firms don't want to lose any serious money for pro bono work."

"You don't make enough money?" said Jack.

Mike smiled. "You know that's not what I said. I mean everyone wants to appear to do the right thing, but few are willing to lose any money because of it. One of our seven deadly sins, greed."

"I have this weird idea, Mike, that the legal profession has a responsibility to society," said Danny.

"No argument from me, Danny, as you well know. I'm not proud of how the profession has responded. Some have done what should have been done. Others haven't."

"I wish," said Jeremy, "that we in the museums and libraries could do more. We do exhibitions on-line and maybe it does some good, and we work with school boards. I'd like to be able to do more."

"All this needs thinking about," summarized Danny, as he swallowed the last of his coffee. "And this isn't even the biggest problem. At the end of the month there's going to be a climate conference in Glasgow. Everyone will agree to reasonable goals, but my guess, I'm feeling pessimistic these days, is that only a few countries will meet them."

"We have to stop being presentist," added Jeremy.

"And we have to stop feeling only about ourselves and our own world," said Lenny. He rose. "Well, I have to take three kids to hockey games, my guy and two friends. Maybe I'll continue this conversation with them."

XLIV

Danny and Louise learned little from the autopsy of Gary Gerrity. "It's likely the second of the three blows that killed him," said Hugh. "Death occurred in the evening, between eight and ten."

They did learn there were no fingerprints on the knife, which came from a drawer in the kitchen, or anywhere else other than Gerrity's fingerprints on the second mug. As well, the floor had been wiped, so there were no foot-prints of the killer. "This person had the presence of mind to bring a rag," said Louise, "and to wipe everything. This murder was planned."

"And, of course," said Danny, "Gerrity knew him or her. No forced entry at all."

In their probing over the next week, Danny and Louise learned that Gerrity had led an unusual life.

First, they called on Amanda Salderson. "How and when did you meet?" asked Danny.

"We met on-line two years ago, on one of those dating services for mature people. We had dinner and started a relationship soon after that."

"Were you happy in the relationship?"

"Gary took care of us, me and my daughter Laura. He helped us through some tough times."

"What do you mean?"

"Laura has a drug problem. She needs support and counselling. Gary helped out."

"How did he help?"

"He gave us money so that we could work on Laura's problem. He helped to pay our rent and gave us some extra. I depended on that after a while. I don't know what I'll do now."

"Do you know who inherits Mr. Gerrity's money?" asked Louise.

"He didn't talk much about it. I guess his relatives. He had no kids. He told me that he put something in his will for me and Laura. Just to tide us over, he said."

"Was Mr. Gerrity involved in any organizations?" asked Danny. "Did he belong to any group?"

"I don't know much. I know he was talking with the people at Recovery House about donating some money. They're a place that gives support to drug addicts in recovery. They help Laura. She goes there two times a week."

"I need to ask," said Danny, "where you were between eight and ten on the night Mr. Gerrity was killed?"

"I cared for Gary. I didn't kill him."

"We ask everyone Ms. Salderson. It's something we must ask."

"I was home."

"Are there any witnesses?"

"No. Laura was out with her boyfriend."

"Did you make or receive any phone calls?"

"I don't think so."

"Thanks," said Louise. "Now, what about his friends? His relatives? Have you met them?"

"No. We always did things alone. I don't know that he had many friends. He talked about his relatives, but he said he didn't like them."

This blank slate didn't get Danny and Nadiri very far. They then went to see the director of Recovery House, Susan Corbyn.

Corbyn was in her forties, dressed modestly, with dark hair that was turning white. She had blue eyes, high cheekbones and a firm chin. She seemed able and intelligent.

"Are you here because of the death of Gary Gerrity?" She asked. "I read about it in *The Star* a few days ago."

"Why do you think we want to speak about Mr. Gerrity?" said Danny

"Because he's disliked here. We were involved with Mr. Gerrity in a very unhappy matter only six months ago."

"Tell us about it."

"About a year ago Gerrity got in touch with me. He wanted to discuss a donation. 'Of a good deal of money' he said. We met and he told me he had cancer and was thinking about his legacy. He said that because of what he learned about Recovery House from Amanda and Laura Salderson he wanted to donate three million dollars to us. I immediately got in touch with the chair of our board, Rod Turcott. We met again and Gerrity said he wanted to learn about Recovery House so that he could direct his funds to particular programs."

Corbyn paused and took a sip from a bottle of water.

Then she said, "Do you want the story blow-by-blow or just an outline?"

"An outline for now," answered Danny. "Perhaps blow-by-blow at another time."

"He was received as a kind of saviour. We scrape through each year and this donation would have given us a terrific amount of relief. He said he needed to get his affairs in order and the money would be available in six months. Then he insisted that Amanda Salderson join the board. Then he asked us to change some programs. Then he asked Rod to get rid of some board members who he said didn't show him empathy or respect. We wasted months on all this fuss. Waiting and waiting for the money. He even dramatically wrote a cheque for half a million, asking us not to cash it immediately."

"This sounds like a very unhappy tale," said Danny.

"Awful. It was undoubtedly a scam of sorts. Eventually, he told me that his cancer had progressed and he would be dead in three months. The short version is that one of our board members challenged him about both his money and his cancer. He got upset and said he would withdraw. We finally had to ask him not to come to this place again. The donation was all a game to him."

"Very odd," said Louise. "What did he get out of this pretence?"

"We're not certain. We speculated. For several months he was treated with great honor and respect. Maybe he just did it for kicks. I don't know. We decided not to beat ourselves up about it and go on with our work. I do feel foolish sometimes in thinking about it."

"I've never encountered anything like this before," said Danny. "He must have alienated a lot of people."

"Of course. He's a rotten human being. But if you think that someone from Recovery House killed him because of this, I'll tell you you're wrong."

"How do you know that?"

"Because the people who work and volunteer here respect life. They have all seen the dark side of drugs. Many have experienced tragic deaths in their families. Do I have an alibi for everyone, Inspector? No. You're welcome to talk to everyone connected with this place. If you exclude clients, that's about fifty people. If you include clients, you'll be talking to several hundred more."

"For the moment, talking to you and Mr. Turcott will do. Before we leave, please give me his contact information. I won't even ask you the question we ask everyone."

"What's that?"

"Where were you three nights ago between eight and ten?"

"You can ask. I was with my husband, having dinner with my sister and her husband. We met at their place for drinks and then went to Indian Street Food on Bayview."

Danny put up his hand, gesturing Corbyn to stop. "No need, Ms. Corbyn. If I understand what you do, you save lives, not the reverse."

"I will be honest with you. I don't...didn't like Gary Gerrity. I did not wish him well. But I didn't wish him dead."

This pattern repeated itself several times as Danny and Louise learned about Gerrity's life.

Over the course of the last ten years or so, Gerrity had befriended five women who had a teenage daughter at risk in one way or another. They had a steady relationship for a year or a bit more and the woman became dependent on Gerrity, financially and emotionally. Each woman had—or had had—a key to his place. Each woman was used by Gerrity in his approach to an institution where he would claim an interest in donating substantial funds.

Hence, as they probed, Danny and Louise realized it was likely that Amanda Salderson had not told them the whole story. She probably knew Gerrity did not have cancer. She probably knew he was not really intending to make a donation of money he didn't have. Her lies had helped his credibility and masked his motives.

The organizations Gerrity fooled for a time included York University, where he had met with the president and others, claiming to want to fund a program and a professorial chair in the mental health of teenagers; Tessa's Place, where he had been welcomed in much the same way as he had at Recovery House; the Faculty of Medicine at the University of Toronto, where he had offered to build new laboratory facilities; and Sport Canada, where he had offered several million dollars of funds to support excellent young developing athletes.

None of the institutions had taken him to court. None had publicized what had happened.

By the end of a week, Louise said, "We're not getting anywhere, sir. The guy had no life beyond his scams and his dependent women and their children. Two of the five women we've seen have alibis. Three don't. They are

Amanda Salderson, Vivian Blackstone who was his accomplice at Tessa's Place, and Margaret Wilde, who was the woman supporting him at York University. Do we talk to everyone at every organization?"

"No. That won't get us far. But I'd like to talk to the heads at Sport Canada, the two universities, and Tessa's Place. Maybe that will get us somewhere."

"I found out when I researched Tessa's Place that Nadiri's partner, Debra Castle, has joined the board? Did you know?"

"Was she on the board when Gerrity did his thing there?"

"No. She just joined a few months ago. On January 1st."

"Then I don't think we have a conflict of interest on anyone's part."

"Really?"

"It's a good rule, even if it gets in the way sometimes. Considering whether there's a conflict of interest is not about Nadiri. It's about being perceived as objective. If Avi was a client at Recovery House, I would have had a conflict. That's what it is."

"I get tired of having rules that assume we're dishonest."

"So do I. But enough of us are dishonest that we need the rules."

"I feel like having a big sigh, sir."

"Go ahead. I sigh regularly. My latest was over a recent conversation with the Chief and the Mayor."

XLV

The search for Eddie Hagan took only a few days. Nadiri and Alvin found him on the Thursday after Thanksgiving when he again came to The Bog. What troubled them was that Hagan seemed to have been prepared for the arrest. He immediately called his lawyer, Murray Helmore, and refused to answer any questions without Helmore present. Moreover, Helmore was a leading criminal lawyer, clever and high-priced, someone Hagan, still low on the hierarchy of the mob, couldn't afford on his own.

Hagan was interviewed the next day at noon. All wore masks. Nadiri opened the questioning. "Mr. Hagan, we have reason to believe you were involved in the burglary of rare stamps from the home of Mr. Riordan Adams on September 8th. Is that so?"

Hagan, about fifty, gray hair in a short pony tail, brown eyes that seemed to always be busy looking for something, dressed in a suit and tie that didn't come from Harry Rosen, said simply, "I don't know what you're talking about."

"We have evidence," said Nadiri, "that you were the person who hired Robert Casey and Christopher Osborne to rob Mr. Riordon's home in the Baby Point neighborhood."

Helmore replied. "What kind of evidence, Sergeant?"

"I can't reveal where I obtained my information. I can only tell you that Mr. Hagan was identified as the person who hired the two men. Mr. Hagan received the stolen goods, worth over twelve million dollars, and he then paid the two men in cash."

"My client has told you he knows nothing about this matter. That is his full statement."

"Mr. Hagan," said Alvin, where were you on the night of September 8th?"

"What day of the week was that?" asked Helmore.

"A Wednesday."

"Most Wednesdays I go to my sister's house," said Hagan. "I have dinner with her family, her husband and two kids. I was probably there."

"You are aware that the burglary occurred on September 8th?"

"I'm not aware of any caper of this kind," said Hagan. "I told you. I have no idea what you're talking about."

"Mr. Hagan, what do you do for a living?" asked Nadiri.

"I manage some properties for a firm."

"What is the name of the firm?"

"It doesn't have a name. It has a number. 48937567 Ontario Inc."

"Who do you report to?"

"Why is this relevant?" asked Helmore.

"We believe Mr. Hagan was acting on behalf of someone who employed him."

"Mr. Hagan has told you he knows nothing about the burglary. Unless you have clear evidence, that is his statement. He wasn't there. He didn't do anything."

"We have a statement that he was involved."

"From who?"

"I am not revealing that."

"Then," said Helmore, "it's the word of your anonymous source against the word of Mr. Hagan. Frankly, Sergeant, to use the overused metaphor, you do not have the smoking gun. In fact, you don't even have smoke, let alone a gun. I am asking you, are you charging Mr. Hagan with anything?"

"He's a person of interest in this case."

"Then I'm going to terminate this interview. You either have hard evidence or you don't. Either make a charge or we leave. We've cooperated. There's nothing more to say."

Nadiri and Alvin were silent, both unable to find enough to hold Hagan. After a minute, Helmore picked up his briefcase from the table and stood up. Hagan followed. "Thank you, Officers," said Helmore. They left.

Nadiri was seething, but she knew enough not to let her frustration get the best of her.

"Where do we go now?" asked Alvin.

"I don't know. I'll be thinking about that in the next hour or two."

Later that Friday, Nadiri requested a meeting with Danny about the case. The three met on Monday morning in Danny's office.

Nadiri filled Danny in on what had happened so far in the case and then added, "I don't know where to go from here, sir. Because Riordan Adams lived, we managed to get the intruders. Because Christopher Osborne thought it would help him, he identified Eddie Hagan. But there it stands. Hagan denies being involved. We might get Robert Casey to also testify against Hagan, and that might give us enough to charge him. We won't get further. I'm convinced Hagan would be willing to go to jail if necessary to protect whoever is above him."

Danny thought for a minute. "I think if the stamps turn up, that might lead us somewhere."

"Yes," responded Alvin. "We've inquired everywhere and at the moment there's no lead. Do we simply stop?"

"You have no more to go on," said Danny. "Before you stop, however, go back to the beginning and do a review. Just to satisfy yourselves that you've done what you could. In the meanwhile, the Crown will deal with Casey and Osborne and something could turn up in whatever arrangement is made."

"I think, sir, the only thing that could turn up is enough solid evidence to charge Hagan. The case will end there if that happens."

"You're probably correct, Nadiri. This one may not turn out satisfactorily."

"You know," said Nadiri, "this reminds me of what is happening in general in society."

"What do you mean?" asked Danny.

"In general, the rich or the people at the top get away with a lot. They don't pay their fair share of taxes. Their companies are protected as well. Even clear instances of flouting the law are overlooked or simply not investigated. Look at Amazon, Facebook, and all the big corporations. Look at how much tax Bezos, Trump or probably even

Rogers in Canada pays. The big guys are protected, not only by the state, but by big expensive law firms."

"We know," added Alvin, "that even in the pandemic the rich got richer and the gap between the wealthy and everyone else grew wider."

"Now," said Nadiri, "to end my rant, Casey and Osborne, each of whom got twenty-five thousand dollars, will go to jail. Hagan may go to jail, though at the moment that's unlikely. The guys or guy who hired them and got twelve million in stamps are clear and free. So the people who hire people who rob and beat up people are not punished. The people they hire are punished. We get the little guys and the big guys are protected by numbered companies and loyal hit men."

"And maybe," said Alvin, "some of these people not punished are seen as model citizens, sitting on boards and contributing to charities."

"I won't tell you you're wrong," said Danny. "We don't always succeed." He paused. "We just keep pushing, doing the best we can."

"Sometimes, sir," said Nadiri, "my best feels like I'm up against a system manipulated by some bad people who get away, in this case, with assault and theft. The little guys get caught. The big guys just keep on going."

"I can't oppose you on this one, Nadiri. I hope the case will end better."

"I wouldn't bet on that, sir," said Alvin.

XLVI

Two nights later, Nadiri and Debra had one of their cooking sessions at Debra's apartment. Debra's cooking was getting better, and tonight Nadiri was showing her how to make a simple but delicious chicken francese, a dish said to be French, though originating in Italy.

As usual, they were getting all the dinner ingredients together, including the rice and asparagus which would accompany the chicken.

"You can do the rice and asparagus while the chicken is baking," said Nadiri. "It will all take less than an hour and we'll have a great dinner."

"Let me try to do this," said Debra, "before you tell me I'm hopeless and straighten me out. It's time for me to take some initiative."

"Good. Where do you start?"

"We have chicken breasts, flour and egg, among several other things. I think we put flour on the chicken, then dip it in the egg, and fry it in my heavy skillet until it's not quite finished. Then we put it on paper towels to drain."

"Perfect. What else do you do now?"

"Does it eventually go in the oven?"

Nadiri nodded.

"Then we put on the oven. 350?"

"Too high. About 300."

"Close. Not bad."

When the chicken was frying, Debra said, "Now, after I take out the chicken, do I use this pan for the rest or another?"

"This one is fine."

"Then I just put in the wine, chicken broth, butter, parsley and lots of lemon juice. A bit after that I use the cornstarch to thicken it. Oh, yes, the usual salt and pepper to taste, whatever that means."

"You know what it means. You like to pretend you're not understanding things in the kitchen."

"True. I like precision in directions. Not things like 'put in some parsley.'"

"But great cooks love improvising. That's what gives a good dish some personality."

"I feel more secure with precision."

"Security isn't what cooking's about. It's about your own take on things. You're ready for that."

"OK. I'll just fool around then. You'll eat it no matter what?"

"Yes. And I'll enjoy it."

When the sauce was done, Debra put the chicken in the skillet, scooped sauce on top and put it in the oven. She made simple rice and cooked the asparagus while the chicken was finishing.

Nadiri set the table and brought the open bottle of wine over to accompany the meal.

"This is terrific," said Nadiri as she tasted the chicken. "It works very well with the rice. I love it. I think you don't need me anymore in the kitchen. Now we should just cook for one another every so often."

Debra smiled. "It is very good. I never thought this could happen. I'm a woman who lived on Kraft dinner and overdone chicken and hard hamburgers for over thirty years."

"Time for you to go solo."

"We'll see. I like having you around to annoy and to give me some direction."

"I'll be here to annoy, but I don't think you need direction."

"Maybe not in cooking, but I need a career direction."

"What do you mean?"

"Covid has changed everything. You know that. I still don't fully know what my job is. I mostly troubleshoot a lot and fill in elsewhere when needed."

"You're reliable. You're smart and steady."

"What the city doesn't realize is that librarians are turning into frontline workers."

"Really? What do you mean?"

"For example, some branches are turning into food banks as the need in the city rises during the pandemic. Did you know that the demand on the Daily Bread Food Bank has increased over fifty per cent? More than a hundred library staff are packing food hampers every day."

"Well, people trust you. Libraries, even when usage is cut down, have been open more than other public places. They're one of the few places vulnerable people can go without being hassled."

"The gap has made us into an important part of the social safety net, but it means we are expected to pick up the pieces for people with addictions, those who don't have enough food, and even people who need help with mental issues."

The two finished their meal and adjourned to the living room with what was left of the wine.

"What are you going to do?" asked Nadiri when they were settled.

"I don't know. I do know that as an administrator I see reports of increasing intimidation, both verbal and physical. Some people's personal space has been violated. Sixty per cent of librarians, who are mainly female, have reported they've been insulted, excluded, or mistreated because of their gender. We actually need to hire public nurses to be in most branches. We need social workers."

"So you're telling me that libraries have become a microcosm of society. All the big issues in the larger society are there."

"Yes, but they manifest themselves on the local level and affect branches and the individuals working in them. There's the same stress that people feel in hospitals or in shelters."

"Let's get back to you. What does this mean for your career?"

"I'm not certain. I'm thinking about pulling back. Maybe I really should just go back to heading a branch instead of trying to plug the holes in the system."

"Don't make a hasty decision because you're stressed and tired about being in a crisis."

"I worry that the crisis is becoming normal. Libraries are one of the places that have changed because we don't have adequate support in the system anymore."

"Can you talk with anybody about this. I mean about you, not the system."

"Yes. Joan Myhalvic heads the social science section. We've not sat down to talk about it, but she's encountered the same issues."

"Invite her for coffee. Maybe you both need to vent to someone else who is experiencing this stress. Start there."

"Sounds good. As you know from watching and reading the news, a lot of people are leaving their old jobs. There's a shortage of workers in many areas, not only in restaurant work and nursing. Thanks for listening. I just need to give this lots of thought." She smiled. "Maybe this is the mid-life crisis for people of our age in Covid."

XLVII

The Gerrity murder case was going nowhere, reflected Danny. However, his second thought was that he had been nowhere several times before and had eventually got somewhere by being determined and tenacious. He decided to go to Tessa's Place first to speak with Molly Muldoon. He had met her briefly once before and was interested in her perceptions. And Vivian Blackstone was one of the three women in Gerrity's life who didn't have a clear alibi.

Danny and Molly met late one afternoon in Molly's office at five-thirty, when the day was almost over.

"Welcome, Inspector," said Molly when Danny appeared at her office door.

"Thanks, Ms. Muldoon." Danny took a seat and followed up. "I've learned we have at least one person in common."

"Yes, I know. The unique Joe Grace, who's a friend."

"He's a most interesting person. A very decent guy. He must have a deep and possibly tragic history."

"You'll have to ask him that. As you may have experienced, Joe guards himself very well."

"That he does. But he's been a good citizen and a real help in two murder cases. We wouldn't have the racist Karl Geistmeier behind bars now if it wasn't for Joe. I must tell you I tried to ask Joe about his life, but he shut me off immediately. That's something I can respect."

"Not everybody does. They find him abrupt and sometimes rude."

"I would prefer direct to rude."

Mollie smiled. "You get him. He has nice things to say about the person he calls Mr. Big."

"That makes two of us. He's one of your many admirers."

"Let's stop there," said Molly, "before we both get big heads. Now, why are you here?"

"Good idea. You will have heard about the murder of Gary Gerrity. I'm here to get as much background as possible. Sometimes we need to learn about the person in order to know where to probe."

"Fair enough." Molly then related the story of Gerrity's relationship with Tessa's Place. "He taught us a hell of a lesson," she concluded. "We were totally taken in for a time. Probably because we very badly wanted the fairy tale to be true."

"How did you find out that he was a fraud?"

"Two board members became suspicious and challenged his truthfulness and legitimacy after a time. They took the lead. Then I played a dirty trick on Vivian Blackstone which got her to tell us the truth about Gerrity."

"Could you have sued?"

"I don't know. We were advised not to bother. Gerrity

had money, but nothing like the millions he promised. We put the whole sorry episode behind us and went on with our work."

"Tell me about Vivian Blackstone."

"She's not a bad person. She was helped by Gerrity. Or rather her daughter and she were helped. Gerrity made them financially and emotionally dependent. We helped her afterwards."

"A related question. Do you know of anyone here who might have wanted to hurt Gerrity for any reason?"

"Define hurt," said Molly with a grin. "I wouldn't have minded breaking his kneecap at the time."

"But you didn't. OK, who might have had a desire to kill him?"

"That question doesn't resonate, Inspector. That's not who we are. People attracted to working here or to sitting on the board are people who give of themselves to try to help others. We rescue people. We don't kill them."

"I get it, Ms. Muldoon. I got the same response from Susan Corbyn at Recovery House and I buy it. Still, let me ask. Is Vivian Blackstone the kind of person who would want revenge?"

Molly hesitated for a time, thinking. "I don't think so. That's not part of her make-up. She'd do anything to protect her daughter, the way any parent would if there was a problem, but I don't think she and Gerrity had any connections after the incident at Tessa's was finished. Let me ask, Inspector. How many of these incidents have occurred? There's Tessa's and Recovery House. Any others?"

"Three that we know of. York, the U of T medical school and Sport Canada. All also involved women of a certain age and need who had vulnerable daughters. That's seemingly how Gerrity spent the last several years."

"What pathology." She paused. "When are you going to ask me the big question?"

Danny laughed. "Really?"

"I always wanted to be part of a murder investigation. My father used to read me Agatha Christie novels."

"Then I'll ask. Where were you on the evening of the murder of Gary Gerrity?"

"Home alone."

"Any witnesses?"

"Nope."

"Any telephone calls?"

"Nope. Am I a suspect?"

"I'm afraid not, Ms. Muldoon. Just as Joe wouldn't be a suspect even if he didn't have a firm alibi. Your character and history count. But I'll follow up anyway. Did you do it?"

"Nope. He deserved misfortune. He didn't deserve to lose his life. You don't kill someone for lying and wasting your time and energy. At least I don't."

"What about Vivian Blackstone?"

"She was hurt and she was used, and she knows it. My best guess is that she's not the kind of person who would commit murder, but as you probably know at least well as I do, people do strange things in exceptional circumstances."

"That they do, Ms. Muldoon. That's why I ask."

"I hope I helped a bit, Inspector."

"You did. But I still need to get a better sense of what happened."

"I'm told you're smart. But I sense you're also very determined."

"I am. The law should deal with the Gary Gerrity's of this world. Not individuals who decide they can kill someone."

"Agreed. But if you spent a week with us, you'd learn that the law doesn't always work as it should. We have woman and children who have been beaten badly and there's little redress."

"No argument. The law has for a long time been made by powerful men. Now we're changing the law."

"Too slowly."

"Always too slowly. The law is often behind societal norms. That's a problem we can work on." Danny stood up. "Thanks. This has been helpful. I wish you and Tessa's every success. As far as I'm concerned you're doing important work."

"Tell that to the Premier."

They shook hands and Danny went on his way.

The next day, Danny and Louise went to York University, to meet with people there. They drove up the Allen Expressway to Sheppard and then took Chesswood Drive to Finch, winding around acres of industrial land and oil depots. They both remarked on how the area seemed to lack any personality or interest, so different from much of the rest of the city. "It could be anywhere," said Danny. "Anywhere in many cities in North America. Detroit, Cleveland, or Milwaukee."

As they turned left onto Finch, Louise said, "You know, I went to York for my B.A. and M.A. For one of those years, there was a strike, something York has experienced much too often. Strikes really interfere with the students' education. I don't think there's a strike happening now."

"It's getting better," said Danny. "People are willing to negotiate. Maybe it's one of the few good things that happens during a pandemic. My cleaning person at home, a wonderful woman who has two daughters at York and works to pay their tuition and support them, told me how damaging any strike is to her kids. I know some faculty at York. Several are friends and I have a lot of respect for them. And the university does a lot of good, both socially and academically. I'm puzzled at how the place got itself into this endless series of strikes. It has really hurt the institution."

"There's something even more bizarre, sir," said Louise as she turned onto the campus. "We can't strike. Under the law. Because we are, as they say, an essential service. They can strike, and that is their right, but when I was here the strikers used the language of the poor and the needy to explain their actions. Strange."

As Louise was parking in the York Lanes lot, she asked, "Who are we seeing?"

"We have an appointment with Tamara Singer. Her title is Director, Principal Gifts and University Development. I called the President's office and they directed me to her when I told them I wanted to discuss Gerrity and his offer of a gift to the university. I was told the president was very busy and unavailable. So we'll start with Ms. Singer. If we then feel we need to talk to the president, I'll arrange to get to her."

They walked a bit and went to the ninth floor of a brutalist structure that looked like it was designed by an architect hired in the time of Stalin's Russia. Through glass doors, they entered a comfortable reception area in the Office of Development. They waited ten minutes and were then escorted to Tamara Singer's office.

The office was large and well appointed. Its windows looked out over the pleasant Commons near the building. Singer was in her forties, dark hair, an attractive face, with a welcoming manner. She was dressed impeccably, like someone in one of the major corporations located in the city. She took Danny and Louise to a comfortable part of the office with a couch and chairs and offered coffee or tea.

"I'm pleased to meet you," she said. "How can I help? I understand you're here to talk about Gary Gerrity and that unfortunate business."

"I assume you know that Mr. Gerrity was murdered?" asked Danny. Singer nodded.

"Do you know," asked Louise, "of Gerrity's pattern of behaviour?"

"I'm not certain I understand you. I've learned that he did what he did to us to other institutions. I've talked with my opposite number at the University of Toronto and we exchanged experiences."

"Tell us briefly what happened here."

"Gerrity came to see us with a woman named Margaret Wilde. They seemed to be in a relationship. He said he wanted to explore donating four million dollars to the university to found a program and a chair in the mental health of teenagers. He noted that our psychology department had several distinguished people in the field. When I asked why that program, both told me that Wilde's daughter had severe difficulties in secondary school and they became interested in the issue. They saw the donation as a way of helping."

"Did he tell you he was ill?"

"Yes. He had cancer and he didn't have a clear prognosis."

"Why did this matter come to your desk?" asked Danny. "Forgive me, I don't know how university administrations are organized. I only know about the academic side."

Wilde sat up straight and moved to the edge of her chair. "This office deals with major gifts. We only handle gifts of at least one million dollars. Gerrity's four million was nice, but we have recently had one gift of thirty million and another of twenty-five."

"Why is the donation process so complicated?"

"The people offering the gifts come with a possibility, not a certainty. We often have conversations with various phil-anthropic people and foundations to suggest how they might help. Negotiation can be a long process. Among other things, there are naming rights, very important these days."

"Did Gerrity suggest he have naming rights?"

"To the Chair. Not unusual."

"Thanks for your help. As a curiosity, do you ever name a faculty or a building after a distinguished scholar?"

"If he or she has donated at least twenty million dol-lars," answered Singer with an ironic smile, "we would consider it."

XLVIII

That same day, Nadiri received the surprise of her career. As if from nowhere, an unexpected call came from Simone Lobedeau of the police lab.

"Hi, Simone," she answered. "I didn't know I had anything going at the lab."

"You didn't," answered Simone. "But now you do. It's very rare. We have identified a gun used in an attempted robbery at a convenience store as the gun which was used in the Marson murder."

Nadiri took several seconds to absorb the information. "That's terrific. Wow. We've come close to giving up on the case. Do you know the owner of the gun?"

"Not yet. Let me explain. I'll get the information to you in writing later today."

"Keep going. Please."

"Last night, there was an attempted robbery at a convenience store in East York. The perp waited until the store was empty, took out the gun, and threatened the owner, who was behind the counter. The owner, a man named Albert Wong, had sensed that the guy wasn't there just to buy a bag of chips or some milk. He was ready with a gun of his own, in his hand, hidden below the counter. He also, with his right foot, hit an alarm that went on very loudly. The perp was so surprised he turned and ran. When he turned his hand hit a stack of cans and he dropped the gun. He didn't wait to pick it up. The police who came to the scene turned it in. It's a nine millimeter Luger handgun."

"How do you know it's the same gun?" asked Nadiri. There are lots of Lugers out there."

"I can't take all the credit," said Simone. "One of the lab assistants suggested we check it. She remembered the Marson case."

"So you checked with all your magical tools."

"That we did. It's the same one used on Marson."

"Did they catch the guy?"

"Not yet. The person in charge is Sergeant Russ Conanter. I've let him know about this and he's expecting a call from you. You'll get my formal report later today."

"Terrific. I'm calling him right away."

Nadiri immediately found Alvin and briefed him quickly. Then she called Conanter. The two introduced themselves and quickly got to the two cases. "Bring me up-to-date on the search for the thief," said Nadiri.

"Sure," answered Conanter. "We have his image on tape and we have Wong's description. He did wear a Covid mask but luckily we have his prints on the Luger. He's Jonathan Menasker, known to all as Johnny. He lives in an apartment in Parkdale and, every so often, as far as we know, he goes to another neighborhood to rob a small retail shop. He's gotten caught once before and did two years."

"Do you think you'll get him soon?"

"If he stays in the city, certainly. Which he'll probably do. He doesn't have a lot of money and he's never lived outside of Toronto."

"I'll look up his file. This is a big break. Thanks Russ."

"I'll keep you informed."

XLIX

Danny was feeling overwhelmed. He didn't mind that, for he was the kind of person who always had several balls in the air which rarely dropped. But now he believed his work on a special task force for the chief on racial profiling, the amount of incidents the squad was looking after, the complications of Covid, and his own personal life were getting in the way of his handling the Gerrity case. 'Perhaps,' he said to himself, 'we're not getting anywhere because I'm not able to devote the time needed to both reflect and act.'

He decided to try another way of handling the matter. First, he met with Louise in order to sum up where they were.

Over coffee in his office, he asked Louise her opinion about the incident.

"I think, sir, we've only gotten so far. I'm not certain why. What I mean is that I believe at the moment we have three main suspects and no one else. Those are the three of the five women who don't have alibis, Margaret Wilde, Vivian Blackstone, and Amanda Salderson. All had keys or could have had keys, all were known to Gerrity and could have had a cup of tea with him, all had issues.

"It's a strange case. I want to look elsewhere, but there's nowhere else to look. Gerrity was a loner, except for his serial relationships with women who had teenage daughters at risk and his pattern of scamming non-profit institutions. He hardly spoke to family. He didn't like them and they didn't like him. He had few if any outside interests. You often talk about widening the net. In this case there doesn't seem to be a wider world."

"So what are we missing?"

"We're either missing proof that one of the women killed him, or we need another lead."

"I agree. But maybe we're missing a lead detective who can give the case the attention it needs. I've been stretched lately, Louise, and I feel I haven't given this enough attention. I don't only mean interviewing people and things of that sort. I mean that I'm not thinking enough about it, or not letting my unconscious work on it as deeply as it should."

"Sir, you've done everything you could do."

"It's good of you to defend me, Louise, but you're wrong. I feel I'm letting the case down." Danny looked up. "I have a proposal."

"What's that?"

"I want you to become the lead on this case. I'm withdrawing. I'll be around, but I'm dumping the case in your lap. You take over. If you need a partner, find out if Ted is free or if he can be spared from whatever his assignment happens to be. He sometimes thinks laterally and that gets him somewhere."

"So I'll pick it up from here?"

"No, I think that won't work. I think you should start all over again. We've missed something. I've missed something. The case needs to be redone. Not reviewed, redone. It's yours from here on. Work on it full-time."

"Thanks, sir. I'll check in with you regularly."

Louise checked with Sara about Ted. He was on a domestic violence case and could be freed.

The two of them met and Louise summed up what had happened.

"Where do we go from here?" asked Ted.

"We don't go from here, Ted. The inspector was firm that we have to start all over again. I still have old eyes on this one. He wants a fresh view. You know nothing about this case. That might be an advantage. Let's start by interviewing Vivian Blackstone, Margaret Wilde and Amanda Salderson again."

L

On the Friday after her first conversation with Russ Conanter, Nadiri got the call she had been hoping for.

She and Russ exchanged greetings and then she said, "I
hope you're calling with good news."

"Only good news, Nadiri. We have him. He was spotted
going into an LCBO in Parkdale. He's now in a cell and
is being charged with attempted armed robbery. He's denying everything and accusing us of persecuting him. I
thought you'd want to be in on the formal questioning."

"You bet. Thanks, Russ. I'll come to you."

"We're doing the questioning at 2:00 this afternoon.
Come at 1:30 and we can talk about strategy."

"I'll be there. Much appreciated."

From his deep voice, Nadiri imagined Conanter to be a
large man, about fifty years old. She was surprised to find
him leaner and younger. He was about six feet tall, seventy-five kilos, and nearer to forty than fifty. He had
brown eyes, a full head of black hair, a Roman nose and a
thin mouth. Nadiri immediately thought he was one of
those people who are a lot tougher than they seem.

"How is your Inspector?" he asked. "I met him a few

years ago. An interesting guy."

"That he is," replied Nadiri. "I was his partner for six years. He's doing fine."

"What I'd like to do," said Russ, "is to start the session with the failed robbery. Then, I'll turn it over to you. I hope you haven't come here prematurely. Menasker doesn't yet have a lawyer, so he could stop the session at any time if he decides things are going badly for him."

"Don't worry about that. The important thing is that we may have the murderer. There are a lot of ways this can go."

In the interview room, Menasker was waiting, masked. He had greying hair, a furrowed brow and hazel eyes which were now darting back and forth. He was dressed in jeans, a denim shirt, and running shoes.

Russ made the introductions on tape, informing Menasker again of his rights, including having a lawyer to represent him. He then opened the questioning. "Mr. Menasker, we have clear evidence that you attempted armed robbery on October 23rd. Do you admit to having committed the crime?"

Menasker thought for a moment and then replied. "I'm not admitting to anything."

"Johnny," countered Russ, "we have the gun, we have your prints on the gun, we have tape from the store, we have identification from the owner. We could go to court tomorrow."

Menasker took a sip of water. "I'm not admitting to anything."

"All you are doing is stalling," said Russ. "This doesn't help anyone."

Menasker didn't respond. He looked to the side and made it clear he wasn't ready to have any discussion.

"All right. Johnny, the charge stands. We'll have to deal with this in the presence of your lawyer."

"I don't have a lawyer. I don't have the money for a lawyer."

"Then the court will assign you one from legal aid. You must have one."

"Do what you do. I admit to nothing."

"There is another matter, Johnny. I'm turning over the questioning to Detective Rahimi."

Menasker was puzzled. He told himself that some sort of trick was being played on him and decided not to speak. He knew from experience that sometimes the police just tried to wear you down.

"Mr. Menasker," began Nadiri, "your gun is a problem. Your gun was used in a murder recently. It was the murder of a dentist, Dr. James Marson, on the evening of July 27th, over three months ago."

Menasker's eyes opened wide. He sat up and, insofar as Nadiri could make out with the mask covering the lower portion of his face, he looked puzzled.

Nadiri continued after several seconds. "You are now a suspect in the murder of Dr. Marson. In addition to the charge of armed robbery, you are being charged with murder."

Menasker stammered. "I…I d…don't know anything about that. Are you kidding me? Are you trying to get me for the robbery this way? I don't know what the fuck you are talking about."

"I'm taking about your gun being identified as not only

being used in the robbery, but also in the murder of Dr. Marson. We have clear proof."

"You're bullshitting me."

"I am," replied Nadiri, "telling you the truth. Your Luger was used in a murder."

Menasker put his hand up, his open palm facing the two detectives, asking for time. His head was lowered as he was processing the information. Russ and Nadiri gave him the few minutes he needed.

Finally, his hand came down and he looked at the two investigators. "I know nothing. Nothing. I know nothing about what you're talking about. I don't murder people. I didn't murder anyone."

"Then," asked Nadiri, "how do you explain how your gun was used in the murder?"

Menasker again put his hand out, asking for time. After about thirty seconds, he said, "I'm going to need a lawyer. I'm not saying another word until I have a lawyer."

"That's your right," said Russ. "We'll get in touch with legal aid." Russ then formally concluded the interview.

Nadiri thanked Russ, and they both indicated they would continue to work together. She then went back to the station and briefed Alvin.

"What do you think?" asked Alvin.

"He appeared genuinely puzzled. Both Russ and I agree on that."

"Could the lab have made a mistake?"

"I'll ask, but I know the lab people will say they are ready to go to court with the evidence. I think it's more complicated than a mistake. Maybe we have to find out the history of the gun in the last few months. It'll get clearer once we question Menasker with a lawyer present. The whole point, of course, is if he didn't fire it, who did?"

"We thought it was the Jane Doe new dental patient," said Alvin. "Could it be someone else?"

"Maybe. Let's wait. Menasker has something to say. We just have to get him to say it."

LI

The next Monday Louise and Ted started with the three women who had no firm alibi. Margaret Wilde was the first available.

Wilde lived in a rented apartment near Yonge and Eglinton, not that far from Gerrity's house. Nadiri suggested that Ted start the questioning in order to get a fresh view. "I may take over at some point, Ted, but you start."

Wilde offered coffee and cookies and they got settled in her living room. "We're just reviewing things, Ms. Wilde," said Nadiri. "We need to go over a few matters."

"How did you and Mr. Gerrity meet?" asked Ted.

"We met on-line, on a site for mature people looking for a companion."

"Did you tell Mr. Gerrity you had a daughter?"

"The site gave some personal information, including children."

Ted reviewed the relationship, not hurrying. Louise was impressed with his manner and his willingness to take his time getting to know Wilde and putting her at ease. After ten minutes they came to the heart of the matter.

"When did you know that Mr. Gerrity was a fraud?"

"I'll be honest with you. I didn't know he was a fraud until after the York University business began. Gary took an interest in my daughter. He helped us financially in some ways. Not big money, but he would give us money to go shopping, take us out to eat, things like that. We began to rely on him. Then, he told me about his wish to go to York and set up a chair and support research into teenage depression."

She took a sip of coffee to compose herself. "I was impressed. He took me with him sometimes to talk with people at the university. Then someone at a dinner told me they were sorry that Gary had such a difficult illness. I had heard nothing about it. I asked Gary and he told me that he had made up the illness when talking to the York people. 'They become more sympathetic and open when they think you're very sick' he said. 'You can control things more.'"

"How did you feel about that?" asked Ted.

"I didn't like it. I started thinking about what was happening. Gary didn't live like a man who had four million dollars to give away. I started noticing things I hadn't bothered about before. Sometimes he would tell me things about his past. I wondered if he made up all his business accomplishments too."

"How did the relationship end?" asked Nadiri

"When York started ignoring him. They told him to make a decision by a certain date and nothing happened. Gary started behaving differently. He was rude, he ignored us. He basically just stopped being involved in our lives."

"How did you feel about that?"

"We were hurt. But Isobel and I moved on. There was nothing else to do." Wilde looked up. "You don't kill someone because they end a relationship in a bad way, Officer."

"We're not suggesting anything, Ms. Wilde. We're just trying to understand the man," said Ted.

"Let's get to your alibi. You say you were here on the night Mr. Gerrity was killed."

"That's right. Isobel was at her father's place, so I have no witness. There's no one who can vouch for me. I had not seen Gary for months, maybe a year. He lives not far from here and some months ago I was going into Metro to get groceries and saw him there. I turned around and walked away. I don't think he saw me."

Nadiri and Ted ended the interview at that point. They thanked Wilde and told her she had helped them to get a better picture of Gerrity.

"Am I still a suspect?"

"You're simply someone who knew this strange man," said Nadiri, "and who doesn't have an alibi that can be confirmed. There are others in this group as well."

"If there's anything else I can do, let me know."

As they walked back to their car, Nadiri told Ted, "You did well. I really liked how you paced it and made her comfortable."

"Thanks. I have a question. What was in Gerrity's will?"

"What do you mean?"

"I remember the Inspector once asking something in Latin. It's about who would benefit from an act."

"*Cui bono* it's called. Who gains?"

"Well, I don't know how much money Gerrity had. But I believe you said he had property. In Toronto. Who got it?"

Louise banged herself on the forehead. "I'm embarrassed, Ted, we didn't ask."

"Maybe I'm just out to lunch. I thought it would be useful to know."

"You're not out to lunch. I let it slip. I'll find out as fast as possible."

That afternoon Louise found the name of Gerrity's lawyer, whose offices were in Gerrity's neighborhood. She called to make an appointment. She pushed to see him as soon as possible, which meant the next morning.

When she and Ted appeared at the offices of Northey, Ignasiak and Associates, they were immediately taken to see Adam Northey. After introductions and Nadiri and Ted's showing of their credentials, the three got down to business.

"The will was very simple," said Northey. "Mr. Gerrity had no spouse or children. The only relatives he had were distant and he had little contact with them. He willed his entire estate, the bulk of which was in real estate that he had inherited, to the Princess Margaret Hospital. I am the executor. The firm is selling the property and arranging for the bequest."

"That's it?" said a bewildered Louise.

"That's it, Detective. I hear the surprise in your voice. I, too, was surprised when he did this three years ago. But the will is legal."

"Did you do any other work for him?"

"We represented him regarding his real estate. Let's say

that Mr. Gerrity didn't seem like the kind of person who might give all his wealth to charity."

"But he did."

"Yes. I asked him all the proper questions. There is no doubt in my mind that this was what he wanted."

"Did he have a will before this one?"

"No. He made a will on our advice. I spent time telling him how necessary it was."

"Is there anything else you can tell us?"

"Not really. He was somewhat eccentric, but that's not a crime."

"Of course. Thanks, Counsellor. We'll get on with our work."

Louise and Ted walked to Helendale Avenue, where they intended to interview the neighbors again before seeing Amanda Salderson in the late afternoon.

"How bizarre," said Ted. "The guy makes a career of fooling non-profits and then he gives his money to charity in his will. Maybe he had a bad conscience."

"You're nice, Ted. I don't like the guy. At all. Why he scammed everyone is interesting, but it probably has nothing to do with the murder. I am constantly surprised in this job about how people behave. Sometimes a nice surprise, sometimes a disappointment. This is just a surprise."

LII

That same day Nadiri and Russ interviewed Johnny Menasker again, this time with a lawyer present and Alvin behind a two-way mirror. Legal aid wisely assigned someone with experience in what was turning out to be a very complicated matter. He was Edgar Lomanson from one of the major criminal law firms. Lomanson regularly did two or three pro bono cases a year, as did many other lawyers, as a way of contributing to the community. Cynics called such activity by people whose earnings were in the range of several hundred thousand dollars a year 'one per cent conscience-washing'. However, Nadiri had encountered Lomanson once before and knew him as someone who gave his best on every case. Lomanson was now in his fifties, with a head of light grey hair, a furrowed brow and grey eyes.

Nadiri started off the questioning. "Mr. Menasker, do you admit ownership of a Luger gun with serial number 8435m?"

"For clarity, detectives," said Lomanson, "what are we dealing with here? There are now two charges against my client."

"We are dealing with both," answered Nadiri. "Mr. Menasker is charged with attempted armed robbery. In addition, he is being held on suspicion of murder."

"I'd like to have some understanding," said Lomanson, "about what benefits might be obtained as a result of my client cooperating with the police."

"You know," said Nadiri, "that we can't guarantee anything. We would be in error if we suggested anything like that. The Crown handles such issues. However, as we have done before, we can add the cooperation of a person in the file. That sometimes helps."

"Thanks, Sergeant. Keep going."

"I asked about the Luger."

Lomanson turned to Menasker and nodded. "I am the owner of that gun," said Menasker.

Russ Conanter stepped in. "Did you attempt to rob a convenience store in East York on October 25th?"

"I did."

"Did you have the gun in your possession at that time?"

Menasker gulped. He looked at Lomanson, who again nodded. "I did."

"Was that the gun which, in your haste to run, you left in the store?"

"Yes."

Nadiri sensed what was happening. The plan was to admit to attempted armed robbery, which now was the lesser problem. She wondered what would happen when they shortly discussed the murder.

"So," said Russ, "you are now admitting to the crime of attempted armed robbery?"

"The gun was there as a threat," said Menasker. "I never would have used it. You need to believe that."

"We appreciate your statement," said Nadiri. "That's something to raise with the judge."

"We would like it on record," said Lomanson, "that there is no instance of any kind when my client fired a gun."

"All I can tell you," said Nadiri, "is that up until this moment the police have no record of the gun being fired by Mr. Menasker. There is one big matter, however, as you know. The gun owned by Mr. Menasker was the weapon used to kill Dr. James Marson on July 27th."

"My client is innocent of that crime. The gun may have been used. However, he is stating it was not used by him."

"Was the gun in your possession on July 27th?"

Lomanson turned to Menasker. Nadiri knew they had had a conversation about how they would handle the charges and the interview, but from Menasker's body language, it seemed that he was hesitant at that moment. There was silence, Lomanson quietly looking at Menasker in expectation that he would answer, Menasker looking away, seemingly trying to make this moment disappear.

After about thirty seconds, Lomanson asked, "Can my client and I have a brief discussion?"

"Of course," said Nadiri. "We'll wait outside."

"What's happening?" asked Alvin as Nadiri and Russ walked into the space where he was watching the interview. At this moment, Lomanson and Menasker had turned their chairs so that their backs were seen, and they were whispering.

"They're confused," said Russ.

"I don't think so," said Nadiri. "They have a strategy. Menasker is not all that confident about it for some reason which we might discover. They decided to give us what we had. He admitted to attempted armed robbery. They had a plan about the murder. Now Menasker is not convinced it should be followed?"

"Why?" asked Alvin.

"I have no idea." answered Nadiri. "If he didn't do it, he's hesitant for some reason."

At that moment, a knock on the door by Lomanson signalled that he and his client were ready. Nadiri and Russ returned and sat down.

Nadiri spoke. "I'll ask the same question, Mr. Menasker. Was the gun in your possession on July 27th?"

"No."

"Do you know who had the gun?"

"Yes."

"Who had the gun?"

"My girlfriend, Wilma Johnson."

"How did that happen?"

"She asked to borrow it."

"Do you know why?"

"She said that one of her employers felt unsafe and wanted to have a gun in her home."

"How is Ms. Johnson employed?"

"She looks after two families. She helps around the house, takes the kids to school, shops, cooks, whatever is needed."

"Do you know the names of these families?"

"No. We don't talk much about her work."

"Do you and Ms. Johnson live together?"

"Yes and no. We each have our own apartment in my building."

"How long have you been together?"

"A long time. About a dozen years."

"Mr. Menasker, do you have a job?"

"I pick up odd jobs now and then."

"What kind of odd jobs?"

Lomanson intervened. "Officers, I believe you got what you needed regarding the two charges. The nature of Mr. Menasker's employment isn't relevant. We have no further information to give you. I am asking that the charge of suspicion of murder be withdrawn."

"Not yet, Mr. Lomanson," said Nadiri. "We'll do our best to verify Mr. Menasker's claim as soon as possible. Then we'll make a decision."

Lomanson nodded. The interview ended.

When the three detectives met again, Alvin asked, "What do we do now?"

"My case is complete," said Russ.

"But ours isn't," sighed Nadiri.

"Let's find Wilma Johnson," said Alvin. "While you were questioning Menasker, I looked her up. No form for anyone with that name and at her approximate age."

"Let's go to Parkdale and find her," said Nadiri. "Finally, we might solve the Marson murder."

As they were driving to Parkdale, Nadiri remarked, "It's November second and there are still lots of leaves on the trees. That's new."

"My wife, Amy, noticed that the leaves are changing

colour," noted Alvin, "but the colours are not as deep as they were when we were children."

"That's a shame. I always thought of the Fall here as the most beautiful time of the year."

"It would be a shame to lose what Amy calls the 'wonderful aesthetic of October.'"

"It's been happening slowly, over the years. A lot of people don't even notice it. There's a climate conference, Cop 26, going on now in Glasgow. The countries represented there need to treat the climate more seriously. There's a problem with politics. Governments worry more about the next election in a few years than about where the planet will be twenty years from now."

"I worry for my kid."

"Rightly, Alvin."

LIII

Louise and Ted worked their way through Gerrity's side of Helendale. They found some neighbors at home, but learned nothing new. They went across the street and still found nothing until they got to #134, the home of Marcia Macintosh, the retired Social Studies teacher who had the reputation on the street as the neighbor who loved to know about others' lives.

Macintosh invited them in, clearly delighted to be part of the investigation. "I already answered questions," she said.

"We're just reviewing things," said Louise. "Sometimes it's good to review matters. You reported to us that you didn't see anything the night of the murder."

"No," answered Macintosh, "that's not what I reported."

"Excuse me, ma'am. That's what I remember and that's what's in my notes."

"Then you are wrong, Officer. I always told my students to answer the question that was asked. What did you ask me?"

Louise was puzzled but knew to be patient. "I asked if you saw anything odd on the street that night."

"Correct. And I answered in the negative."

"Can you help us, Ms. Macintosh?" asked Ted. "Tell us where we went wrong."

"I wasn't asked if I saw anything. I was asked if I saw anything odd."

"And you answered," said Ted. "Can we ask you now if you saw anything?"

Macintosh smiled. "Good question as a follow up. Yes, I did."

Louise felt she was about to burst, and worked to contain her frustration. Carefully, with a smile, she said, "What did you see?"

"I saw the woman who was regularly with Mr. Gerrity enter the house about nine fifteen. She left a little after ten."

"Did she lock the door when she left?" asked Louise.

"Yes. With a key."

"You can definitely identify her?"

"I don't know her name. I've seen her often. I could identify her."

"Was she carrying anything?"

"Yes. She had a cloth bag which she probably used as a purse."

"Was there any identification on the bag?"

"It was a Hudson's Bay one. You know. Green, red, yellow and something else. It had the colours of Hudson's Bay on it. Like the jackets some people wear."

"Before we go further," said Louise, "is there anything else you can tell us about that evening on the street or regarding any other matter that might be relevant?"

"No. It was a quiet night. I customarily read in the evening in this room." She pointed to a wingback chair which was near the window facing the street. "In that chair."

"Thank you, Ms. Macintosh. This is very important. We will need to have you sign a written statement summarizing what was just said. Can you come to the station with us now? We'll drive you home afterwards. It will not take long."

"Yes, I can do that."

"Thank you," said Ted. "You are being a very good citizen to do this."

"Thank you, Officer. I always told my students to do their civic duty."

They took Marcia Macintosh to the station, typed up a statement and had her read it. She did so carefully and made two corrections, deciding she preferred certain words to others. Then she signed it.

After driving her back, Louise said, "Well, that's two things we didn't do. We didn't think about the will and I didn't question Macintosh carefully enough. The Inspector was right. We needed to start over."

The interview that afternoon with Amanda Salderson became important. Louise got hold of Danny on the phone and briefed him about what had occurred with the lawyer and Marcia Macintosh. She asked if Danny wanted to be at the interview. "No," he replied. "I gave you the case. You and Ted are doing just fine. Keep going at it."

They went to Salderson's apartment at four in the afternoon. She had coffee brewing and some muffins ready. "Help yourselves, Officers," she said. "Tell me how I can assist you. I thought you had gotten whatever information you needed in our last interview."

"Thanks for the coffee," said Louise. "We like to review things and we found some information which may be useful."

"What's that?"

"You told us that you were home on the evening of the murder but there were no witnesses. As I recall, you also said your daughter was out with her boyfriend."

"That's right. I wish I had a witness but I was alone."

"Ms. Salderson, first can you give me the name and the contact information for your daughter's boyfriend?"

"What does that have to do with anything?"

"It's useful to check things. That's part of how we work."

Salderson adjusted her posture. She seemed to be uncomfortable. "His name is Joe. Joe Iococcia, or something like that. I'm not sure how to spell it. I don't have his phone number."

It was a small two-bedroom apartment and no one else seemed to be there, but Louise asked, "Is your daughter at home?"

"No, she's at school. George Brown. She's studying to be a nurse."

"We'll need to talk with your daughter, Ms. Salderson. How do we contact her?"

Salderson took a sip of her coffee and didn't respond.

Louise, after a time, followed up. "Does she have a cell phone? Everyone her age has a phone."

"Yes." Salderson stopped stalling, realizing it would do her no good. "I'll give you her number."

"Thank you."

Salderson rose, trying to signal the end of the interview.

"Sorry, ma'am, we have some more questions," said Ted. She sat.

Louise continued, "Do you carry a purse, Ms. Salderson?"

"Not a regular purse. I usually carry a cloth bag. I have several. I find it can be both a purse and a shopping bag when I'm out."

"Do you have a cloth bag with the Hudson's Bay colours on it?"

She was visibly uncomfortable. "I have one, I think. I don't use it a lot."

"Is it here?"

"It's in the closet in my bedroom."

"Can we see it?"

There was a hesitation. Then, "I'll go get it."

She rose. So did Louise. "I'll accompany you," she said.

"No need, Officer. It's light."

"I'll accompany you, Ms. Salderson."

They went towards the bedroom. "Ms. Salderson, you will show me where the bag is," said Louise. "I will carry it. You are not to touch it."

"Get out of my home," she shouted. "You have no right to do this."

"Ms. Salderson, you are under arrest on suspicion of murder. My colleague will be calling for a car to take you to the station. We will not touch anything in this apartment until we receive a warrant to legally investigate. We will seal the apartment once you leave. You have the right to call a lawyer and get counsel."

"You have no right to arrest me."

"You're wrong. We have clear evidence that you lied to

us about your whereabouts on the night of the murder. Sworn evidence, Ms. Salderson. We know you were present in Mr. Gerrity's house at the time of the murder."

She crumbled. "The bag is in the closet," she said as she retreated to the living room and sat.

Louise went to the bedroom closet and easily found the bag. With gloves on, she took it by its two handles to the window to get some light. In it were many things, including a large rag with what looked like blood on it. She touched nothing.

They were silent until the car came from the division to take Salderson to the cells in the station. Arrangements were made for her to be questioned again the next morning. She had no lawyer. Legal aid was arranged. The bag was taken to the lab.

Louise again called Danny to inform him what was happening. "I'm relieved," he said. "You did well."

"Give Ted a lot of credit, sir. You were right in two ways. We needed new eyes and we needed to start again."

"Let's sum up together when it's over, Louise. You and Ted finish up. Then we'll talk."

The interview with Salderson was straightforward.

She appeared with a legal-aid lawyer in her mid-thirties, Amy Hivion, whom Louise had encountered a year ago on another case and for whom Louise had respect. She was, Louise thought, very competent, non-confrontational, and represented her clients well without some of the drama enjoyed by other lawyers. Ted put on the tape and they began.

"Ms. Salderson," said Louise, "you are aware of the

charges against you relating to the murder of Mr. Gary Gerrity?"

Salderson nodded. She was visibly upset, barely holding together. "My client," said Hivion, "is aware of the charges."

"I need to tell you, Ms. Salderson, we have a witness who saw you enter and leave Mr. Gerrity's home at the time of the murder. You had a key and you locked the door behind you when you left. As well, we have sent your bag to the laboratory and they will be analyzing the contents, including the rag which seems to have blood on it. The blood might be enough to get a DNA sample. That DNA sample might match the DNA of Mr. Gerrity."

"What else do you have, Officers?" asked Hivion.

"We have the fact that Ms. Salderson lied about her whereabouts on the night of the murder. She told us she was at home. As well, she told us her daughter was out with her boyfriend. In the time between yesterday and this morning, we located the boyfriend who said he was at work as a bartender that evening. Ms. Salderson's daughter has not cooperated."

"May I have a conference in private with my client?"

"Yes. We'll leave you here. Knock on the door when you're finished."

Louise and Ted went outside. Sara Bellucci had been watching the interview through the two-way mirror and joined them.

"What do you think?" asked Ted of the other two.

"I don't think they'll grandstand," said Bellucci. "Hivion will talk with her and then they'll try to get the best deal they can to make things easier for Salderson."

"I hope so," said Louise. "Holding out doesn't make sense. Salderson is caught. And if the DNA comes in, her guilt is a certainty."

They chatted some more, imagining several scenarios. Ten minutes later there was a knock on the door.

When they got settled again, Hivion spoke. "My client is deeply distraught. She asked me to speak first on her behalf. She admits to the murder of Gary Gerrity. She does, however, want a number of matters entered into the record which help to explain the matter and which mitigate the charge."

"We don't do the charging Counsellor, as you know."

"We'd like some matters to be on the record."

"Of course. Proceed in any way you see fit."

"Mr. Gerrity was abusive," said Hivion. "He was abusive psychologically, putting Ms. Salderson and her daughter in a dependent relationship. He was also abusive physically."

The physical abuse was new and took Louise by surprise. She followed up. "In what way was Mr. Gerrity abusive physically?"

Hivion turned to Salderson. "You should answer this question."

"He hit me. Twice. Once he slapped me in the face. Here." She pointed to her left cheek. "He did it after a meeting. He told me I wasn't supporting him enough in my manner. He pushed me into the wall of his kitchen after another meeting. For the same reason. He also threw hot tea on my chest once. For the same reason."

"I have a question or two," said Louise. "Is there anything else you want to put on the record?"

"There was verbal abuse as well," said Hivion. "On a regular basis." She turned again to Salderson and asked her to speak.

"In private he used the word 'bitch' a lot. He would not use my name. Instead, he used bitch."

"Please give an example," said Hivion.

"That night when I came, he said 'Get me some tea, bitch'. He would say 'Let's go, bitch' when he wanted to go somewhere. He used other words."

"Anything else you want to add? asked Louise.

"Not now," answered Hivion.

"I have something else. Ms. Salderson, in your first interview you said that Mr. Gerrity told you he left something in his will for you and your daughter. Did that play any role in your deciding to kill Mr. Gerrity?"

Hivion put her hand on Salderson's arm to stop her from speaking. She spoke. "Mr. Gerrity was abusive and insulting. He hit my client. That's what we are telling you here. We have nothing else to say. We'll talk to the Crown about other matters."

Louise thought about pushing the issue but decided not to do so at this time. "If that's so, then we can end this interview. Ms. Salderson, you are now being formally charged with the murder of Mr. Gerrity."

Salderson was escorted out. Hivion stayed and bumped elbows with Louise and Ted before leaving.

"That's a good lawyer," said Louise to Ted later. "She did what she could to help her client. Who knows? Maybe she'll manage to get murder turned into manslaughter."

The lab results came in four days later. They did manage to get a DNA sample and it did match that of Gerrity.

A few days later, Danny met with Louise to sum up the case.

"You did a fine job. I'm glad I backed off."

"Don't give me all the credit, sir. You told us to start from the beginning. I would have just carried on."

"I felt that I was missing something because I had too much else on my plate. The case needed to be looked at, as the lawyers say, *de novo*."

"We missed something, sir."

"I want to speak with you about that. You're often my partner. And by now you're a veteran. I think you need to be more active sometimes. Don't trust me implicitly. I'm fallible, like all of us. And I'd like to think I can handle being wrong on occasion. Especially if the criticism comes from my long-standing partner. It's OK to call me out, Louise. In fact it would make us a better team."

Louise was taken aback. After a minute, she said. "I never thought of things that way. You make sense. Sir, I wasn't hesitant because I'm a passive person. I think it's because I have a lot of respect for you."

"I know, Louise. But when I criticize you, you know it doesn't mean I don't have confidence in you. You must do the same with me. Criticism is good. It's not a lack of support. In fact, it's part of support."

"You're right. I'll adjust."

Louise continued. "Still, don't give me too much credit on this one. Ted was really good. He's the one who thought about the importance of looking at the will. He has a really good interviewing manner and he's patient. He got more from Macintosh than I might have."

"That's good to know. He's still a regular constable we bring over to help us at times. I think it's time he considered joining the squad when there's an opening."

LIV

Wilma Johnson was easily found. She answered the phone while in her apartment in Parkdale. Nadiri and Alvin went to see her at ten in the morning the next day.

Johnson was dressed neatly and simply, a blue blouse, a black skirt, and flat sensible shoes. Like most Torontonians in these days, she answered the door in a mask. She had black hair with a few grey strands and light blue eyes. Nadiri judged her to be about five feet four inches and sixty kilos.

The apartment on Jameson Avenue was small but not tiny, on the seventh floor facing west. When Nadiri and Alvin were seated in the living room, Johnson asked, "Coffee? Tea?" Biscuits were on the coffee table.

Both accepted a cup of coffee. While Johnson was in the galley kitchen, Alvin went to the bookcase. In it were mainly mysteries, a few romance novels, cookbooks, and several books about children and their development.

When seated over coffee, Johnson, looking very relaxed, asked. "Why are you here? Does it have to do with the murder of James Marson? A terrible thing. The marriage was dissolving, but still….It affected the children deeply."

Nadiri wondered if her ease was genuine or if she was an excellent actress. She decided to start with generalities and build to the important matter. "What kind of work do you do?" Nadiri asked.

"I look after two young families, the Marsons and a family of four nearby, the Pounders. I do almost everything. I cook, I clean, I take the kids to school, I do laundry, I help out in any way that's needed. I've been doing this for the Marsons since the kids were born. I don't have kids of my own, but I've helped to raise these four."

"Do you find it satisfying?" asked Alvin.

"Mainly," responded Johnson. "I get a lot of affection from the kids. I feel I'm making a contribution to their growth."

"Were you trained for this kind of work?" asked Nadiri.

"No. I graduated from a collegiate, had some odd jobs and was drifting. I needed steady work. A friend who worked as a dental assistant to Dr. Marson recommended me for baby-sitting. It turned into a permanent job. I've tried to learn a bit about child development. I'm very fond of the children." She paused and then said, "You're not here to ask about my job. Can you tell me why you're here?"

"Fair enough," said Nadiri. "We're here to ask about a gun."

"I don't have a gun."

"The gun we're asking about is owned by your boyfriend, Johnny Menasker."

"I know Johnny owns a gun. I also know he's in trouble again because of an attempted robbery. He promised he was done with that." She shook her head. "He wasn't."

"It turns out the gun used for the robbery was also the gun used in a murder."

"Oh, my god," responded Johnson. "Johnny murdered someone?"

"We're not certain. We have the gun, but we don't have a clear sense of who the murderer was. There's more. Mr. Menasker informed us the gun was in your possession at the time of the murder."

Johnson hesitated, clearly trying to put together the information given by Nadiri. The silence continued for thirty seconds. Then, Johnson spoke. "Are you talking about the murder of Dr. Marson?"

"Yes," said Alvin. "He was murdered on the evening of July 27th. The gun was the Luger owned by Mr. Menasker. He claims he gave it to you."

"He did give it to me. Caryn, Ms. Easton, had told me she felt insecure in the house alone with the two children. She said she would be happier if she had a weapon. She said that in Kentucky, where she was raised, there were always guns at home for protection. I asked her if she knew how to shoot and she said most everybody in Kentucky was familiar with guns and knew how to shoot. The next time I saw Johnny, I asked him about his gun. He gave it to me and I gave it to Caryn."

"When did she return it to you?" asked Nadiri.

"About a week after the funeral. She said that after what happened to Dr. Marson, she had changed her mind about having a gun in the house."

"There's another important question we need to ask,

Ms. Johnson," said Nadiri. "Where were you on the evening of July 27th, from about seven to nine?"

"That's easy," said Johnson, showing no hesitation. "I was in the Marson home, looking after the children."

"Can you prove that?" asked Alvin.

"Ask the children. They'll remember that night."

Nadiri then said, "Do you have anything else that might help us to confirm your alibi? Did anyone call you at the Marson home? Did someone come with a delivery?"

"Neither of those, Officer. I do have my diary. My hours with the two families aren't fixed. I work about twenty hours a week for each family, sometimes more, rarely less. So I keep a clear diary of when I'm expected, sometimes with chores listed. Otherwise I'll miss something or make two commitments for the same time."

"Do you have the diary here?"

"Yes. It's in the kitchen. I'll get it." Johnson rose, went to the kitchen area, and returned quickly with the diary in hand. She gave it to Nadiri.

Nadiri opened the notebook to the end of July. Johnson had told the truth about how it was kept. There were many notations, some with an M and some with a P as the heading. Listed were various tasks, from providing meals, picking up children from school, doing laundry, shopping, etc. For July 27th the list read:

M and P – take young ones to school.

P – clean in morning

M and P – Pick up kids at school

M – shop for dinner

M – look after children, 6-10

"Can you tell us when Ms. Easton returned on that evening?" said Nadiri.

"She returned a bit before nine. She said that her dinner with a friend ended earlier than expected."

Nadiri took a deep breath and then said, "Ms. Johnson, may we take this diary now? It's very important that we have it in our possession for a while."

"If you need to," replied Johnson. "Can I write down the lists I have for the next week or two?"

"Yes. Please do so here, in our presence."

"I don't know what's happening," said Johnson. "Can you tell me what's going on. Is Johnny in more trouble? Am I in trouble?"

"We can't yet reveal anything more," said Nadiri. "Let me just say that you have been very helpful and we appreciate your cooperation."

"I'm afraid of what I'm thinking."

"We will inform you what is happening soon," replied Nadiri. "At the moment we can't discuss this any further."

When they got to the car, Alvin asked, "When do we see Caryn Easton?"

"As soon as possible," said Nadiri. "I'll call and set up a meeting for this afternoon."

LV

Nadiri and Alvin arrived at the home on Dawlish Avenue at two o'clock. Caryn Easton answered the door, invited them in and offered coffee. Both Nadiri and Alvin politely refused.

When they were seated, Caryn said, "Are you here with new information. Has something come up?"

"We'll get right to the point, Ms. Easton," said Nadiri. "To answer your question, yes, we do have new information." She paused. "We need to review a bit. Remind me where you were on the night Dr. Marson was killed."

There was no hesitation from Caryn. "I told you. I was here with the kids."

As the two detectives had rehearsed, Alvin now joined the conversation. "We have information," he said, "which indicates you were not here until a little before nine p.m."

Caryn took some time before responding. "Who told you that?" she asked.

"Our information is reliable," answered Alvin. "We need to know where you were that evening."

Caryn gave it some thought. "Until you tell me more, my story remains the same."

Nadiri changed the subject. "Do you own a gun Ms. Easton?"

"No."

"Are you familiar with guns?"

Caryn tried a smile. "I told you, Sergeant, I grew up in Kentucky. Everybody there is familiar with guns."

"Have you had," said Alvin, "a gun in your possession at any time in the last six months?"

Again, Caryn did some thinking. "I did borrow a gun for a time. I was afraid after James' murder to be alone in the house with the kids. I borrowed the gun from our housekeeper. After a few days I had seconds thoughts about that and I returned it."

'Not bad,' thought Alvin. 'But not good enough.' He then said, "We have information which indicates you had a gun in your possession at the time Dr. Marson was murdered. Moreover, our information that you were not at home on the evening of his murder is very solid. Can you tell us what kind of a gun it was?"

"I don't remember. It was a pistol."

"You're familiar with guns," retorted Nadiri, "but you don't remember much about the gun you borrowed?"

"I didn't look. And I returned it after a few days."

Nadiri decided it was time to end the game. "Ms. Caryn Easton," she said, "we are arresting you on suspicion of the murder of your husband, Dr. James Marson." She then cautioned Easton as Alvin called for a vehicle to take Easton to detention. After the caution, Nadiri said, "We have arranged for someone from social services to pick up your children at school and to look after them while you are detained. If you wish to make other arrangements, you will be given the opportunity to do so once you are booked."

"You're going to be seen as fools," said Caryn, with venom in her voice. "I'll get a lawyer who will show how stupid the police are."

Nadiri told herself to resist the temptation to reply. Alvin took her lead.

On the way downtown, Alvin said, "So we'll get credit for solving the crime, even though we really didn't do it. It was dumb luck and Wilma Johnson."

"The lab deserves most of the credit," said Nadiri. "They were smart to tie the two events together and test the gun. It's like one of those goals in hockey where the person making the assist deserves the goal, but the person who put his stick out in front of the assist gets the first star. Let's remember to give the credit where it's due."

LVI

The next Tuesday evening, Nadiri went to the first in-person get together of her group of friends since Covid had begun some twenty months earlier. They were ten in number, friends since they were together in high school growing up in Thornhill. They cherished the relationships and the group because they could be themselves. Sometimes they just brought one another up-to-date; sometimes one of them raised a serious matter, seeking opinion and advice.

During the pandemic, they had met monthly and had done so via Zoom until now. Zoom, thought Nadiri, was inadequate for such a group of vital and alive people. You couldn't have several conversations going at once, no one could just bounce into a discussion. The artificiality of conversation was maddening on Zoom. Even with Omicron on the rise, the group decided to 'go live' again and have a meal together. All, at around forty years old, were double vaccinated, waiting for the opportunity to get a booster. This evening, they were meeting at a restaurant on the Danforth selected by Nikki Drakos, one which had a table in the back that could accommodate them and also, as Nikki informed them, very good Greek cuisine.

When Nadiri arrived, Nikki, who owned a small dress shop nearby, and Mariana Lopez, in the philosophy department at York University, were already at the table. Nadiri showed the management proof of having two shots and her identification. She kept her mask on until she got to the rear, where she hugged her two friends.

The three ordered wine and Nikki was given the task of selecting appetizers for the table. She chose tzatziki, hummus, keftedakia, and taramasalata, with lots of pita.

Soon the table was full and several conversations were going, people catching up on each other's lives. The talk was a bit noisy and very spontaneous. 'This is what life should be,' thought Nadiri, like most people worn down by Covid fatigue.

As the meal progressed and the main courses were served, Celia Rogdanovivi, a lawyer in a small firm, got the attention of the table. "Now that we're here," she announced, "I'd like to get a sense from you of what's happened to women in Toronto these last two years. A few months after Covid there was a lot of talk about big issues. Now I sense everyone's just accepting the consequences."

Angelina Conforto, a vice-principal in the Toronto District School Board, plunged in. "It's not good. Women's shelters are overwhelmed. The mental health of women who are abused or who have to stay home and juggle domestic and kids' matters is going through the roof, with not enough support from the health system. Eating disorders are up. I think Covid has moved us backwards."

"I'm going nuts," said Barsha Gupta, who had three young children. "I'm like a lot of mothers with small kids.

I'm a teacher, an organizer, a food provider and everything else. I'm worn out. If there's another school closedown, I don't know how I'll cope."

"We're seeing a lot of people who need legal help because of the pandemic," said Celia. "They need to file for support, or get help with landlord problems, or deal with a spouse who is abusing them. And these people can't afford it. We do even more pro bono work. One of my partners is doing pro bono work persuading other law firms to do more pro bono work. Most of our work is with women."

Barsha looked at Nadiri. "Is there more crime?"

Nadiri smiled. "Well, there's less street crime, because there are fewer people on the streets. But in general there's more violent crime, a lot more cyber-crime, and a big increase in domestic violence. There are jurisdictions in America where the police are arresting fewer people in order to try to control the spread of Covid in prisons. I think women have borne the brunt of all this, especially women with families."

"I also think the mental health side of Covid isn't given enough attention," said Marina. "I know psychologists and psychiatrists are overwhelmed with referrals and requests."

"All right," said Celia. "Has anything good happened?"

Patti Brown, who worked for the Ministry of Finance at Queen's Park, now entered the conversation. "Some good things have happened. All political parties agree on the importance of government support and government accountability. There's help for people unemployed and for families. Remember, most provinces, not ours yet, have partnered with the federal government on the day care issue."

"What hasn't happened," said Martha Neilson, a head nurse at Toronto Western Hospital, "is a recognition that the medical system can't keep carrying the burden. We're losing nurses, doctors are burnt out and not performing as well as they should because of the load, we've postponed lots of surgeries. People are suffering and dying because the system is clogged. I have to make decisions about which needy patient gets what they need. It's frustrating. No, it's more than that. It's demoralizing and debilitating."

"My problem personally is a worry Covid is never going to end," said Maya Notundu, an executive at the Royal Bank. "We used to talk about getting back to normal. Now, incoherence and fear are the new normal. In July we had two weeks when we thought the pandemic would be over shortly. Then came Delta. Now comes Omicron. Are there enough letters in the Greek alphabet to handle what comes next?"

"I wonder," said Nikki. "There are twenty-four letters in the alphabet, and a few won't be used, like nu and xi."

"How come?" asked Martha.

"It was thought nu would be confusing," answered Nikki. "And xi is a common Chinese name, including that of the leader of the Communist Party who is head of state or, if you accept my understanding, the autocrat for life of an authoritarian state."

The women had finished their main course and the waitress came, which stopped the general discourse.

After the table was cleared, several new mini-conversations started. Nadiri listened to Nikki and Mariana, seated on her left, talk about their professional lives for a while. Then she turned to Celia on her right and asked, "OK, Celia. You left a big position at a Bay Street law firm three years ago because you felt you were helping corporations pay little tax and rich folk get away with whatever they were doing. Is the world more just?"

"Tough question," answered Celia. "I'll answer a bit indirectly." She paused for a bit. "Many important things are delayed. Surgeries are delayed, cancer treatment is delayed, culture is delayed. We just had a conversation about what has happened to women, and social justice, if it ever comes, is delayed. Food banks here can't keep up. The rich world gets richer and vaccines are rare in the poor world.

"Another 'd' word. Our lives have been diminished. We can't even anticipate any longer. People want Christmas. Now Omicron may kill it." She put up her hands in a movement indicating she would stop. "Enough ranting," she said.

"What do we do about it?" asked Nadiri

"I've thought hard about that. For me, it's become simple. Do your best. Don't be complacent. I've given up trying to solve the world's unfairness and its problems. I do what I can and hope that I can look at myself in the mirror when I wake up in the morning. Your boss would say that. He's right."

"You do sound like Danny, Celia. I sometimes feel hopelessly inadequate in the face of what needs to be done."

"I always feel that way. I try not to dwell on it and instead maybe do a little good. I'm really glad I left the big law firm. They're still only for the corporations and the wealthy. They rationalize their work by saying everyone needs legal representation. But if every lawyer behaved like them, ninety-five per cent of the population wouldn't have it."

"No insult intended, but I know of few professions with more self-regard than the law."

"It's time we asked what we are really doing. Something happens between going to law school with high ideals and when you're forty and finding yourself representing some guy, usually a guy, who makes money by loaning it at high interest rates to the poor, or from slums he owns, or from shifting his money offshore."

"How many ask that question and take it seriously?" said Nadiri. "Covid has hurt us. We need to reacquire a sense of urgency about important matters."

As they were finishing their dessert, Nikki addressed the table. "OK people. This is wonderful. Do we meet in person next month?"

"That's a question we can't answer today," said Maya. "Now Omicron is coming. We don't know where it will be next month."

"Please, we can't close down again," lamented Barsha.

"We don't know. We just don't know," said Mariana. "Perhaps the virus is a message from nature. Let's take it seriously."

"It's my turn to find a time and place," said Nadiri. "I'll do that, knowing we might have to go back to Zoom if Omicron spreads as fast as they tell us it might."

"Do we cancel Christmas again?" asked Nikki, in a voice that was a sigh.

"We don't know that either," said Mariana. "I overheard Celia's short rant. She talked about delay and diminish. How about yet another 'd' word. Destroy. Lots that is valuable is being destroyed. We need society. We need each other. In person, not on a screen."

"Let's not end so pessimistically," said Celia. "We have each other and most of us have families. Let's cherish that."

LVII

Toward the end of November, Danny received a phone call from the Chief. They exchanged greetings and then John Kingston revealed the purpose of the conversation. "Danny, this call is more social than professional. As chief I've received an invitation from Masai Ujiri to attend this year's Giants of Africa luncheon on December 5th. We have a family birthday celebration that day, and Sandra will divorce me if I'm not there. Could you represent the department at the lunch?"

Ujiri was the president of basketball operations for the Toronto Raptors. Under his leadership the Raptors won the championship of the National Basketball Association in 2019. More than that, now a Nigerian-Canadian, he was deeply involved in many activities helping African youth. His public work had made him a favorite son in Toronto, someone who supported human rights, tolerance, and economic development. Danny had never met him, though he admired him from afar.

Danny thought about the request for a few seconds, for he avoided the public side of the department's responsibilities as much as he could. But it was John Kingston asking him, someone who gave him great support. And the event was supporting the charitable work of Ujiri. Hence, he replied, "I think I can, John. It's at the end of Chanukah, but the holiday doesn't get in the way."

"Good. You can take Gabriella as well."

"That won't be possible. That week Gabriella will be in Minneapolis, conducting. I'm on my own."

"Thanks. I'll let the organizers know you'll be coming to represent the department. You'll get all the details from them in an email."

Danny attended the event honouring Nelson Mandela, and had an interesting afternoon. In addition to meeting Ujiri and having a pleasant short exchange with him, he had conversations with Precious Achiuwa, a Raptors player from Nigeria, Nomzamo Mbatha, a human rights activist and actress from South Africa, and Marci Ien, the MP for Toronto Centre, the riding next to Danny's, and Minister for Women, Gender Equality and Youth. There were others, including some civil servants and journalists he knew. He stayed for the six o'clock Raptors basketball game against the Washington Wizards. He was seated next to another well-known Torontonian, the Raptors superfan, Nav Bhatia, who had never missed a home game of the Raptors since they began as a franchise in 1995. They talked basketball, told one another about their families, and took pleasure in watching the Raptors win 102-90.

On Wednesday, December 8th, Masai Ujiri announced he had tested positive for Covid. Toronto Public Health asked anyone who had attended the game on December 5th to self-monitor for Covid signs for ten days, to go for testing should they have any symptoms, and to self-isolate while results were pending.

Danny decided to get tested the next day. He learned from the CBC news that Bhatia would miss his first game on Friday night because of the announcement and his decision to test and isolate.

Danny was supposed to pick up Gabriella at the airport in the late afternoon on the 9th. Instead, he called her and explained what had happened. "The pandemic is still with us," he said. "Omicron seems to spread quickly. It's better to be cautious. Until I get the results of the test I'm self-isolating."

As he sat in his kitchen on that Thursday having a sandwich for lunch, taking a break from Zoom exchanges related to his work, Danny recalled his optimism while dining at Elena's with Gabriella six months earlier, on Canada Day, 2021. This was before Delta, a short moment when the world thought there might soon be an end to the sad effects of the pandemic. Now, Delta was leaving while the world was saying hello to Omicron. He shuddered, telling himself to be patient and to try to humanize as much as possible those things that were still in his control.

Finishing his lunch, Danny was moved to avoid Zoom for a little longer. He went to the living room and picked up his violin. He played a few scales to warm up and then, though there was no accompanying harpsichord or piano, he played the slow movement of Bach's Sonata #5, a piece he often thought about when he was sad. He noted, not without some self-irony, that he was playing it better than ever, with no one to listen.

Then, in an attempt at transcendence, he played some of the solo part of the first movement of Beethoven's Violin Concerto, the opening theme and the cadenza. 'If he can do this while going deaf, we can keep persevering,' he said to himself. He wasn't certain he believed he could, but he vowed to act as if he did.

Acknowledgements

Thanks to Fran Cohen for her careful reading and her wise suggestions. Martin Sable provided his usual clear legal advice. Thanks also to Emily Posthumous of the Toronto Public Library and to Meagan Gray of the Toronto Police Services for helping with information about working during Covid. Brian Current provided insights into what happened to musicians during Covid. Mike O'Connor was his usual helpful and creative self in designing and producing this book.

As always, I remain grateful to Jan Rehner, who listened, made many important plot and character suggestions, edited with care and insight, and made this a better book.

About the Author

Arthur Haberman is a retired professor of History and Humanities. He lives in Toronto and loves the city and its people.

CPSIA information can be obtained
at www.ICGtesting.com
Printed in the USA
BVHW031324030223
657817BV00001B/115